CAN'T STOP LOVING YOU

ALSO BY MIRANDA LIASSON

Heart and Sole
A Man of Honor

The Mirror Lake Novels

This Thing Called Love
This Love of Mine
This Loving Feeling

CAN'T STOP LOVING YOU

MIRANDA LIASSON

Montlake Romance

This is a work of fiction. Names, characters, organizations, places, events, and incidents are either products of the author's imagination or are used fictitiously.

Text copyright © 2016 Miranda Liasson
All rights reserved.

No part of this book may be reproduced, or stored in a retrieval system, or transmitted in any form or by any means, electronic, mechanical, photocopying, recording, or otherwise, without express written permission of the publisher.

Published by Montlake Romance, Seattle

www.apub.com

Amazon, the Amazon logo, and Montlake Romance are trademarks of Amazon.com, Inc., or its affiliates.

ISBN-13: 9781503941533
ISBN-10: 1503941531

Cover design by Eileen Carey

Printed in the United States of America

For my parents, who filled my childhood with books and love.

CHAPTER 1

The only reason Arabella D'Angelo set foot inside her cousin Lucy's wedding was family guilt—of the big, whopping Italian variety.

"We go as a family," her father, Vito, had announced—more like *pro*nounced in his heavily accented English. So there they were, Bella sitting there with her good friend town veterinarian Ethan Cohen, who'd been more than happy to stand in as her date. She couldn't think of a better person to help buffer the awkward comments of her former high school classmates, many of whom had come into town for the wedding.

On one side of her father, her sister, Gina Maria, gave her a sympathetic glance. Gina's husband, Manuel, kept glancing at his watch, probably thinking that the clock was ticking on the babysitter, and if they could just get home before exhaustion set in, there might still be time for Saturday-night fooling around. On the other side of Vito, Aunt Francesca sat, her posture rigid, looking like she'd come straight from the confessional.

"This wedding feels more like a funeral," Aunt Fran said, draining her wine. "Remember the weddings we used to go to in Italy when we were young, Vito? Dancing, celebrating, good wine, not this cheap stuff."

"I can't comment on the dancing, Francesca," Vito said, glancing at his cane, "but I have to agree with you on the wine."

Only her younger brother, Joey, looked happy. Probably because he was eighteen, and thanks to his many cousins, he'd have all the booze he wanted, plus a chance to hit on the junior bridesmaids. What wasn't to like?

"Bella, go bring a plate of cookies for us, huh?" her father called out. He was old school; the parents command, the kids hop to it. Or rather, the *female* kids. His body might be recuperating from back surgery, but he hadn't lost his army drill-sergeant tone. Post-op pain had simply bumped his demeanor from a nine to a ten on the surliness scale.

Bella got up and ruffled Joey's hair, which earned her a duck and a what-the-hell look. She pointed a finger at his face. "Behave yourself," she warned.

"Yeah, yeah," he answered, carefully smoothing his hair back into order. "Just like you taught me. Schmoozing, boozing, and some making out with the ladies."

She shot him a severe frown, but his ability to charm mutated it into a half smile. Bella could have smacked her baby brother upside the head and made him do the cookie run, because over her dead body would he become the kind of man who allowed himself to be waited on hand and foot by women, but the opportunity for her own escape was too tempting. "Sure, Pop. Ethan and I will go." She nudged her friend. "Right, Ethan?"

"Anything for you," Ethan said with his usual pleasant smile, reluctantly setting down his own glass of wine.

"Such a nice guy," her father said, throwing a hand up into the air. "How come you don't marry him?"

"She doesn't love me," Ethan said with a shrug and a wink. As they left the table, he added so only Bella could hear, "Although God knows I've tried to get you to."

She turned to face him and put a hand on his arm. "I do love you. I'll always love you. You're my best friend."

A stab of guilt gutted her. She kissed him on the cheek. The psychologist in her wondered what to do about Ethan. They'd had a thing a few years back, which had ended amiably, but every time he broke up with his current girlfriend, he kept wanting to get back together.

"My father loves you so much, he's forgotten you're Jewish," she said.

"No, he hasn't. He just knows I love you enough to convert and raise the kids Catholic."

She rolled her eyes. "Thank you for coming tonight. I'm not sure I could've faced this crowd without you." Ethan had helped her get on her feet again after the worst crisis of her life, and she owed him everything. They'd been drawn to each other because of their mutual history, but the spark just wasn't there. Now, he was still smarting from his last relationship and she was on the brink of making some major life changes, although she hadn't told her family yet—or Ethan, for that matter.

Despite her best efforts, she just hadn't met any men who were... normal. Not even halfway. Of course, living for all these years in their sleepy tourist town of Mirror Lake, Connecticut, hadn't exactly given her a potpourri of guys to choose from, even if her friends had made it their main mission in life to fix her up.

On impulse, she diverted Ethan away from the cookie table and hung a sharp right toward the bar.

"Godfather's not going to like this," Ethan said, glancing behind his shoulder at where her family sat.

"My dad can wait a little." A few minutes later, they stood near the cookie table, Ethan holding two full shot glasses.

"What is it with you I-talians?" he asked, stressing the long *I*. "I've never seen so many homemade cookies in my life."

Bella popped a *palle di neve*, a snowball cookie, into her mouth and gave a shrug. "It's what we do. People get married, we bake."

He handed her a shot glass full of whiskey and clinked his own glass to hers. "Mazel tov," he said.

"*Salute!*" she replied and chugged down the drink. It burned, hot fire sliding down her esophagus, but not enough. She wished for numbness, something one or two shots could never give her. Having half her high school class here was making her nervous. Bringing back all kinds of memories she'd rather forget. Not to mention she kept scanning the room, looking for a tall, sinfully handsome man with gypsy-black hair, olive skin, and a wicked, barely-there smile that used to make her knees go weak.

He wouldn't even look the same, she was certain of it. Nine years since she'd seen him last was a long time, and the boyish features she remembered were surely long gone. He'd probably gained thirty pounds. Gone bald. Suffered from the pox. She could only hope.

"You all right?" Ethan flashed her a concerned look. "It's like a damn reunion here. You sure you don't mind hanging around with the only Jew from Our Lady of the Lake High School, class of 2004?"

"It's all right, as long as you don't drink too much like at the last wedding and ask the DJ to play 'Hava Nagila.'"

"I'll try to behave." He set their empty glasses down on a nearby table. "By the way, you look drop-dead gorgeous in that red dress. Roman will appreciate that."

She gave him what she hoped was a stern look. "Ethan."

"I know he's here . . . somewhere. His mother brought her lab-mix rescue into the clinic the other day and told me he was coming." Ethan seemed to be watching her reaction carefully.

She had not dressed to impress Roman Spikonos. She was over him. He was long ago. However, there was nothing wrong with wanting to look your best if you just happened to run into your first love twelve years after you broke up with him, was there? And no other combination inspired confidence more than a lipstick-red dress and heels.

"Oh, hello, Bella, dear," her elderly third cousin from Delaware said, giving her a hug. "So beautiful, sweetheart. And this is your boyfriend?"

"My best friend, Helen," she said, kissing her on the cheek. "Ethan Cohen."

"That's not a typical Italian name," Helen said.

"Our name was Cohenini but we shortened it when we came to this country," Ethan said without missing a beat.

"Oh," Helen said. His reply must have satisfied her, because she turned to Bella. "You're over thirty now, aren't you?"

"No, *not quite* thirty, actually," she said.

"I thought you were thirty-one," Ethan said. An "oomph" escaped his lips, the result of a strong right elbow to his ribs.

"Wait right here. Loretta and I have a nice young man for you to meet!"

"Italian matchmaking," Ethan whispered. "A favorite pastime of your people. Second only to arranged marriages."

"Watch it, or they'll take *you* on as their next project."

"I'm telling you, Bella, I'm a great catch. Besides getting along so well, we have all the same living habits. You're organizationally challenged, and I am, too. It could be a perfect match."

"Organizationally challenged? My life is very organized!"

"Professionally, yes. But let's face it, you're messy. Someone unkind might even say you're a *slob*."

She couldn't help smiling. Ethan was the kindest person she knew. He knew almost everything about her and still loved her. She wished she could love him big and bold and awful, with the kind of love that rips your soul apart and leaves you knowing there's no one else for you in

5

the entire world. She'd felt that once, when she was very young. Except she almost hadn't survived the soul-ripping part.

As for Ethan, her inability to love him like *that* wasn't for lack of trying. If she were foolish enough to wait to find a man who had rocked her world like the one who had when she was eighteen, she'd be a white-haired old woman living in a run-down Victorian buried alive under the wardrobe items she'd failed to put away. With seven stray cats to keep her company.

She wasn't going to be that woman. Her girlish expectations had only led to tragedy. It would be far better to find a nice man—but not Ethan; he deserved better—who didn't make her feel like she had a fistful of exploding firecrackers in her stomach. She was determined to be more sensible. Lower her standards, accept someone decent if not thrilling. This was real life, right? Besides, there was that *thirty problem* right around the corner.

At least her three best friends were chomping at the bit to help her. As an early birthday present, they'd vowed to help her meet the man of her dreams, each promising to introduce her to a nice guy they knew personally. Why she'd agreed to that cockamamie scheme, she had no idea. Only her sister and her closest friends knew this—but she was thinking of leaving town for good. Joey was leaving for college next year and . . . she intended to leave, too.

One of her mentors from grad school had let her know about an opening in her practice in Chicago and asked if Bella would be interested in applying for the job. It was a great opportunity, and the icing on the cake was that it was in the city where she'd always dreamed of living.

Not that her life wasn't very fulfilling. She was a psychologist, a damn good one. She loved her job. The practice she and Maggie McShae, her best friend and business partner, had started was building nicely, and they got along well as friends and partners. Together they'd made their office on Main Street beautiful and relaxing, full of feng shui and calming influences that hopefully made clients want to unburden themselves of all their problems. It was evidence that she'd finally succeeded at something, after all those years of struggle, of feeling like she was the object of everyone's scrutiny.

Lucy, the bride, whizzed past, a vision in white, towing her groom behind her. She was six months pregnant. Bella's father hadn't said anything about *that*, short of sharing an eye roll with her long-suffering aunt. He hadn't passed any judgment, either, something he was very fond of doing. Seemed like Bella was the only one who felt his quiet disapproval drape over her like a veil, as it had for years.

And, oh, Lucy looked so happy. Glowing, really. Bella saw it in the way she looked at her new husband, how he held her as they approached the dance floor, how he gently caressed her baby bump, like Lucy and the baby were precious to him. Like they couldn't wait to get their life together started. Bella couldn't help but feel her stomach seize up into a ball of knots.

Twelve years ago, there'd been no wedding for her, only a pregnancy. In high school, no less, and she'd lost the baby at nearly five months. The town had long since stopped talking about it, but bits of it persisted in sideways glances from judgmental old ladies, and in the awkwardness that lingered on the edges of her conversations with people who didn't know her very well.

That incident had shaped her, forged her character, taught her who her real friends were. It had toughened her and made her extra guarded with her heart. Another reason to leave. Here in Mirror Lake, she'd never quite escaped the label of *that girl who got pregnant in high school, poor thing*. Just once, she yearned to know what it was like not to have to steel herself against people's curious questions, or their sympathy, or any preconceived notions they might harbor. She wanted to know what it felt like to be *normal*, unblemished by past mistakes. Here, her slate would never quite be erased clean. And that was the biggest reason of all to get out.

"Bella, hi," someone called from behind her. She turned to find Christy Abrams, one of her old soccer teammates from high school, standing in the bar line. "You look great," she said.

Christy still had a sunny, welcoming smile. She now wore her strawberry-blonde hair in a chic chin-length cut with highlights. Cute. "You, too."

"Well," she said, smoothing down her dress over her hips, "never quite lost that baby weight after the last one. Dave and I have three now, two boys and a girl. Here're their pics."

Christy flipped through her phone, displaying shots of freckled kids with various gaps in their wide grins. "They're beautiful," Bella said, and she meant it. A pang hit her, an old one. The baby she lost would have been almost twelve years old now. Twelve! Still hard to think about, but maybe tonight was just stirring up those old painful memories.

"We live in Jersey. Dave runs an architectural firm, and I do the accounting. I heard you've got an office downtown. Got any kids?"

"No, no kids." She was careful to keep the smile on her face from turning melancholic.

"Oh, I'm sorry. I didn't mean to—"

"Hey, no, it's all right. Really. Oh, you're next," she said, pointing to the space in front of her in the bar line. "So nice to see you."

"Great to see you, too. I'm sitting by a bunch of the other soccer girls—Janet, Corinne, Stacey—come on over, okay?"

"Oh, thanks. Sure. Sounds fun."

It didn't sound like fun. She hadn't seen them in light-years. After she'd gotten pregnant senior year, she'd had to leave her Catholic high school, and they'd all stopped being her friends. Not that she blamed them or even held any grudges after all these years . . . it was just awkward for everyone. And for a girl who'd done everything perfectly up until then, it had been a hard blow.

A blow that was long past. She'd gotten through it, all of it, and had come out on top. She had nothing to be ashamed of. She was successful now. A great education, a great job. But she was lonely. She wanted to find that special someone, have a family and a yard and a dog. Did it only seem that all of her classmates had three kids and counting?

Helen was back, towing Cousin Loretta. "Come this way," she commanded. Before Bella could protest, the two women had steered her away from Ethan, who signaled to her that he was going to talk to a nearby group of old friends, and toward a table where a man in a green tweed sports coat waited. He smiled as they approached. With horror, she realized it was Les Vanderhaven. The guy who'd had a crush on her all through high school. He'd settled a couple towns over and she rarely saw him, except that he did her family's taxes and she knew from her aunt that he still occasionally asked about her. She must've stopped moving because the women actually nudged her forward.

"Les, dear, she's ba-ack," Helen said in a singsong voice.

He looked a lot older than thirty, and not just because of his receding hairline. His middle was paunchy and he looked so . . . pale. Belly-of-a-fish-washed-up-on-the-beach pale. Like he never saw the light of day in that CPA office of his.

Ew. Bad visual.

"Hey, Les, great to see you," she said, giving him a hug. He'd always struck her as being a little hapless, and that impression still held.

"Bella, hi! God, you look great! Your aunt told me you were coming tonight and that you weren't dating anyone. Wow, you look fabulous!" He raked her up and down in a way that told her he was still interested, and that gave her the creeps.

Les stood. "Hey, how about we get a drink?"

She was about to say no when he grabbed her arm and started walking. "You know I've been divorced for a year," he said, pushing up his glasses. "Melanie left me for a tax attorney. Except they embezzled some funds from the nonprofit they worked for and they're both serving time. Go figure."

Hence her nickname about town, Felony Melanie. "I'm sorry about that, Les." She was sorry, but she'd also had about enough. She pulled out her cell and pretended to check it. "Oh, Les, I've got to take this call. Sorry I can't get a drink with you. Take care, now!" She left him and exited out one of the ballroom doors, running into Gina Maria coming back from the ladies' room. "Hey, G, would you mind getting Dad that cookie plate? I'm going to get some air."

"Sure. Okay. God, my shaper undergarment is killing me. If it wouldn't expose all the wedding guests to my boobs, I'd rip it off and throw it in the trash can."

"You look pretty, Gina."

"I'm never going to get this pregnancy weight off."

"That's what Christy Abrams just said, too. It's only been three months. You're a new mom. Give yourself a break."

Gina made a dismissive gesture with her hand and looked at her hard, in the way only an older sister can. "You all right?" After Bella reassured her sister that she was fine, just on the lam from Les, Gina lowered her voice and steered her aside. "Hey, I just wanted to tell you that Roman's here somewhere. There's a bunch of single women in the bathroom talking about how gorgeous he is. Just so you know."

Bella forced a smile to show her how little it mattered. Really. "I always knew we'd run into each other eventually. I can handle it." Of course she could. She was mature now, tough, strong. On the other hand, maybe she'd just step outside now and never return. "I'll be back in a little while, okay?"

"Manny and I are looking to get out of here as soon as Dad's had enough. We'll drop him off at home and get him settled."

"I can do that. Really. You two enjoy date night."

"You sure?"

She couldn't be more positive. "Dad wants to leave early anyway. He keeps obsessing about how there's too much work back at home and he can't let the Nicolettis get ahead of us. And I'm more than happy to cut out of here early." Their family business, D'Angelos' Nursery and Garden Center, was one of two that served Mirror Lake and surrounding communities. The rivalry between their center and the one owned by the Nicoletti family was legendary, and it was fueled by an old feud that had originated in Italy and traveled across the Atlantic to perpetuate in the descendants of both families.

But for now, Bella needed to escape. And she'd better hurry, too, because she could hear Les calling her name. She snaked through the back hallway, past the restrooms and the kitchen. Fortunately, she'd worked here, at Gianno's Party Center, as had her siblings in their youth, and she knew the back corridors better than anyone. Walking quickly down one that led to the back parking lot, she exited out the heavy metal door, which was propped open by a wooden dowel.

She turned left out the door, planning to head to a bench she'd spied earlier on her way in from the parking lot. The early-September evening held just a touch of coolness, a faint harbinger of the change of season to come. Rounding the corner of the building, she bumped smack into a solid wall . . . but not one made of brick. More like rock-hard muscle, approximately six feet two of it. One that wore a dark-gray suit that clung closely to his broad shoulders in all the right places and smelled amazingly spicy and good. She looked up—way up—into the dark, dangerous eyes of the man she'd once loved passionately, the very same one her father had wanted to murder just as badly. And probably still did.

"Oh. Sorry," she managed. Her throat seemed to suddenly constrict to the size of a pin. She was lucky to talk at all because taking in air suddenly got complicated.

Oh, she'd had ages to rehearse this moment. Which she'd done countless times, usually on the sleepless nights of those early years, too numerous to count, when the dull, constant ache for him had kept her tossing and turning until dawn.

But she'd survived. She'd accepted. Life had moved on, and she had, too.

"Bella," Roman Spikonos said quietly, his voice sounding as smooth as Crown Royal, but with a gravelly edge, deeper than what she remembered. She'd always joked he had a cowboy voice, which was silly because he was as Connecticut Yankee as she was.

Backlit by the buzzing fluorescent bulb that hung off the brick building, his features looked hard. It wasn't just the steely square jawline, the unsmiling, too-full lips, or the pitch-black hair that seemed to gleam almost moonlight blue in the unforgiving light. Or that nose, as straight and classically Greek as Michelangelo's *David*. At first she could swear his coffee-brown eyes widened with surprise, but he quickly snapped them back to neutral. Yep, those eyes, which had always had the capability to go soft with feeling—they were his most impenetrable feature.

His hair used to be longish, curling recklessly, but it was now cropped in close, thick layers. In his suit, he could've been mistaken for a tycoon. Gorgeous, but not the man she'd known so long ago.

He was holding a drink. The impact of their collision had caused it to slosh over the sides. Her first impulse was to wrench it from his fingers and gulp it down fast, but the civilized part of her somehow held back.

Roman's gaze lit on her face. Examined her intently. Seconds or minutes passed, she didn't know. Everything seemed to stop, even her breathing.

She'd run into him once before, just once in all this time. They'd both been with other people, and it had been awkward. It had taken her a long time to forget their last meeting, hell, to forget *him*, but she had. They were adults, and the past was the past. No reason they couldn't be cordial.

Right. But thank God she'd worn the red dress.

Les's voice echoing down the hallway stunned her back to reality. "Bella? You back here?"

Roman frowned. Glanced from the door to her. "I—came out for some air," she whispered, edging quickly away from the building. She did need air, but not because Les was chasing her down. More like because the impact of seeing Roman was the equivalent of being hit in the chest with a baby elephant. Surprisingly, Roman followed her as she hightailed it to the parking lot. Without hesitation, he grabbed her hand and pulled her down between two parked cars.

His hand was large, encompassing, his grip no-nonsense and firm. In control, like the rest of him. It was nowhere near sensual, like a lover's clasp, yet she felt the heat of him down to her bones, and it set off that same old ache, familiar yet unwanted. When he tugged it away, she almost breathed a sigh of relief. She eyed the way his jacket pulled over the muscles of his broad back, the fit of his pants on his fine ass, the contour of his leg muscles as he squatted. Memory had served her poorly. The man was a thousand times hotter than he'd been in high school, and he'd topped the hotness charts back then.

Les called out again. She couldn't see him, but she imagined him standing there, pushing up his glasses, surveying the parking lot. Bella, squatting between a Chevy and a Toyota, felt like she really was in high school again. Funny how not even five minutes in Roman's presence could do that to her. As soon as Les went back inside, pulling the heavy door shut with a scrape against concrete and then a clang of metal against metal, she stood up and summoned her maturity. "Sorry. I was just standing around talking when . . ."

"Lester accosted you?"

"It was more like my cousins led me right to the lion's mouth, but same effect."

He grinned. "Some things never change."

"He couldn't still have a thing for me."

"Why not? You're still beautiful." He took a sip of his drink and offered it to her.

Too intimate a gesture. It made her blush. Thank God it was dark. "What is it?" she asked, looking at the amber liquid. Did it matter?

"Seven and seven."

An old-fashioned drink. That suited him. He'd never cared about being in fashion or following the crowd. Despite her better judgment, she found herself reaching for the glass. Putting her lips to the cool edge. *Where his had been,* that perverse voice inside her said, but she shut it up by taking several gulps, even though she'd meant to take only a sip. The ice was mostly melted and it was a bit watery, but it did the trick. "Thanks," she said, running her fingers over her lips and handing it back.

"No problem." He was still eyeing her, but his face was a brick wall. No emotion got through. No sadness, no anger, no . . . anything.

A muscle in his jaw ticked. A frown drew his dark brows into a V. Even his posture reeked of tension. Suddenly, she knew what was wrong. At least, she used to be able to read him so easily. If she still possessed that ability, she was willing to bet the farm that he was still angry. After all these years.

He had reason to be. He'd wanted to marry her at eighteen—marry her!—and she'd told him no. She'd lied to get him to leave. It was the hardest thing she'd ever done.

But she'd *wanted* to marry him. Lord, how she'd wanted to. The old, familiar pain still sliced at her, threatening to drop her to her knees.

No. Not after all this time. Everything had turned out as it should have. She'd finished college *and* grad school *and* somehow got her baby brother raised up to eighteen in mostly one piece. Not shabby accomplishments, if she could say so herself.

She'd resolved her own anger a long time ago. After all, what had happened between them had upended her family. Forced her out of high school. Getting pregnant had caused adulthood to punch her in the gut with a fierceness she'd never experienced before or since. But none of it was any more his fault than her own.

Had his life been the same? Somehow, she doubted it. He'd gotten away from here, went off to lead the life of his choosing. And never looked back.

But no, she wasn't angry. Most of the ache had passed. If anything, she was sad at the losses, the choices she'd had to make, the innocence she'd lost.

Last she'd heard he'd been working in a craft beer brewery in upstate New York. He was probably just here visiting his mother. No wedding ring, but that didn't surprise her. The man was gorgeous, with Hollywood looks, and he was in the prime of his life. From what she'd heard, he changed girlfriends like women do shoes.

"So, you're doing well?" she asked. That seemed a neutral way to start.

"Own my own business. You?"

"I'm a psychologist."

He raised a brow, like that had surprised him. Had he really not cared to know what had happened to her over the years? With his mom in town and being a psychologist herself, a colleague, that was hard to believe. "You like it?"

"Very much."

"Sorry to hear about your father. His back."

"He's doing better. I moved back home to help out for the next couple of weeks. Fall's a busy time at the garden center, you know. Fall activities, pumpkins to harvest from the back fields, that kind of thing."

He nodded. "Nice of you."

"Sorry to hear about your granddad." Both his grandparents, who owned Apple of My Eye Orchards, the business right next to her family's, had passed away—his grandmother two years ago and his grandfather last winter. She thought he'd say something like he was selling the orchards, but he just nodded his head and went silent.

So much for chitchat. Careful, polite, and sugary, but underneath lurked a trove of sadness and hurt. Like frosting over burnt cupcakes. She should have stuck it out with Les.

"Well, I should be getting back." She peeked over the hood of one of the cars. "Looks like the coast is clear now."

He didn't say anything, but there he went, looking at her again with those eyes, judging or assessing her, she couldn't tell. With his gaze came an awareness, way too electrifying, that she struggled to ignore. Accompanied by blood surging in her ears, dizziness, and tingling, worse in some places than others. Oh Lord, she couldn't remember any of the specific reasons she'd fallen so hard for him in the first place, but her body sure did, and it was letting her know, loud and clear. Either that or she had a neurological condition. "Want to get a cup of coffee?" he asked suddenly.

What the . . . ? She paused. For too long, probably. Shock and indecision warred. It would be so tempting to go off with him, sit and talk like old times. She'd wondered time and again how he'd fared. People would see them leave together, and that would feed the gossip mills for at least a month, but she didn't really care about that. Still, her family would wonder where she'd gone. And hadn't that always been the choice? Her family or him?

She had much to say. So many years of feelings she could never let out, questions that were never answered. Now a rare chance to speak her piece had just dropped into her lap.

She'd never been one of those people who always had a tart reply ready on her tongue. Maybe she'd imagined this meeting many times, but words and thoughts evaded her.

"Look—" he said.

The door opened once again. "Arabel-la," Les's voice called out in a singsong tone. "I know you're back here. And I brought some wi-ine."

Going back to the wedding suddenly held the appeal of clotted milk. To hell with her purse, her family, and all the friends she hadn't spoken to in years. For once, maybe she could make an unexpected choice. She of all people understood that her inability to move on might possibly have a lot to do with the devastatingly handsome man facing her right now. Maybe it was time to confront the past, confront *him*, and get some things out on the table once and for all. She faced Roman, whose gaze still possessed a searing intensity that raised gooseflesh on her arms. "You know, I think I will take you up on that coffee, after all."

CHAPTER 2

Roman led Bella to his gleaming black pickup and opened the passenger door. She swung up into the cab, her red dress swirling around her, the parking lot lights catching the reflection off all that glorious black hair. Those pretty legs. His breath hitched and it literally pained him to breathe.

Seeing her again, smelling her flowery fragrance, brought way-too-distant memories catapulting back, and that was not a comfortable or comforting feeling. Plus she herself looked as skittish as a jackrabbit, ready to bolt at any minute. Yet he couldn't help the feeling that kicked up inside of him, excitement that he was with her for the first time in twelve years. Anticipation. *Hope.* Irrational, yes, and illogical, but he couldn't seem to help it.

Offering to get coffee with her had been an even dumber idea than going to that wedding. But then, he'd always seemed to put his foot in it ass deep where she was concerned.

Was he still trying to come to her rescue, even knowing she no longer needed it? It was a trait he couldn't seem to help. He found himself wanting to get her to smile. Hear her laugh after all these years. They'd had some good times. Really good times.

Things were different now. He'd loved her once, a lot. And she clearly hadn't felt the same. His mission now was to find a way to make peace with her, since he was here to stay, although he was pretty sure she didn't know that yet. Then he'd tuck her back into his memory, where she belonged. Locked down tight. Maybe returning was a good thing. Maybe it would flush her out of his mind for good.

He felt a sense of innate danger, an instinctive pull in his gut, which was ridiculous. Of course their relationship had been an intense experience. It had been *high school*. What wasn't intense back then?

She didn't say anything, but there she went, looking at him again with those eyes. Skeptical, guarded. He'd been watching her all night, he'd admit that, because she'd somehow become even more beautiful in the years since he'd seen her and he simply couldn't help himself. Apparently what was left of his eighteen-year-old self just hadn't caught up to reality yet. Hadn't remembered the heartbreak, or the hurts that were just too great to ever get over.

"Do you mind the windows down?" he asked, trying to fill the silence. "Don't want your hair to get mussed or anything."

"Oh no. I love the windows down." She always had. She'd never cared about mussing up her hair, and he'd loved that about her. Nor was she ever one to pick over a couple of lettuce leaves like so many of the women he'd dated. For being as slender as she was, she could always eat him under the table, too, and he wondered if that was still the case. She'd always had a zestful appetite for life.

With her, it was always superlatives. *I love this chocolate cake! Will you take a look at those stars tonight! I had the most amazing day!* She had a way of pulling him into her excitement, too. For a kid like him who came from such tragic circumstances—two alcoholic parents and siblings he'd been separated from at the age of eight—she made even the grayest day seem special in some crazy way.

"How's your family?" she asked. A neutral topic she'd picked on purpose, no doubt.

"My mom's good. Yours?"

"Well, Dad's . . . Dad. He hasn't changed much." She might have sounded sad or irritated but she quickly skirted over the topic of her father. "Gina's been married eleven years, has a three-month-old, and Joey's a senior this year."

Roman wasn't looking forward to telling Vito that he'd inherited the orchards next door. The orchards his grandparents had farmed for the past fifty years. Now was his chance to do them proud but put his own spin on things, something for which he'd been preparing for the past eight years, ever since he'd left the army. He wanted Bella to know his plans first, before he told anyone else. Didn't he owe her that much?

He found himself rolling the truck to a stop. It was a dead-quiet back road, old State Route 1, nothing around but cornfields and darkness. It smelled like loamy earth, and more like summer than the upcoming fall, the scent of coming rain heavy in the air.

"Why are you stopping?" she asked. "Are you out of gas?"

He might have picked up the slightest edge of panic. A you-aren't-a-serial-killer-are-you kind of tone. "No," he said, drumming his fingers on the steering wheel. "More like out of patience. I can't stand all of this small talk." He turned off the ignition and faced her. "Don't look so outraged. We used to be able to talk. We used to be able to tell each other anything." He needed to try and clear the air. Plus he needed to tell her that he was back for good.

She snorted, still eyeing him warily. "Oh, come on, now. Did you expect me to pick up where we left off twelve years ago? Neither of us wants to go back there."

"I want to know how you're doing. How you're *really* doing. I want us to make peace with each other. To be friends." He remembered a time when she'd laughed a lot. Now she seemed so . . . serious. It made him sad. "Look—" he began.

"No, Roman," she interrupted. "Don't 'look' me. I'm having a hard time understanding why you're suddenly so anxious to pull the friend card."

"You say that like you're blaming me for leaving town. As I recall, you didn't exactly care if the door hit my ass on the way out."

"You offered me marriage out of guilt. I didn't want you to *have* to marry me. I wanted you to stick around because that's what people do when they love somebody."

He'd asked her to marry her because he'd *loved* her, but there was no way he was saying that now. "Yeah, well, people who love other people don't tell someone loud and clear to get lost."

"My father threatened to kill you. What else was I supposed to do?"

He loosened his tie with a fierce tug and unbuttoned his collar. She looked pissed as hell, those elegant brows drawn. *Livid*.

Suddenly, their entire relationship came back in one word. *Tempestuous*. They were both passionate people. Neither one of them had ever been good at holding back their emotions.

She shook her head adamantly and folded her arms, indicating the discussion was closed. "You don't know anything about anything. I think you'd better take me back to the wedding."

"Fine." He tried his best to keep the irritation out of his voice as he turned the key, put the truck in gear, and headed down the country road. "Hope your buddy Les has moved on to someone else."

She shrugged. "I left Ethan by himself. I need to get back anyway."

He bristled at the name of his former friend and basketball teammate. He knew they'd had a thing a few years back. Hell, maybe they still did if they'd come to the wedding together. "He's your date?"

"What's wrong with that?"

"Not a thing." *Everything*. Ethan was wrong for her in every way possible. He was sedate and affable, pleasant enough, but where was the passion? Bella needed a man who brought out her spirit, not one who would subdue it. Roman couldn't believe she would date Ethan . . . sleep with him. The thought made him wince.

His jaw felt tight enough to split a nail. Plus he had a massive headache, thanks to the hot-blooded Italian chick whose temper had not cooled in a dozen years. He drove straight down the road, knowing there was a turnaround ahead.

Suddenly something four-legged and hairy flashed in front of the truck. Fox? Coyote? He swerved and braked, barely missing the creature, a move that sent the truck careening off the shoulder and bumping into a shallow ditch.

Clouds of dust settled. With the motor cut, the early-September night was all crickets.

"Shit," he said, but thought a lot worse. "Are you all right?"

He looked over to reassure himself that she was. At the same time, she pointed out the windshield, accidentally poking him in the eye.

"Ow," he exclaimed from the sudden stab of pain. His vision fogged with tears.

"Oh my God, I'm sorry," she said, leaning over to help him.

"Geez! You may be mad at me, but do you have to stab me in the eye?" He blinked a few times, keeping her at arm's length. Somehow he felt safer with some distance between them.

"It looked like a dog," she said, which told him her priorities. "He ran into that field over there. Are you sure you're okay?"

"Don't worry, I still have a second eye." He held a hand in front of one eye and then the other. Yep, both still working.

"I didn't poke you that hard," she said. "Did I?"

His next expletive wasn't so PG.

"What's wrong?"

"I think I lost my contact."

"It *is* a dog," she said, looking out his window. "He's just sitting there. I think something's wrong with his leg."

He blinked and squinted to see. "It looks like a limping raccoon."

Bella rolled her eyes; he saw *that* clearly. "Now I'm really worried," she said. "That just confirmed you're blind."

"I think the contact might have fallen on the floor."

Bella bent down to look. "Wow, it's really immaculate down here. What, do you vacuum every day?"

"No, I just like to keep my things clean."

"There's not even a piece of fuzz anywhere. You're still just as neat as ever."

"Some of us see that as a virtue, not a negative. At least I never lost my cross-country jersey right before the district meet among the mountain of clothes on my bedroom floor."

She popped her head up. "That was one time. And it didn't even impact you."

"Maybe you don't remember I was the one who drove you all the way to Crooked Creek so you could borrow one from that kooky girl who graduated the year before us."

"She was *nice*, Roman. She helped me out in a pinch."

"She had to take it out of her framed T-shirt box. We practically had to pry it out of her hands."

The sudden sound of Bella's laughter was snorty. Sonorous. Unexpected. Exactly as he remembered. It made him laugh, too.

"That *was* pretty funny," he said.

"Yeah. It was," she said. He would've given anything to see the expression on her face, but everything was too blurry.

"Aw, the dog is walking off." He heard the click of the door handle as she released it.

"Before you go running off after a stray animal, will you check my shirt? Besides, you really shouldn't go out there by yourself."

She threw her hands up in the air. Of course. Never a half reaction with her. "I wasn't about to leave you without your stupid contact. You're just as bossy as ever."

"I'm not being bossy. I'm looking out for your welfare."

"Like you did twelve years ago?"

Whoa. The silence that followed that zinger was long and thick. She'd let him have it, he'd give her that one.

Baggage. They had so much of it, airfare would cost a fortune.

"I—I'm sorry," she said before he could muster a response. "That was uncalled for." She pulled out her phone, turned on its flashlight app, and started running the light over his shirtfront.

"Thanks," he managed. He just needed to find his contact so he could get them the hell out of here.

"Could it be in your eye?" She turned the light on his face, temporarily blinding him.

"Hey!" he said, tilting the light away.

"Let me look and make sure it's not in there," she insisted.

He relented with a sigh. "I don't think it is, but okay." And he had another problem. She was very close, so much so that he could smell her perfume, and it was sweet and wonderful enough to make him think of nuzzling her lovely neck. That would certainly distract him from his blindness.

She knelt on the seat and spread his eyelids apart with her fingers, commanding him to look up, look down, while his eyes teared up again from the brightness. Every nerve ending came alert from her touch. Even though it was no-nonsense, not exactly caring and gentle, but definitely competent, warm, and soft. It threw him off his game. Worse, it made him *remember.*

Through his tears, he snuck a good look at her, intent as she was on her task. She had beautiful eyes, big and wide; they were a rich mahogany color, darker than his own. God, that artist with a bold hand, had given her striking features, strong brows and cheekbones, and full lips perfect for kissing.

"I don't think it's in there," she finally announced.

He breathed out in relief, except she wasn't done with him yet. She ran her hands over his shirt. Her fingers were on him, flicking over the material. He could feel the heat from her hands. As she bent her head, silky curls hit his face, his neck, and he couldn't help closing his eyes and inhaling the fragrance of her hair. More subtle and sophisticated than the in-your-face berry scent of her teen years but amazing nonetheless. Dammit, how could she still affect him after all this time? Even when he was so pissed off?

"It's not on your shirt. I'm checking your pants."

Oh, that would be a very bad idea right about now. "Maybe you're right," he said quickly. "We—we should just go get the dog." Oh, bollocks. Did he really just say that? But what other choice did he have? He couldn't have her groping around down there. She might just discover some—er—developments that he definitely did not want her discovering.

Outside, they heard a whine. Thank the Lord, because that made Bella finally take her hands off him and look out the passenger window. "Hi, sweetie," she crooned. "You're okay. I'm coming right out." She turned back to Roman. "He's crying like he's hurt," she said. "Do you think the truck—"

"No. I missed him. But he seemed to be favoring a leg when he ran across the road. He's probably hurt."

"We've got to find this contact." She bent her head low and ran the light over his pants legs. Fortunately she started down by his knees.

He had to work hard to distract himself from her touch before she saw the visual result herself. "Do you have to do that?" he asked, swallowing hard.

"Do what?" She paused and looked up at him, but he was too blind to read her expression clearly. He could guess it was wary, though. "Oh, for God's sake," she said. "Do you really have that inflated of an ego that you think I'm trying to—"

Of course he didn't think she was trying to hit on him, but he had to distract her somehow. He put his hands up in defense. "I'm just calling it like I see it."

"If you actually think I'd try and—"

Suddenly he groaned, but not from the fact that she was touching him. Red-and-blue lights were flashing in his rearview mirror. Could this night get any worse?

"Oh, for crying out loud, Roman—" Her head was still low, and suddenly he felt a sudden pinch on his thigh. "Wait, I think I found it."

"Forget the contact, Bella. Now." He reached down and tugged her upward.

"What's going on in here?" a deep voice asked.

"Got it!" Bella said, popping her head up. The look on the face of Mirror Lake's finest, Tom Rushford, the police chief, was priceless, as he stood outside Roman's door with a flashlight.

"Well, I'll be," the cop said on a breath. He was more than a little speechless.

"It's not what you think," they both said in unison.

"Wow, after all these years," Tom said. "Who knew?"

"We are *not* together," she said, pushing off from Roman's thighs and sitting up. "And if you start that rumor I'll—I'll make Joey contaminate your next mulch load with earwigs."

"What have you got to say for yourself, Roman?" Roman could swear Tom was biting the insides of his cheeks to keep from laughing.

"A mangy-looking dog ran in front of the car, and I hit the brakes. She poked me in the eye and my contact dislodged."

"Oh, okay." Tom let his flashlight hover over Roman's lap, which Roman quickly covered up with his hands.

"All zipped up. See?" Roman said hastily.

"All righty," Tom said, checking his phone. "Well, I'd love to help you two out with that dog, but I'm getting another call. You two behave yourselves, you hear?" He gave a knowing wink and left.

As soon as Tom drove off, Bella was out the door. Roman reinserted his contact and hopped out of the truck.

Right around then, rain pelted down in big, fat, unrelenting droplets. If someone would've told him just an hour earlier that he'd be ruining his suit running around some farmer's field in the rain watching Arabella D'Angelo try to coax some skittish wounded dog to come home with them, he never would've believed it.

"Don't get too close to it," he said. "Maybe it doesn't have its shots."

She responded by taking off her heels and edging closer to the dog.

"Fine. Ignore me. You always did what you wanted anyway," he mumbled.

"I heard that," she called over her shoulder. He couldn't help smiling a little.

She crooned sweetly to the dog, who was sitting under a big oak. "Such a nice puppy. It's okay, buddy. We're going to take care of you."

He practically snorted. "We" was definitely not going to translate into "him." She was welcome to do what she liked, but all he wanted to do was get the hell out of here. "It's really raining now, Bella. Let's call it a night."

She turned around, her curls misty from the rain. "Give me another minute. Go wait in the truck if you want." She kept sneaking closer to the dog, creeping through the low grass. She'd always been tenacious. Clearly that trait had grown a hundredfold in the years they'd been apart.

Finally, she stood two feet away from the animal, who emitted a low whine. Wet, he looked even more mangy than before. Nothing but a tangled mass of dark hair, brown or black, he couldn't tell. Skinny, basically pathetic. Just the project of compassion she loved to take on. It wasn't surprising she'd become a psychologist.

As she inched closer, the animal got up, although with difficulty. The skittish thing was getting ready to bolt, Roman sensed it. Maybe it was because he himself had once been alone and afraid, a mangy kid himself. Not that that experience would necessarily translate into having any kind of camaraderie with a wounded dog. Suddenly, the sky broke loose, the rain changing from drops to soaking sheets.

Out of patience, Roman flung himself forward and grabbed the animal, one arm around the neck, another around the belly. The animal let out a yelp, and he feared it was going to take a chunk out of his hand, but it was out of steam. Against his chest, the animal was listless, trembling. Cold.

The trembling part got him. Someone had made this creature fear him, just as his parents had with their own children. "I got you, now," he found himself saying. "Just stay still."

Bella walked over and shone her light on the dog, oblivious to the fact that her clothes and hair were ruined. "His left leg is all messed up." Sure enough, there was a clot of blood and a gaping wound. "He needs the vet hospital."

Roman shot her a look. "Of course he does." Because what else could possibly make this night more hellish?

She rolled her eyes. "Look, just drop us off and I'll find a way home. Then you're off the hook. Okay?"

Off the hook. Like she thought he'd been after he left her that day she'd come home from the hospital.

But she'd thought wrong. He'd never been off the hook as far as she was concerned. How shallow did she think he was?

He carried the dog, who probably weighed forty pounds tops, toward the truck, planning to toss an old blanket that he kept in the back over the bed.

"I'll hold him on my lap," she said, wiping wet hair from her eyes. Her dress was soaked, her makeup running. Her hair was drenched too, but she had too much for it to ever go completely flat.

"No way." That ball of mud in his immaculate cab?

"It's really raining, Roman. And the poor thing is shivering something fierce." She trained those big brown Italian eyes of hers on him, her how-could-you glance accusatory.

He blew out a sigh. "Fine. Get in." She hopped in, tossing her shoes to the floor and making a futile gesture to squeeze out her hair. At any other time, he'd be thinking how her muddy feet were ruining his nice carpet, and how she and the dog were dripping all over his upgraded leather upholstery. But those things barely crossed his mind. How could he possibly think that this soaking wet, tangled mess of a woman was beautiful? After all these years?

An old saying his grandpa used to say came to mind and almost made him laugh. *I wouldn't kick her out of bed for eating crackers.*

He put the hairy bundle in her lap, then reached around and pulled the blanket out and tossed it over the shivering dog and her. Then he shut the door and walked around to start his truck.

CHAPTER 3

"It's all right, sweetheart," Bella crooned to the dog as they sat in the waiting room of the animal hospital, which was located about ten minutes outside of town. She was trying to use the words to calm herself down, too. Roman being back in town was bad enough. But having a run-in with a hurt dog in a muddy field with him and ending up here instead of back at the wedding was something else entirely.

The hospital was staffed by both of the town vets—Ethan and his senior partner, Cole Hansen, who was just a few years older than Ethan. The vets from Crooked Creek, the next town over, provided coverage, too, and one of them was on call tonight.

Bella used Roman's phone to call Ethan to let him know why she'd gone AWOL and to send word to Gina to take their father and Aunt Fran home. She felt bad shirking her duties, especially when Gina was having a rare night out with Manny. Ethan hadn't said much, but she could hear an edge in his voice when she'd told him about Roman.

There had always been animosity between him and Roman, ever since Bella began dating Roman in high school, and it had only worsened in the years after Roman left. Roman sat there pretending to flip through magazines while she was on the phone, but she could see his brows lift in judgment. She considered telling him there was nothing between Ethan and her, but why should she? She didn't have to justify her life to him. The life he'd been completely absent from while Ethan had not.

She finished her call and took a seat next to Roman on the vinyl-covered bench, as far away from him as possible without being too obvious. He sat there, his long legs stretched out, his pants dripping water onto the tile floor. The years had made him taller and more muscular, traits she tried hard not to notice. She shivered a little in the air conditioning and crossed her arms for warmth, but she was soaked to the bone. A big glob of mud ran down her leg. The hem of her dress had caught on something in the field and torn. They looked like they'd just come straight out of an episode of *Storm Chasers*.

At one time, they would have laughed hysterically at such a comedy of errors. But the tension was too heavy and thick for either of them to crack a smile. So she focused all her attention on the poor animal, who needed it anyway. It was a lot easier to comfort a beast who didn't talk back. The other beast was way too vocal.

Suddenly she felt a heaviness drape around her shoulders. Roman's suit jacket. It was warm, and dry on the inside at least, and smelled spicy, like him. She looked over at him in surprise. He was sitting there, his long fingers flipping up his cuffs, exposing the muscle of his tan, lean arms. She caught his eye. "Thank you," she said.

"No problem." He gave her the briefest glance, then kept fiddling with the cuffs, trying to make them perfect, no doubt. Order had always been his way of dealing with the messiness of life. He hadn't changed a bit. Neither had his way of looking out for her, of being considerate, or his ability to get to her with the smallest act of kindness. But she tried to push all that out of her head.

"You know, you didn't have to do this," she said. "Stay, I mean. Ethan offered to swing by and take me home. You should go." That was actually a little fib. She'd felt bad enough explaining to Ethan why she'd abandoned him at the wedding and wasn't coming back. He'd kindly offered to get her purse and even wanted to drive out to the hospital, but she'd told him no. That was all she needed, to have him and Roman butting heads.

"Look," Roman said, "you may not think I have staying power or whatever it is you believe about me. But I'm here and I'm not leaving. Got that?"

"You don't need to prove a point." Which seemed to be exactly what he was doing. He didn't care about the dog. He was just being his usual stubborn self. Trying to win his side of the argument.

"I'm not proving anything. I'm just going to stay here with you until this thing is settled."

She stopped arguing, because he had a history of digging in his heels just as hard as she could. "Look, maybe this all happened tonight for a reason. Maybe it's the universe telling us to make peace."

He snorted. Oh, the man was impossible.

She threw up her arms. "Fine. At least I tried."

His turn to sigh. He straightened up, pulled his legs in, and looked straight at her. God, he had gorgeous eyes. That Greek heritage. Big, chocolate-brown eyes. A woman could get lost, what with all that sexy brooding going on in there . . . and for a second she thought she detected a softening in them.

"What happened between us was a long time ago, Bella. I don't harbor any ill will toward you. It was unfortunate, but it's in the past. We were just kids, and we both grew up. End of story."

"You're so—different." His words sounded matter-of-fact. Emotionless. Somehow he seemed to have compartmentalized all that feeling into a couple of tiny, flat sentences, without a hint of pain or sadness. It was . . . odd. There was even a psychological word for it. *Denial.*

"Of course I'm different. I'm twelve years older than that boy who left here that spring night."

The impulse to say *I'm sorry* rose to her throat. For all the pain they both went through. She'd gotten pregnant over Christmas of senior year and had miscarried at five months, just before graduation. Not only did she have to leave school, she'd had to let her scholarships and her spot at her top college go. And worse than everything else, she'd had to let *him* go.

She still remembered the stricken look on his face the day he left. Oh, she *was* sorry, for that and for all of the anger and upset it had caused—not just in their families but between them, too.

If only their baby had lived, things could have been different. Her father would have had to accept Roman, and eventually, everything would have settled down. The pregnancy had been an accident, one that had altered the entire trajectory of her life, but she wasn't sorry for that. She'd *wanted* that baby. As much as she'd wanted him.

There was no way she could tell him any of her thoughts. Not now and not here, in a veterinary waiting room that smelled vaguely of Pine-Sol and wet dog. Or was that wet-dog smell coming from her? Instead, she kept it brief and painless. "Like you said, we grew up."

Roman looked about to say something, but the door opened. Ethan himself walked in, wearing scrubs. He took in the two of them together. Their state of dishevelment. Roman's coat around her shoulders, which she promptly dropped.

Ethan gave her a cool nod. "You came in yourself," she said. He wasn't on call. He didn't have to be here.

"Of course I did. I brought your purse. I hope you don't mind, but I fished your keys out and drove your car here."

Ethan turned to Roman. "Glad to see you're back in town." He didn't offer a handshake, just a businesslike nod. He talked mostly to her. "So, okay, about your dog. Looks like somebody did something bad to her. That injury on her right leg is a burn. We cleaned it up and bandaged it. She's malnourished and she's got fleas. And she's dehydrated. My sense is she got dropped off along the highway somewhere and was left to fend for herself. We're going to keep her overnight and give her fluids and antibiotics."

Bella's eyes teared up for the poor animal. "Well, on a positive note, at least we know she's nobody's dog." Out of the corner of her eye, she could see Roman grimace, on behalf of the dog or because he thought she was being a sucker for a sob story, she didn't know.

"If you want," Ethan said, "I could walk you back and let you see her." She got up to follow him, but he waited for her at the doorway to the animal holding area and motioned for her to go ahead of him.

The dog was sleeping in the bottom of one of a handful of crates lined up side by side along one wall of the white-tiled room. Down the line of crates, which was a little reminiscent of a row of jail cells, there was a German shepherd with an IV bag and a little white dog balled up on a towel fast asleep.

"When can I take her home?" she asked. "You did say she's a she, right?"

"Vito's not going to like this," Ethan said, curling his fingers through the cage and leaning on it.

That was for sure, yet she found herself chuckling. Since her father's surgery three weeks ago, she'd been working and caretaking nonstop, and she was tired. Plus her apartment in town was sitting empty while she was living back at home and she knew she couldn't have a dog there. Yet some ornery part of her stood up and made her dig in her heels. She looked into the big, sad eyes of the still-damp mutt. She wasn't going to give up the dog.

"I'm taking her home. Besides, I need some stress relief right about now. The psych literature says pets are good for stress."

"She may create a lot more stress than she takes away, you know that, don't you? She wasn't treated well. We don't really have a good idea of what her manners are like yet."

Bella squatted down next to the crate. The dog stirred a little, lifting her head and assessing her with soft brown eyes that were more than a little wary.

Ethan bent down next to her. "You need to know two things. Number one, the dog's going to make it. Number two, you know I love you, right?"

"Of course." They'd known each other since they were kids. She couldn't imagine life without his friendship.

"I'd probably be more if you were okay with that."

She touched his cheek. "We're way better as friends, and you know it."

"If you say so. Be careful, Bella."

"What are you talking about?"

He shrugged, tipping his head toward the waiting room.

"Roman? Oh, come on. I would never—no. Don't even think that." She should have stopped there, but when she was nervous, she rambled. "He's just here to drive me home. You know Roman, he's always been . . ." *Passionate* was the word that came to mind.

"In love with you?"

"Responsible. I was going to say overly responsible."

"You're shaking a little."

She'd never lied to Ethan, and she wasn't going to start now. "Seeing him again has been a bit of a shock, as much as I knew that someday he'd be back."

He gripped her shoulders. "I'm here for you if you need me. Got that?"

She rested a hand on his arm. "I'm sorry about leaving you at the wedding. Les wouldn't let up, and Roman asked if I wanted to get coffee . . ."

"I don't care about that. But, Bella, you should know—"

Someone cleared their throat, and she turned around to see Roman standing in the doorway. She dropped her hand.

"I wondered if it was all right to see the dog?"

"Sure," Ethan said, getting to his feet, "come on back."

Roman eyed the animal from afar. "He going to be okay?"

Ethan sighed. "It's a she. And yes, she's going to be fine."

Roman's eyes traveled around the room, taking in the four crates in front of them, the four on the opposite side. Monitors, IVs, equipment. The desk against the wall. "Nice place."

"Thanks, but let's forget the small talk for now, Roman." Ethan's voice was uncharacteristically sharp. "I thought you'd at least have the decency to tell Bella what you're really doing in town. Don't you think she deserves to know?"

"What's this about?" Bella looked from Ethan to Roman. A tiny muscle in Roman's jaw twitched. They looked like two MMA fighters about to face off.

"I was about to tell you before all this happened," Roman said, nodding toward the dog. "I've inherited my grandparents' orchards. I'm here to take over their business."

"The orchards," she said in disbelief.

Not that the fact that he was taking over the orchards was so remarkable. It was just that they happened to be next door to her family's thirty-year-old garden center business.

Her family had wondered what would happen to the orchards now that both of Roman's grandparents were gone. One of the longtime employees had told them Roman had no interest in running the business as an apple farm. The rumor was that it was going to be sold.

She clenched her fists to her sides as the motivation behind his actions became crystal clear: his initial friendliness, his offer to get coffee. "So that's why you wanted to make peace," she said, lighting into him. "To assuage your conscience. So I could make it easier for you with my dad that you're going to be working next door." Because saying her father would not be pleased was like underestimating Armageddon.

"No. That didn't have anything to do with tonight."

"Maybe you'd better go," Ethan said.

"I'm taking Bella home," Roman said.

"No need for that," Ethan said. "Her house is on my way."

Maybe she should feel flattered that two men were fighting over her, a situation that had happened exactly never. She glanced at Ethan, leaning against the desk, scowling. And Roman, brows knit, arms crossed, irritated as all get out. They hadn't even been in each other's company for a full fifteen minutes. If this was any indication of how her hard-earned peace in this town could be so easily spoiled, she was in big trouble.

She lifted her keys and her purse from a nearby countertop. "Tell you what. I'm driving myself home. You two can ride together. I'll stop by to check on my dog tomorrow."

She walked past both of them, retracing her steps to the waiting room, glad to finally leave Roman Spikonos behind. He was still stubborn, argumentative, and impossible. And now she could add *sneaky* to the list. Forget the fact that he was still one of the sexiest men she'd ever seen, still capable of stirring up every emotion and *doing things* to her insides, things that made her heart pound and her breath catch and gave her whole body the jolting shock of static electricity times a thousand. But all that had gotten her in a whole heap of trouble before, and she was determined to never head down that path again.

CHAPTER 4

Twelve Years Earlier

"It's destiny," Bella's friend Jess said over flat, bad pizza in the cafeteria. She pushed her phone toward Bella. "See for yourself."

Jess read their horoscopes every day over lunch in the high school cafeteria. Today had been no exception. "The present astral configuration indicates that you will meet a dark and handsome stranger who will alter the course of your life." Jess looked at her pointedly before reading the next line. "Be careful about chance meetings." Bella rolled her eyes. There weren't any "strangers" at Our Lady of the Lake. She knew everyone. Besides, she had the highest GPA in the senior class. She was too smart to believe in nonsense.

Two periods later, Bella reached out her hand to accept the chemistry test Mrs. Martin was handing her. She kept a polite but humble smile on her face, as usual. She always got the highest grade, not that she was bragging or anything, but it was a fact of life. When she glanced at the top of the paper and saw the ninety-six, she knew this time was no different.

Well, why should it be? She'd studied her butt off. She always did. It would give her dad something to smile about when there wasn't all that much to make him happy since her mom had died. She liked making him proud.

After her mother's death from ovarian cancer Bella's freshman year, Aunt Francesca, her single aunt who lived in Newark with her paternal grandmother, had taken a few weeks' leave from her school librarian job to come help take care of them. But she had work and caring for Nonna, so they knew from the beginning that her time with them was limited.

Bella didn't fully understand it at the time, but her dad had gone into a depression, overwhelmed with the garden center and the care of three kids. Gina and she were already in high school and at the peak of teenage angst, and her little brother Joey was only three, poor little baby.

Bella, even at the age of fourteen, felt a great responsibility for her brother. After all, she'd promised her mother she'd take care of him. She'd sworn, given her word. Gina, three years older, was a senior when Mom died and busy with her own life. But Bella had a special relationship with her baby brother from the moment her mom had placed him in her arms. Maybe it was the duck fuzz on his sweet little head, or the way his tiny fingers sought one of hers and wrapped around it for dear life. Later, it was his big brown eyes that could fill with crocodile tears, or his fun-loving, endlessly charming personality that had *her* wrapped around *his* little finger for life. For whatever reason, Bella had easily slid into the role of being his second mother.

One night after Joey had fallen asleep, Bella looked up to find her father in the doorway. His thick black hair was sticking up on one side from sleeping, and he had his ratty navy bathrobe on.

"Hi, Pop," she said. She was sitting up in Joey's bed reading one of her own books for a few minutes, Joey sleeping cuddled up beside her, smelling of little kid shampoo and Dove soap. She read to him every night because she wanted him to feel loved, and wanted to somehow fill the impossible void left by their mother.

Her dad walked up to the bed, his hands in his robe pockets. The light from the lamp hit his weathered face, casting shadows on the dark circles under his eyes and the deep vertical creases between them. He'd always been the more serious parent, the worrier. Mom had made him smile, had lightened him up, and now that she was gone, God only knew what would happen to him. "You're a good girl, *bella mia*," he said, touching her cheek. "A very good girl. And you are beautiful like your mother."

She knew she wasn't. Her mom had been amazing, with wavy dark hair, big caramel-colored eyes, and the most beautiful skin she'd ever seen. She'd gotten her mother's hair, but at age fourteen, it was an annoyance, and came with unwanted hair in other places like her brows and upper lip that she had to work hard at getting rid of. She'd inherited a bigger nose from her dad's side of the family, and she was nowhere near as petite as her mom had been.

"I got the highest grade in my advanced English class," she said. "My teacher wants me to enter a national essay contest." She wanted him to know there was no need to worry about her, that she was fine. Gina's grades, on the other hand, were a disaster. Lots to worry about there.

Now, at the beginning of senior year, a few months from turning eighteen, Bella had already aced the SAT and was practically certain of a scholarship, and she knew exactly where she wanted to go. She hadn't decided yet whether to become a molecular geneticist, a physicist, or a biochemist, but all three were possible from Loyola University in Chicago.

She'd read all about Chicago on the Internet. People there were Midwestern—friendly. It was clean. Exciting and beautiful, and Lake Michigan was practically like an ocean, with a beach and everything. She'd jog around the lake every day and eat deep-dish pizza. Become a city girl. She'd get far away from Mirror Lake and the expectations of her traditional Italian family. A loving family, yes, but one that favored and fawned over the sons.

She saw it with her cousins, and she saw traces of it even now with Joey, who was six. Her father didn't seem to expect the same effort around the house as he did with her and Gina. Joey was still young, but Bella feared the pattern was being set. And her father could not cook at all. If it weren't for Aunt Fran, who had taught Bella to cook some basic things and was constantly sending new recipes, they'd probably starve. She'd had it with waiting on menfolk.

She did worry about leaving Joey, who'd just started school. Gina, who was three years older, took night classes at UConn in Storrs and, during the day, was learning how to keep the books for the garden center. Plus she'd been dating Manny Ramirez since junior year. She wasn't really around very much.

But nothing would stop Bella from leaving. Surely her dad would be okay with Joey, right? Even though he was an old-school parent and would probably starve to death without her cooking or get a heart attack from eating too many drive-through burgers.

Mrs. Martin's voice interrupted Bella's thoughts. "The high grade on this test was a ninety-nine, folks," Mrs. Martin said. "So if you got a grade that didn't come anywhere near that, seriously consider coming to extra help on Tuesday and Thursday mornings before school." A few groans sounded around the room.

Someone had gotten a ninety-*nine*? Without trying to be obvious, Bella glanced about the room. Kaitlin Morris? Doubtful, because she was just complaining that ever since she'd started dating Nate Thompson she'd slacked off on her studying. Paul Zigosky? Ziggy was a red hot, but he hadn't beaten her yet, and here it was October. Bruno Santoro? He was looking at her like he usually did, all brooding and lusty like, and she happened to catch his eye. It didn't really faze her, because he did that to all the girls, hoping to get lucky with someone desperate enough to fall for his charms. She smiled politely and turned back around. Unless he'd had a brain transplant, he hadn't gotten the grade. Even if he possessed the aptitude, academics was a vastly undermined part of his personality.

That left the quiet, super-hot guy in the back who'd transferred in from Mirror Lake High at the beginning of the year. Bella felt the hair on the back of her neck prickle, like she could feel him staring at her, as she'd already caught him doing several times. Or rather, how he'd caught *her* doing. She forced herself not to look.

If anything, Bella considered him cocky, a good-looking guy who knew it and who attended Our Lady of the Lake for one reason: the hope of a basketball scholarship, since their team was phenomenal. That sort of utilitarian purpose made her avoid him—the guy had *jock* written all over him, and with the way he checked out the girls with those big brown eyes, you might as well add *trouble* to that list, too.

Confidence seeped from his pores—he wasn't afraid to voice his opinion. Once he even made a point of agreeing with Mary Alice Hutchinson, who had a stuttering problem and had been forced by Mr. Baxter to answer a history question. After that, all the girls fell in love with him a little, especially Mary Alice.

His hair was always perfect—longish layers of shiny black silk, falling perfectly into place in a way that was just mussed enough to look carelessly styled. Even the Our Lady of the Lake uniform, a regulation polo and khaki pants, looked drool-worthy on him. Especially the pants, which caressed his narrow hips like a glove.

He had the Mediterranean complexion, dark and swarthy. His eyes were the color of black coffee, and his nose—perfect, straight, *Greek*. His lips were full and sometimes quirked in the shape of a secret smile, which he'd shot in her direction several times. Like he was sharing a private joke with only her. Thinking. Waiting to make his move.

Which he probably would. Lots of boys at Our Lady of the Lake noticed Bella. She knew she was pretty—not in a vain way—but she was friendly and outgoing and just about everyone liked her, and she was okay with all of that.

She also rejected the advances of a lot of boys, mainly because her father didn't approve of anything but group dating. The ones who were bold enough to ask for more she politely and pleasantly turned down. It actually made her smile to herself a little, thinking what would happen if she ever dared to bring a Greek boy home to her traditional Italian father. Yet one more reason why leaving town for college was a necessity.

Several times they'd locked gazes. In the hallway between classes. In the cafeteria. He'd been lingering after school, leaning against the retaining wall at the front of the building when he watched her and her girlfriends walk by. But he never asked to walk home with her. Or sit with her. And he never talked to her. But somehow she always knew when he was around.

The bell rang, and since it was Friday, relieved sighs and a couple of cheers went up as the stampede flocked to the door. Bella stayed a little longer in her seat, fumbling with her books. It had to have been him who broke the curve, and she had to know. As he approached, she saw a paper jutting out from the others that he clutched with his books next to his hip. Positioned right at eye level so she couldn't miss it. A blue-inked ninety-nine stood out.

Her gaze traveled up, up his lean torso, up his substantial height to his face, only to find he was looking straight at her. With a knowing, amused expression, those too-full lips turned up in a wicked smile. As if he knew all her secrets. Not that she had any significant ones, but he made her feel like she might one day be capable of having some.

His gaze scorched her—no, seared right *through* her—leaving a burning trail *everywhere* and catapulted her into an uncharacteristic moment of panic. Her mouth went dry, her stomach tumbled, and her hands actually shook. Shook! What on earth was happening to her? She busied herself stuffing her notebook into her bag. He pulled out the test paper—purposely!—folded it, tucked it into his book, and strolled out of the room. But just before he cleared the door, he gave her a wink.

Jess's horoscope had been right. Something had just happened, something unlike anything she'd ever experienced, and somehow, Bella knew that things would never be the same.

―――○――

Besides knowing Roman Spikonos was a transfer student, Bella knew only two other bits of information: his mother was a child psychologist in town, and the girl he dated, Reagan Swift, was a drama queen. Literally. Slated to star in both of the drama club productions this year, rumor had it she'd been accepted to Interlochen but her parents had decided to save their money for Juilliard. She possessed the voice of an angel but the personality of a shrew.

Truthfully, Bella didn't want to know more. Because any boy who dated Reagan probably needed his head examined. Besides, Bella was too busy. She had big plans, and she was way too focused to let a boy mess them up. Even a boy she couldn't stop thinking about.

On a Thursday afternoon a few days after the chemistry test incident, Bella finished cross-country practice and ran to the bleachers to grab her things. She had to hurry home and get supper started. Plus the garden center was all geared up for the busy fall season and she'd have to spend several hours hauling pumpkins and hay bales and cornstalks for the fall displays. Not to mention she had a history test tomorrow.

"Hey," Roman Spikonos said as she gathered up her gym bag.

She looked at him. Really looked, because he'd actually *talked* to her, and when she met his gaze, a funny thing happened. Her legs turned boneless. Her mind wiped itself blank. Blood whooshed in her ears, and she turned hot and cold and dizzy all at the same time. She'd never met a boy who'd caused such full-blown chaos inside of her . . . like she was coming down with the flu. All the more reason to get away from him as fast as possible.

Her brain kicked in and she remembered that sometimes he picked Reagan up after practice. Of course. But she'd skipped practice today for a vocal lesson. *Then what in God's name was he doing here?*

"Congratulations on getting the high grade in chem," she managed.

He shrugged. "Luck, I guess."

"You needed more than luck to ace that test," she said.

Another shrug. "You walking through town?"

She nodded and climbed down the bleachers to the field, slinging her book bag over her shoulder. Every muscle felt unnatural, like her legs had suddenly turned into rubber bands, and she was terrified she'd miss a step and go sailing through the air and land flat on her face at the bottom in a broken heap.

Roman lived a block off the square in a quaint old Victorian his mother had refurbished, and it was large enough for her to have her office there. Bella knew it because she'd gone there for therapy for several months after her mother died. Her father would never have admitted his daughter had a problem, but Aunt Francesca had made him send her.

The house wasn't very big but it was charming, one of her favorite houses in town. It had green and deep-red trim and a scalloped roof and a big rose garden in the tiny front yard. And her office was bright and cheerful with big windows and loaded with photos—she hadn't realized at the time that the boy in many of them was Roman. A fairy cottage, she'd always thought. Magic. Very different from the big old Craftsman-style bungalow behind the garden center where she grew up.

Although their landscaping was impeccable, and they always had gorgeous flowers overflowing from baskets hanging on the porch and growing in the little garden, Bella's house hadn't been updated since her mother got sick ten years ago. It always seemed a little sad to her, even though she made an effort to bring in cut flowers, and last year she even bought some colorful throw pillows from Target for their old couch. But it was always like it was missing some essential thing . . . her mother's touch.

He walked beside her in silence. She could usually stare boys down until they squirmed. She could disarm the cutest of them without blinking an eye, but now she found herself holding her breath, unable to properly breathe, feeling winded just from walking. She barely dared to look sideways, out of nerves, but when she snuck a glance, she discovered he was quite tall, head and shoulders above her; she'd have to tilt her head back to fully see his face. She wished she would've said she had a meeting at school or that she was waiting to walk home with her friends Sam and Jess or *anything* to avoid this awkward discomfort.

When they left the field and began walking down the short road that led to Main Street, he slowed. "I have to ask you something."

Oh no. She knew what *that* meant. He was obviously very confident, and clearly expected her to say yes, but she was going to cut him off at the pass. Plus he had a lot of nerve, cheating on Reagan, even if she wasn't very nice. "I'm sorry, but I—I don't really date. I'm too busy with my studies and being class president and—"

She paused, cursing silently that she'd stammered. What was it that had her so tongue-tied? It was part of her spiel, and she knew it by heart. She usually nipped this kind of thing right in the bud.

Her father would never allow her to date a Greek boy, someone flagrantly named *Roman* of all things—there sure wasn't a Saint

Roman in the Catholic lexicon that she knew of, and she'd definitely looked. Especially one raised by an agnostic adoptive mother. No sense in even imagining it. Besides, clearly he liked his girls dramatic and high maintenance and, let's face it, slutty, and she wasn't any of those things.

"I'm not asking you out," he said.

She couldn't help the gasp that escaped her. "You're not asking me out?" she repeated. After all those hot stares, those stealthy glances across the chem lab? She couldn't believe it. Anger percolated up through her chest, which appalled her. How could she be angry? Worse, she felt a little . . . hurt. Disappointed. Oh, what was wrong with her?

"You know this is a new school for me and all," he said. "And . . . um, I just need a little bit of help in English lit."

"English lit?" she repeated, trying to get a handle on what he'd just said.

"Yeah. I'm struggling a little with the readings."

"Oh." Mr. 99 Percent needed help in English?

"Mrs. Lawrence thought you might be interested in helping me. I could pay you."

She didn't have time for tutoring. Especially not gorgeous guys who made her stammer. Ones who performed three points better than she did on chem exams. Was this a trick?

"It's not a big time commitment if that's what you're worried about," he said. "I'm working in my grandparents' orchard, and it's busy. I'd have about a half hour before school if you'd be willing to help me a couple days a week. Just until I catch up. I could pick you up at your house in the mornings and drive you to school, if you want. Then you wouldn't have to walk. It would save you some time."

How did he know she walked to school? Nine-tenths of a mile there and back every blessed day. Well, Mirror Lake was small, so it wasn't like he'd have to go out of his way to know that, right?

She gathered at least part of her flailing composure. "Wh-why do you need tutoring?" she asked.

His lips quirked up in a smile that made her heart dive into her stomach like a careening paper airplane. "I just don't get English. All that old language. And I can't risk it fu—er—messing with my GPA. And basketball practice lets out at five, I think the same time as cross-country, so I could give you a ride home if you want, too." He paused, long enough for her to physically feel his gaze wrap fully around her like a blanket. His voice was all business, all school library, but those eyes . . . they were in the bedroom. Totally.

She tore her gaze away. Stared off at the storefronts, most of which had colorful displays of yellow and burgundy mums with decorative cabbages and gourds and pumpkins. She hated getting up early. God knows she was up late enough as it was, by the time she did the garden center stuff and homework and made everyone's lunches . . .

"Please," he pleaded.

She hadn't meant to look again, but her eyes were drawn back to his face like a wreck on the side of the road you don't want to stare at but you do anyway. And once she did, she was a goner. It was his damn eyes. Those gorgeous, warm brown eyes looking at her like her destiny. She was helpless in the face of all that charisma. "Okay, fine. I'll do it."

"Great." His smile widened, displaying gorgeous white teeth, only imperfect enough to make him human.

"How about this?" she bartered with the miniscule amount of sense she had left. "I can walk to the end of my driveway and you can pick me up there. It . . . wouldn't be a good idea to come up to the house, okay?" The driveway was long and wound through a wooded area before it reached the road. Her father would never notice anything was different.

"So that's a yes?" he asked, those eyes of his drilling into her like she'd said yes to something entirely different. Something a lot more fun than tutoring.

"It's a yes," she managed, hoping she would be able to speak coherently in front of him during their lessons.

He blew out a breath. "Okay. We start tomorrow morning. Don't be late."

CHAPTER 5

Being back on his grandparents' property made Roman want to pound things. Like his own head, for feeling so frustrated. His return to Mirror Lake wasn't supposed to be like this, coming back to the orchards he loved without his beloved grandfather there to instruct and guide him in all the millions of tasks needed to keep the farm running.

He concentrated on pounding the old barn roof that he was sitting on top of now, ripping off old shingles one by one in the September heat. One of many jobs that desperately needed completing around the 130-acre farm. Gramps had been heartbroken from losing Gram last year, then he'd died last spring of a sudden heart attack, and the farm sure showed signs of his absence.

"Hey, watch it! That thing almost hit my head!" Roman looked up from his work to find a man with aviator sunglasses standing in the yard below him grinning widely and flicking shingle dust off his tattooed arm.

"Well, I'll be a son of a bitch," Roman said, tossing down his hammer. "Lukas." He blinked twice, just to make sure he wasn't hallucinating, then climbed down to embrace his older brother, whom he hadn't seen since Lukas had left Mirror Lake to become a national singing sensation.

"Welcome back," Lukas said. They hadn't lived together in the same town for years, but they'd always shared a special bond. Lukas had been a wild child, always causing problems, sometimes with the law. When they were just kids, he'd stolen a baseball glove for Roman and taken the rap, a move that got both of them separated and sent to different foster homes. Lukas then drifted from home to home, finally settling down in high school as a result of being placed with a kindly older couple.

Roman would never forget how his brother had fought for him and had tried to keep up with him despite their different placements. Their younger two brothers had each gone to separate homes at the ages of six and four. Roman's adopted mom had tried to keep them in contact, but both younger boys had been adopted into very wealthy families who weren't exactly eager to continue the connection, and eventually, they'd lost track of each other.

Last year, Roman was happy to help Lukas locate their oldest brother, Nico, who'd become addicted to heroin and lost custody of his son. Roman had helped Lukas get papers signed last spring so Lukas and his wife could adopt Stevie, and last he'd heard, Nico was in rehab.

"The place looks . . . interesting," Lukas said, glancing around at the dilapidated barn.

"It's a work in progress, that's for sure."

"What's your plan for the place? I heard you were working in craft beer in upstate New York."

Roman nodded. "And brandy. I'm building a distillery. My grandfather wanted me to farm the land, but my heart was never into that aspect of it. I'm looking now for some business partners."

"I'd love to hear more about it. Actually, I stopped by to invite you to come for dinner . . . meet my family," Lukas said.

"It would be an honor," Roman said. Lukas had recently married Samantha Rushford, an art teacher and coincidentally one of Bella's best friends.

"How's living next door to trouble?" Lukas asked, tilting his head over to the D'Angelos' place.

"Do you mean Vito or Bella?" Roman asked.

"Well, last I heard Vito wasn't that pretty and Bella was."

"She still is," Roman said, thinking of how her sass, her smile, her compassion for mangy animals—which didn't extend to him, he'd noticed—stirred him as much as those filled-out curves in that pretty red dress. As a woman, she'd become more complex and even more intriguing than she'd been as a girl. Yet his complicated past with her had made him leery of settling here and opening old wounds.

"You always smile like that when you think of a woman?"

"I wasn't smiling," Roman said, making sure to scowl.

"Right. Well, good luck with that."

"I'm just looking to make peace. That's all. I just want to be able to coexist in the same town again."

Lukas smiled affectionately at him. "If anybody can do it, you can. Listen, I've got to go, but I wanted to let you know I've started to search for our other brothers."

"Andreas and Jared."

Lukas nodded. "I sent an e-mail to an Andreas Poulos, who's a financial guy on Wall Street. The PI thinks that's our Andreas. He's still gathering info on Jared."

Lukas and Roman shared the same last name because Roman's adoptive mother, Marjorie, insisted he keep it until he was old enough to decide for himself if he wanted it anymore, but their other two brothers had been adopted and given different surnames long ago.

"Great. More brothers," Roman said a little facetiously.

"You're not eager to find them?" Lukas asked.

"No—it's not that. Just that I'm not sure I can handle myself right now, let alone long-lost family." Especially as far as Bella was concerned. Whom he couldn't seem to stop thinking of.

"Hey, the longer you live in this town, the more you get hooked on how important family is." He gave Roman a little shoulder punch. "See you around."

"Thanks, Lukas." He paused. "It really is great to see you again."

As Lukas drove off, Roman realized he was spending more time thinking about seeing Bella again than pondering his long-lost brothers, which probably wasn't the healthiest thing. Well, he knew of only one way to put her out of his head.

Time to rip up more shingles.

Midmorning, he was still up on the barn roof going at it when he saw his mother's black MINI Cooper pull up the drive.

Marjorie Ganz walked briskly over to the barn in her usual no-nonsense way and stopped, craning her neck up to the dilapidated old roof.

"Oh, hello, sweetie," she said, grabbing ahold of her sunglasses from atop her head and pulling them on. "I brought you lunch, but I have to get back to work in a few."

He swung down the ladder and embraced the woman who had been a mother to him since he was eight. Marjorie was a rail-thin, practical woman who favored black in nearly everything—less time wasted on choices—and was a hard-core vegan. Not to mention she was a child psychologist who took on the most hopeless cases, the ones no one else wanted. Which was why desperate parents often drove from hours away in hopes that she could help their children. He'd been one of those kids, minus the parents, of course. For some reason, her compassion for him had extended beyond the office—and she'd adopted him. Changed his life. She'd tried to adopt Lukas, too, but he was quite a handful by then, was in and out of various homes, and at the time of Roman's adoption, was living with a family out of state. But she'd made sure they stayed in contact. His mom was one of the quirkiest, smartest, most interesting people he knew—and one of the most loving. Lucky him.

He took the container she was forcing on him and peeked inside, finding something that vaguely resembled a sandwich.

"It's a kale and chickpea flatbread with homemade mayo," she said, pushing up her glasses over her gray, one-length hair. "I'm sorry I missed the wedding this weekend, but I felt the environmental crisis conference was more critical."

"Of course," he said. She was always saving the world, whether it was through her practice, sitting on the boards of several children's organizations, or all her work on the environment. She'd also been single for as long as he knew, which was a little sad. She had a lot to offer someone if they could crack through her intellectual exterior.

Her gaze drifted over to her parents' old house.

"At some point we have to go through it, you know," Roman said. The house was empty of people but full of memories. That might make it difficult to stay there, but they were really good ones. He was damn grateful to have landed in the family that he had.

Marjorie waved a hand dismissively. "Honestly, Roman, I'm happy to have you do it. It's just stuff, after all. And God knows, someone can use it."

No matter how glib she was, how free thinking and non-materialistic—and a world-class recycler to boot—he and she both knew it wasn't *just stuff*. Every one of the dozens of tchotchkes held a memory, and those were enough to break their hearts.

"Maybe you can come over for dinner and we can spend a few hours . . ."

"Oh, you're a dear, but honestly, Roman, I can't bear it. Everything in there is yours to do with what you want, okay?"

Gee, thanks, Mom. Roman never realized before how difficult it was to be an only child. After all, when he started out in life, he'd been one of five. A memory surfaced, of roughhousing and horsing around with his brothers. He felt the emptiness that always hit him when he remembered good times, and he wondered what had happened to his brothers. The likelihood of them all being reunited one day seemed slim, and of actually being brothers again, almost impossible.

Starvation finally won over and he dug into the veggies, which actually weren't half bad. Too bad he'd need to eat half a field of kale to feel full.

"So, how are you?" Marjorie asked, clearly pleased he was eating. "Any girlfriend?"

He quirked a brow. His mother conserved words like she did everything else, and she cut right to the chase. "No, and that's the way I like it."

"Now, honey, you know what Dr. Brennan encouraged you to do. You have to fight that tendency to be too self-sufficient."

He'd seen Dr. Brennan, a colleague of his mother's, at her insistence for years. The man may not have been able to cure him of all his deeply embedded flaws, but after all that therapy, Roman now possessed an uncanny ability to know what they were. "*You're* self-sufficient," he pointed out.

"Yes, but I have an entire network of friends, even if I don't have a significant other right now."

"I have friends, Mother." Oh Lord. He sounded like a teenager.

She sighed. "I'm worried about you. Children of alcoholics often become workaholics. And you've always been a bit threatened by intimacy, which is also pretty typical of a child with your background. I don't want you to be too isolated out here."

She waved around at the property, from the woods separating his land from D'Angelos' Garden Center next door, to the rows of apple trees that were planted about one hundred yards from the house and ran in tidy rows all the way down to the lake. *His* property. The thought both excited and terrified him. He hoped he would do his grandparents justice. "I want you to have a happy life, honey." She reached out and squeezed his arm. He eyeballed her in a way that all sons have done to their mothers for ages and hugged her back.

"Thanks, Mom," he said.

Oh, to have a single hippie mother who knew way too much about him and knew all the psychological language to describe it in great detail. He wished she'd find a relationship so she could direct her intensity elsewhere.

His stomach growled. He cracked the lid on the chickpeas again. Looked like a McDonald's run might be in his near future. Or maybe not. The nearest drive-through was twenty minutes away, and he didn't want to take the time. Warily, he tried not to inhale and took another bite. Ugh. Not working for him. But he pretended to like it for his mom's sake.

He looked up from the food to see a scruffy brown dog amble out of the woods. The dog's nose was to the ground, hot on some trail. *It was that damn dog.* The mangy one. Bella's newest project. Now looking a bit polished around the edges—i.e., brushed. Her foreleg was wrapped and her ribs were still visible, but the limp was better. Maybe. The beast galumphed along, happily sniffing along the grass like it was covered with beef gravy.

"Is it a stray?" his mother asked, putting her sunglasses back on and squinting.

"Unfortunately not." Roman put his fingers in his mouth and whistled. "Hey! Come here." The dog looked up, saw Roman coming toward it, and promptly trotted farther up the property. If it kept going through the trees, the beast would run into the lake in another five hundred yards or so. Against his better judgment, Roman ran after it. As if sensing danger, the dog picked up its pace.

"Honey, you have to entice it," his mother said, rummaging in her car. She stood up with another container in hand. "Here, take some quinoa and pretend-cheese dip."

Now *that* would certainly do the trick. *Not.* A figure running out of the woods saved Roman from answering. It was a woman, wearing a T-shirt and calf-length jogging pants that hugged every sweet curve, her thick hair tied back in a ponytail.

"Gracie!" Bella called, cupping her hands over her mouth. Surprisingly, the dog stalled. For a second. Then it tore off toward the lake.

Gracie? She'd named that ratty-looking mutt *Gracie*?

Bella looked around and saw him and his mother. "Oh, hi, Dr. Ganz, nice to see you." She jogged over and gave his mom a quick hug. He, on the other hand, got nothing but a finger wave. "My dog got loose, and I've got to run after her," she said to Marjorie. She cast Roman a wary look. "Sorry about that, Roman." She promptly took off after the dog, dangling a leash at her side.

"I always liked Bella," Marjorie said, getting into her tiny car. "Looks like she could use a little help."

Roman rolled his eyes, then kissed her on the cheek, closed the car door, and ran off through the trees after Bella.

"So you kept the mutt," he said when he caught up, trying not to notice her shapely ass. She must still be a runner like she was in high school. Running was something he enjoyed as well.

"Perceptive as always." They jogged along together for a moment before she said, "You don't need to help me. I can get her myself."

He eyeballed her from the side. She had a nice stride, strong, light on her feet, and they kept up a natural pace together. As they had at one time with other things.

"It's no problem," he said. "I'd hate for her to end up in the lake." That was a stupid thing to say. What kind of dog would plunge into the lake to get away? A dumb one.

It was a warm early-September day, the kind that tricked you into believing it was still summer, except for a faint dryness at the tips of some of the branches and the sparse scattering of a few dead leaves on the ground. The sweet scent of ripening apples was light in the air.

They ran through the rows of trees, down the gentle slope of the land, until at last the lake stretched out in front of them, wide and blue as the September sky. Usually it gave him a sense of peace just looking at it, but not today. Not with the dog plowing right into the water and Bella standing there near the dock, hands on those glorious hips, cajoling the beast to come back.

"That dog has a mind of its own," he said. Stubborn, like her, but of course he didn't say that. "What kind of pet is it going to be?"

She tsked. "I don't know, Roman. Sometimes people don't have all the answers right away. It's called *discovery*."

"Marriage is discovery. A job is discovery. Having a pet should be simple." Just like the decision to stay away from her should be. All he needed to do was head back to his work. Leave her to grab the stubborn animal on her own. As she'd pointed out to him multiple times, she didn't need his help. Ever again.

"Gracie, come here," Bella called, in a tone of voice that wouldn't scare a mosquito off an elephant. The dog, who was happily paddling away from shore, didn't even acknowledge her.

What the hell? He'd never seen an animal swim with such determination. And that was the closest thing to a compliment he could come up with right now for a dog too stupid to know it was swimming too far out.

Bella began pulling off her running shoes. "I'm going to get her."

He put a hand on her arm. "Do not go in there."

She tossed off her T-shirt to reveal—oh God—a sports bra. Purple with wavy geometric designs. Not that he'd really even noticed the designs in light of her gorgeous rack, which he was staring at like an idiot. He must've frozen for a second, because she shrugged her arm away and walked onto the dock.

"Let's at least try calling her back," he said.

"You go right ahead," she called from over her shoulder. "I'm going to grab her before she gets too far out."

She ran to the end of the dock, then bent over, crooning to the dog, who blissfully ignored her. Then she poised on the edge. "Wait," he called, running over to her. "Don't"—a splash rent the air—"—jump." Too late. She'd already swum over to the dog, and was trying to wrap her arms around it. Of course she didn't hesitate. Or wait for help. Some things never changed.

But the water was neck deep, and the dog was wiggling in her arms. Roman peeled off his own shirt—oh, what the hell—and jumped in, too. He managed to take the dog from her and swim with it into shallower water, then carry it to the shore.

He took the leash from her and hooked it around the dog's collar. As he gave Bella a hand out, he caught her glancing at his bare chest. He couldn't help quirking his lips up in a smile because she was blushing vigorously, like they were eighteen again and he'd just whispered something suggestive in her ear.

But the joke was on him. Maybe it was the soft warmth of her hand as it brushed his, or the way she looked all wet and curvy and delicious, because his lungs suddenly felt tight, and need rushed through him, just like in the old days. The intensity surprised him; for a moment he wanted to tug her forward until their wet bodies were flush and kiss her hard in the hot sun.

Thinking like that was not productive. Helping her also made him feel protective of her, and he wasn't going there, either. Old habits died hard, he guessed.

The dog and he both slogged out of the lake together, Bella a few paces behind. Then the dog shook itself so that Roman got pelted with a spray of water. Which didn't even matter because he was all wet anyway.

Laughter rang out into the warm September day.

Figured the first time he'd hear her laugh it would be at him.

It was that same snorty laugh, though, that he hadn't heard in a long time. Not ladylike at all. He'd forgotten how much he liked it.

He turned around. Narrowed his eyes. Tried to look menacing. "You think that's funny?"

She bit her cheeks to stop. That made her defined Italian cheekbones stand out, which reminded him yet again how beautiful she was. "Just a little."

Then thanks to a benevolent God, she waded out of the water, which treated him to quite a spectacular view. Slicked back hair, water dripping onto her shoulders and down her curves, she looked like some kind of fantasy mermaid emerging from the ocean. This time she caught *him* staring, and he tried to avert his eyes. He really did.

Instead he said, "Water's great. Sure you don't want to go back in?" Then impulsively, he scooped her up. He shouldn't have done it; there was no excuse for it. Yet there she was in his arms, objecting mildly, beating on his back in weak protest. The familiar warm weight of her, the wet, silken strands of her hair against his chest, the sound of her laughter, felt so damn good. Like freedom. Like he was young again and the sadness that had separated them had never been.

For a moment, his breath caught as he stared at her. Water beaded on her lashes and her olive skin. Her dark hair lay slicked back against her head, showing the elegant widow's peak in the middle of her forehead. Somehow he got lost in the feel of her cool, slippery skin, the scent of her shampoo—lemons, maybe?—mixed in with the fresh breeze off the lake. Not a stitch of makeup, but her beauty made him speechless. Her laughter faded away and she stared back at him, her dark eyes wide.

Suddenly he remembered what it was like to kiss her; hell, he remembered her sweet, unique *taste*. And in that single, sunny moment, he remembered what it was like to love her, unabashedly and sure, before the tides had turned and all their hopes and dreams had come tearing down.

The dog woofed, breaking the trance. Somehow, Roman must've dropped the leash, because the animal was sitting on the shore, sopping wet and looking more ragtag than ever, waiting for its mistress. Or maybe it was just tired of adventure and finally ready to head home.

"I'm coming, sweetie," Bella called to the dog. Reluctantly, Roman set her down. She waded the rest of the way out and busied herself with the dog. Avoiding his gaze, she said, "Thanks again, Roman. See you later."

Right. Well, it was just as well. He waded out himself, his wet jeans dragging on his hips.

As soon as he reached the shore, he saw the little group gathered there. Bella's teenage brother, tall and lanky, already towering a head above their father, and Vito, looking just as pissed off as that fateful day when Roman had seen him last, standing straight with his meaty arms folded as if ready to confront the devil himself. And Bella's Aunt Fran, wearing an apron and carrying a wooden spoon, more gray than twelve years ago, but with the same regal bearing, the same pearls dangling from her ears.

He reminded himself that this was his property. How much trouble could the old man cause? A tightness clogged his chest, maybe reminiscent of that last day, when he'd allowed the man to intimidate him. To scoff at him. To write him off as a good-for-nothing.

That wasn't going to happen again. Roman was a man now. One who didn't scare easily, and one who didn't run from his troubles. He slowed his steps a little, reminding himself that no matter how strained his relationship was with Bella, he would never lose his temper with her father. Out of respect for *her*.

Vito assessed the situation. Took one look at his soaking-wet daughter, the dog, and Roman, also dripping.

"I thought you knew better than to get back with him," he told his daughter, his voice rife with disappointment.

Roman's neck prickled. Bella's color was high, but this time from embarrassment. He pressed his lips together so the not-very-nice reprimand on the tip of his tongue wouldn't spill out.

"Gracie got away," she said. "Roman helped me fish her out of the lake."

"Go get some decent clothes on," Vito said.

"No, Pop. I'm not leaving," she said. Roman almost cheered.

"I'm about to get angry, and I don't want you hearing that, okay?"

"You can't get angry with him anymore, Pop." She tugged at her father's arm, trying to get him to back down. "All that is in the past. He owns a business now. He's our next-door neighbor, so cool it, all right? Besides, it's almost time to leave for your PT appointment."

Roman cleared his throat. "Mr. D'Angelo, I'm here to run my grandfather's farm. I hope we can be neighborly to one another." He came forward, hand extended. But the old man didn't budge.

Instead, Vito made an unpleasant sound. A grunt.

"Pop, he was helping me with the dog." Bella walked over to her brother. "Let's go home."

Vito shifted his weight and addressed Roman. "Your grandparents were good people and good neighbors. I respected them, no matter what happened between you and my daughter. But I will not conduct my business next to you."

Roman didn't care about the old man. He focused on Bella, who had hesitated before entering the woods. They'd had enough ugliness twelve years ago. Somehow, he had to prevent this from getting out of control. For her sake.

"Pop, come on." She was pleading with him. Roman hated to see it.

"Leave me to my business, Bella," Vito said.

Bella looked at Roman. He saw the apology in her eyes even before she mouthed, *I'm so sorry.* To her father, she said, "I can't be a part of this. I'm going back home. Come on, Joe."

Joe took the leash from his sister and followed, not saying anything. He didn't even look at Roman.

"Vito, stop!" They all turned to see a tiny powerhouse of a woman stalking over in her black skirt and Doc Martens. Roman's mother, who clearly hadn't left when she was supposed to. "You haven't changed in all these years, have you?" she said, stopping in front of Vito. "Not one bit."

Vito rolled his eyes. "Marjorie, don't you have something better to do? Like run your peace talks someplace else."

Unintimidated, Marjorie got in Vito's face. "Give these kids a break. What harm does it do to be neighborly?"

"I understand these things," Vito said. "Once you are addicted to a drug, you can't stop. Why put the temptation next door?"

"Oh, for God's sake, Dad," Bella said. She frowned at Roman, clearly not liking the idea that he could be her crack or something. Despite the tension, he almost laughed.

"They're adults, Vito," Marjorie said. "Leave them be."

"I will not. Look what happened the first time."

"Give them some credit. The condom broke."

"Mom! TMI there," Roman called, looking over at Joe, who was biting back a chuckle.

"Look," Marjorie said, "I appreciate all that you did for my parents. Now I'm asking you to extend the same courtesy to my son."

"I can't do that, Marjorie, I'm sorry. I liked your parents. They were good people. But this—this is too much." He turned to Roman. "I can't stop you from what you're doing, but I'm not going to make it easy for you. I respected your grandfather, but not you. I control the pond for irrigation. And from now on, it's off limits. I catch you stealing my water, and I'll report you to the police. You hear that?"

"Vito, no," Francesca said.

"I'm going back to my lunch," he said and stalked off.

Despite the fact that the old man was trying to ruin him and his grandfather's orchard, Roman found himself smiling a little. Because

Bella looked so mortified. Because he wanted her to know that her father no longer had any power over him. He didn't, really. And he certainly didn't care to expend the energy to maintain an old vendetta that was best left behind them. He just wanted very badly to make her feel better.

She caught his gaze and gave him a quick, succinct nod. One that said, *He is the way he is, but he's not me.* Her aunt patted Bella on the shoulder as they all entered the path in the woods, the dog leading the way.

Roman put his arm around his mother. "Maybe you should've worked for the UN or something."

Marjorie rolled her eyes. "He acts like an old man, and he's only fifty. I just don't get that."

"Maybe he'll chill out with time." He doubted it, but he wanted his mom to feel better, too. They began to walk up the sloping hill back to the house. "Out of curiosity, what exactly did Vito ever do for Gram and Gramps?"

She sighed. "He's a good cook, did you know that? He'd bring over food. And home-grown vegetables. And when Gram's dementia got bad, she started wandering over there for a while, and he always helped her back home. He's not a bad man. He's just very protective of his daughter."

Roman saw his mom off, then went inside to change out of his wet clothes. And thought about Bella. He'd forgotten how she could do spontaneous things and take him along for the ride. Today he'd seen a glimpse of the fun-loving, spunky girl she'd been. Not the cool, guarded, serious woman from the other night.

But he had to be careful. He couldn't allow the thought of her to take him over, as it had once upon a time. As she still might be capable of doing, as it seemed every nerve in his body had the tendency to go haywire in her presence. Maybe there was something to that crack idea, after all.

No, their past was said and done. It would be ridiculous to get to know her again, let alone start something. Especially with a stubborn Italian man next door who hated his guts.

There were plenty of nice women in Mirror Lake, and he was certain he could run into a few on a late-summer's night when the air was just starting to get a chill. In fact, that could be just the remedy for his ails.

And he had to stop trying to be a nice guy. That was one of his problems. An overly developed sense of responsibility. Rescuing people who didn't need or want rescuing. He had to fight it. He would just do his business on his own property and stay clear of Vito D'Angelo and his sassy daughter.

Bella's and his past was more twisted than a soft pretzel. Too much water had passed under that bridge. Too much hurt—no, *devastation*. He'd be a fool not to realize that no matter how much his body lit up like the Rockefeller Center Christmas tree in her presence still, after all these years, some hurts were far too deep to ever be forgotten.

CHAPTER 6

Twelve Years Earlier

"Do you always study?" Roman asked one morning as he sat in the library next to Bella, sharing her copy of *The Scarlet Letter*. He'd forgotten his . . . on purpose, and he was enjoying smelling her freshly shampooed hair and watching her concentrate intently on the page they were discussing from a closer vantage point than usual.

She looked up, surprised. "No, of course not."

"Well, what else do you do, Ms. Smarty-Pants?"

"I work. At the garden center."

"I mean, what do you do for fun?"

"What do *you* do for fun?" she countered, a little irritated. He waggled his eyebrows, and her face reddened. "Why do you date Reagan? She's no good for you."

"Why do you care?" he asked, still smiling. Actually, he'd just broken up with Reagan. How many times had Roman heard that kids raised in homes where both parents were alcoholics often gravitated toward relationships that were the equivalent of emotional roller coasters? And they sought people they could "fix."

He wasn't sure any of that was really the case with Reagan. He'd started talking to her because she was pretty and friendly and had a great rack. Okay, so he was shallow, but, hey, he was an eighteen-year-old healthy male.

But if girls were photographs, Bella was Technicolor, and Reagan was a washed-out, sepia-toned version. There was no comparison.

"Why do you want to be with someone who thrives on creating drama?" Bella continued. "Life brings its own drama. Relationships should be—peaceful."

He laughed. Maybe because this eighteen-year-old girl sounded like his old psychologist. "Peaceful?" Not the first word he'd choose. Wild, hot, crazy—now those were more along his lines. "That sounds a little geriatric."

"Yeah, well, my aunt has an expression. 'Choose your friends. Don't let your friends choose you.'"

He reached up and fingered a curl that had dropped out of her bun. It sprang back from his light tug. "You have amazing hair," he said. He felt his own cheeks redden. This girl made him act like an idiot. He cleared his throat and tried to focus on the book in front of them. "Do you always give guys you like advice?" he teased.

"Who says I like you?" she asked. But when she glanced up at him, their eyes locked. Her breath hitched. His own breathing was stiff and labored, an iron lung in his chest. This girl was *doing* things to him, making him feel out of control, a feeling he hated. Yet he was completely hooked.

"*Do* you like me, Bella?" he asked quietly.

She blushed, but she didn't look away. It was he who finally broke the spell, pretending to study the book on the library table between them.

He wanted to tell Bella he'd broken up with Reagan, but Reagan hadn't taken it very well. He just didn't want her to do anything stupid.

Not that he expected her to direct her wrath toward Bella, but he wouldn't put such a thing past her. He knew enough about the darker side of life to understand that was possible.

He just had to hurry up if he was going to ask Bella to homecoming. Time was getting short. All the guys had already let him know Bella never went out with anyone, but that didn't scare him off. Somehow, he felt it in his bones that she'd say yes to him. He figured he had until the end of the week. Judging by how much everyone liked her, every day he worried someone else was going to get to her first.

Frankly, Bella was right. The drama with Reagan was ballbusting. She was easily offended at some remark her silly friends made, and that usually blew up into a massive fight, where she wouldn't talk to certain friends or others for days. Or she was constantly trying to corral them around her like she was a queen and they were her court.

"Anyway," Bella said, flipping through the book. "Back to the ending. What did you think of it?"

"They're buried under the same tombstone. How melodramatic." He rolled his eyes. He liked science and math. He didn't like being touchy-feely about books.

She shut the book. "It's not melodramatic. Dimmesdale made his confession publicly and claimed his kid as his own and then he fell dead, with a big *A* emblazoned on his chest." She traced a giant *A* on her upper chest with her finger.

"Which he inflicted upon himself."

"No. The guilt burned it from the inside out."

"What?"

"It gnawed on him from the inside out."

"You are crazy, woman."

"He confessed. He made it right. And they're buried together under the same tombstone. That proves that even after death, their love continues."

He shut his notebook. Forget Hawthorne. She was mesmerizing. All sparkling eyes and lush, full lips, and he wanted to kiss her. Now.

"It's a tale of human frailty, Roman. Of undying love. Of forgiveness. Of good over evil. There are endless things to talk about. Surely you can write a three-paragraph essay." She was so . . . passionate . . . And her belief was contagious. Maybe somewhere, love did last. I mean, it hadn't so far in his life. He and his four brothers were taken away from their parents and each other when he was only eight. Maybe it was possible for love to survive the roller-coaster ride of life and for people to love each other in a way that didn't kill them. But damned if he knew.

"Maybe you should be trying out for the play," he said, grinning.

She looked up from studying the book. Most girls didn't exactly play up their intellectual assets, especially in front of guys they were trying to impress. She wasn't embarrassed to say she loved *The Scarlet Letter*, even though most of the kids in the class, including him, didn't really get it. He was impressed that she was who she was. Nothing phony about her.

She turned red and flipped her hand in a dismissive gesture. "No, not me. I just love feeling the story. Reading a book is even better for me than seeing it acted out." She looked at him carefully. "I heard about your audition yesterday."

He shrugged. Everyone was talking about his accidental audition for *Grease*, where he sang a duet with Reagan to help her try out for the part of Sandy, which of course she got. "I did it as a favor."

"Well, you did a great job. You're a perfect Danny."

He stared at her for a moment. "If they offer me the part, I'm not taking it."

"Why not?"

"I'm not into being in the spotlight." His brother Lukas, who was a few years older, had loved to sing and dance and ham it up, but not him. He had nothing against those things, but not in front of a theater full of people.

"What, are you kidding? You in jeans and a white T-shirt, your hair slicked back . . . every girl in the school will want to date you, and every guy will wish he were you. You'll have insta-fame. You can't pass that up."

"That's not important to me. Actually, I was wondering . . ."

Just then, Ethan Cohen came up to them. They were on the basketball team together and they'd started hanging out a little. Roman knew he was a longtime friend of Bella's.

"Hi, Bells," Ethan said. He glanced tentatively at Roman, then back to Bella. "What's going on?"

"Ethan, this is my—" She hesitated. He suddenly realized he'd given her no reason to call him anything else but a friend, and that was just the wrong label, period. Because from the moment he saw her, he'd wanted more. And somehow, he wanted Ethan to know it, too, as soon as possible. "This is Roman. Spikonos," Bella continued. "He transferred from Mirror Lake High."

"Yeah, for basketball," Ethan said. "We met in conditioning." He eyed Roman, not in an unfriendly way, but it wasn't his usual warm, happy-go-lucky Ethan way, either. Like maybe he'd suddenly perceived a threat.

Nah, Roman's imagination was just kicking into high gear. Ethan had been nothing but friendly to him since he'd arrived. Roman had transferred because Our Lady of the Lake had the best team in the state. It gave him the best shot at a basketball scholarship to the school of his dreams, UC Davis, where he wanted to study business. And something sort of unique. Brewing science. They had one of the best programs in the country, and if he could get a scholarship, he'd go in a heartbeat. He wasn't meant to be a farmer, and if he stayed here, his grandfather would make sure he became one.

Some of the guys on the team had resented a hotshot transfer, but Ethan had been welcoming from the start. Roman was hoping they could be friends. Except there might be something standing between them. Five foot five inches of pretty girl something.

Ethan turned back to Bella. "I have something important to ask you. Do you have a minute?"

Roman thought Ethan looked nervous, a little pale. Like he was getting his courage up. Or maybe he'd just spent too many hours working in the animal shelter after school. But when he wiped sweat off his forehead, Roman's heart sank.

"Now?" Bella moved to get up, told Roman she'd be right back. He pretended to be struggling through the remaining homework questions, but they may as well have been written in ancient Greek for all he comprehended.

Bella stood with Ethan just outside the library while Roman tapped his pencil eraser on the table. Shook his foot. Finally he scrawled something quickly on the bottom of a page in his notebook. *Bella, will you go to homecoming with me? Please. R.* Then he ripped it out.

As he passed Bella, he bumped against her, not failing to notice the flowery smell of her hair and how soft her skin was. He put his hands on her shoulders to make sure she was okay . . . and because he couldn't resist the chance to touch her. "Excuse me," he said, tucking the square of paper into her palm. "Headed to the restroom. Be right back."

Lame, he knew. But what else could he do?

When he got back after wandering the halls for a few minutes, Bella was still talking with Ethan. Roman's gut was seized up and churning, and his palms were clammy. The room looked a little unfocused. He'd never had this reaction with a girl before. Ever. This didn't feel like a crush; it felt like death. And he didn't like it at all.

She probably hadn't even read the note. He'd waited too long, blown his chance. He didn't even bother sitting down, just began gathering up his stuff, getting ready for the day to start.

"Bella was just telling me you two are going to homecoming," Ethan said. He wasn't smiling. In fact, he looked troubled. Guarded.

"That's . . . great news." Then he picked up his book bag, said, "See you guys around," and walked away.

"Did Ethan just ask you to homecoming?" Roman asked.

"Yes, but it was only because he had an argument with Barb Hannity. They'll probably make up and he'll ask her after all."

"Does Ethan . . . like you?" He suddenly felt guilty. Maybe he should have let Ethan ask her. But he and Bella were just friends, right?

"Ethan? We've known each other since we were babies. Our mothers were best friends. They even did a photo album of the two of us together when we were toddlers. I think they imagined one day we might end up together, but it's not like that."

"What about you?" she asked. "Are you sure you don't want to go with Reagan?"

"I'm sure," he said, reaching for her hand on the table. It was small and smooth. And it fit perfectly in his. Just touching her sent tingles up his arm and drove every unpleasant thought out of his mind. "So will you go with me?"

"Yes, I'll go with you," she said, flashing him a smile. "There's just one condition."

"What's that?" he asked. Anything. He'd do anything.

"We don't discuss old books."

"Oh, I don't know if we should take that topic off the table. They're growing on me." So was she. A lot. In fact, he'd talk about the entire literary canon with her if it meant they could spend more time together.

"You're such a liar," she said, squeezing his hand and getting up to go to class.

And just like that, he was in love.

In the next few months, Bella's father took right to Roman, despite the fact that Roman was of Greek heritage, that he had been raised by a liberal single mother, and most important of all, that he was dating his daughter.

Roman wasn't afraid to get dirty, and the magic words "Can I help?" seemed to bring out an unexpected side of Mr. D'Angelo. Roman helped him load hay and tomatoes, unload corn, and fix tractors. He hauled and lugged and assisted when watering systems broke down and pumpkins needed harvesting.

"I like your friend Ethan, but he doesn't know an emitter from his shoelace," Vito said one day to Bella. "But this boy," he said, tilting his head toward Roman, "he's good with his hands."

Roman did his best not to look at Bella. Yet he couldn't help it, and there she was, smiling and casting him a knowing glance that made him immediately look back down at the spark plugs he was helping her father change.

Roman had never experienced anything like this. He wanted to spend every minute of his free time with Bella. And he didn't mind her family. Her little brother was cute, a natural charmer, and Roman didn't have to try very hard to win him over. Roman understood how strict Bella's father was, but he was eager to prove that he respected his daughter and would do anything to please her—and him.

So months passed with Roman doing his best to act the gentleman. He'd made out with lots of girls before, had gotten to various bases, but with Bella he'd really tried to be different.

"Bella, sweetheart," he said, gently grabbing her hands away from his crotch and holding her wrists one night when they were parked in his car at the scenic lookout. "Stop. You're driving me wild."

"Roman, we need to talk," she said.

That was probably the last thing he was capable of right now, but he nodded and let go of her and adjusted his pants, because his things were very tight down there. He forced himself to sit up straight and take a few deep breaths. "Okay. Let's talk."

"Well, I appreciate that you're very respectful of me, but I'm crazy in love with you and I want to ask if you'd like to . . . like to take our relationship to the next level."

Would he like to take this to the next level? He was crazy about Bella, too, more than he'd ever been for any girl. He would have done anything for her, including keep his hands off her if that was what she wanted. Or at least try to.

"Wait a minute," he said, suddenly grabbing her by the arms. "Did you just say you were in love with me?"

"Yeah. I did. I'm sorry if you're unhappy about that, but it's the truth." She cast him a wary glance. Grabbed her sweater from the seat like she was going to open the door and bolt.

"Wait." He reached out to rub his palm over her sweet, soft cheek. Cupped his hand around her neck and pulled her closer. Looked into her eyes and whispered, "I love you, too."

The thing was, Marjorie had told him in her usual blunt way on more than one occasion that his penis was a loaded weapon, and he should be very careful where he put it. He understood that. He was grateful that she'd adopted him and thankful for her unfailing love, and he'd never do anything less than make her glad she'd taken him in and changed his life for the better.

So he knew the decision to make love wasn't an impulsive one. He was aware of the responsibility. And he wanted to plan something special.

One cold December evening just before dusk he drove them to the Mirror Lake Nature Center, which was basically a little-kid hangout. It was right next to the lake and as he predicted, it was deserted at that time of day.

Multicolored Christmas lights hung in a string along the roofline, lighting their way as they followed the little pathway to the back of the building near where old Mr. Richardson kept the birdfeeders stocked. Sure enough, an old rowboat was tethered to a skinny maple trunk, just as Roman had left it earlier. He put an old cooler and his duffle bag in the boat and braced himself on the bank, waiting for Bella to climb down.

"It's *December*," she said, as if he needed reminding he was freezing his ass off.

He blew out a breath, which immediately turned into a little white cloud. "But the lake's not frozen yet."

"Where are you taking me? It's cold." She burrowed her chin further into her scarf and wrapped her arms around herself.

He held out his hand for her. "Somewhere with no little brothers, or parents, or cramped cars. Somewhere special." She took his hand and sandwiched it between her purple mittens.

"You didn't have to fuss," she said. "I don't care where we go as long as we're together, Roman."

"I know you don't care," he said. But *he* did. He wanted this night to be special. The first thing he did once they were both settled in the boat was flip a little battery-operated switch. In the almost dark, the outline of the old boat lit up with strings of tiny white lights, a quiet glow in the mist that reflected off the black marble surface of the water.

"Very pretty," she said.

He looked at her, pleased that she was smiling. "Yes, you are." Then he started to row, steadily, rhythmically, the oars cutting the almost-still water, the blue rectangular cooler sandwiched between their legs. Halfway across, he stopped and let them drift for a minute.

"It's different," she said, staring out at the water. "The lake." Christmas lights dotted most of the houses on shore, continuing the illusion of magic. "I've never been out here in December."

"Neither have I. Until now." He searched her face, scouring it for any sign of doubt. "Are you sure you want to do this?"

"Yeah," she said, a faint smile turning up her lips. "But I'm afraid I'm not going to be any good at it."

He laughed. "You can't possibly do anything wrong." He was the man. It was his job to ensure they did things right. Wasn't it? "And I did tell you I haven't done this before, either, didn't I?"

She leaned over and kissed him. "Guess we'll figure it out together."

He ran a finger along her cheek, which was cold but so soft. Looked deep into her eyes, which were a little watery from the cold. "I'd do anything for you, Bella. Anything. You know that, don't you?" He was so full of love for her his heart hurt. He couldn't remember feeling happy like this ever before in his life. Couldn't believe this had happened to him of all people. He, who'd had such a sad and lonely childhood, who even now tended to be a little too solitary, a little too guarded. But she'd changed him. Made him less afraid about opening up. Took away all that old sorrow and filled his heart with the pure joy of being with her.

He banked the boat on a woodsy part of the shoreline. Tied it to a beat-up old dock. Judging by the absolute darkness, there weren't any houses around, at least not occupied ones. She helped him carry the cooler up a sloping, neglected lawn to an old cabin.

He set the cooler down in front of the door. "You have to wait out here a minute, okay?"

She looked around. It was pitch black except for his flashlight. "Are you kidding?"

"Hey, at least there're no bugs." She hated bugs. Any kind, but especially spiders. "Be back in a sec."

It was a little scary out there, so he let her stand inside the cabin door if she promised to face the door and close her eyes. There was a solitary bare lightbulb hanging from the ceiling, which he flicked on while he worked. He'd rowed out here earlier, gathering firewood and kindling, and he now he lit a fire in the fireplace, got it going nice and strong. Then he unzipped his bag and did some more setting up.

"Okay," he said at last. "Turn around and open your eyes—oh, wait! I've got to turn off the light." He ran back across the room and flicked off the switch. Returning to her side, he took her hand. "Now look."

She opened her eyes, which instantly went wide and even got teary. "Oh, Roman," she said, looking from him to the scene before them. The fire was crackling along brightly, and he'd lit a dozen candles in little glass cups. Interspersed between the candles were pieces of paper. Bella walked over near the fireplace, where he'd set up an air mattress and blanket. Then she read the message spelled out on the papers. *I LOVE YOU BELLA.*

"I love you, too," she whispered.

Then he pulled her into his arms and kissed her. Her lips were soft and moist, and she fit into his arm so perfectly, his sweet Bella. He knew then that they were meant to be together, that he'd never love anyone as much as he did her. Their kisses became urgent, their touches more frantic. They made love in front of that fire, and it might've been a little clumsy and awkward, but it was also sweet and incredible.

He was so afraid he was hurting her, and she kept saying, "No, you aren't, keep going," and then suddenly he was inside of her and she'd relaxed a little. Finally so did he, and when he made himself look at her to make sure she was okay, she was smiling up at him, and he swore that as long as he lived he'd remember that look in her eyes, that look of complete, pure trust. He knew in that moment he'd do anything for her, give her anything, scale mountains and deserts and oceans for her happiness.

As gently as he could, he began to move against her, being so careful not to cause her any more pain, until finally she tugged him more fully against her, wrapped her arms and legs around him tightly, and said, "It's good, Roman. Go faster." And he felt her smile against his cheek until passion took over and swept them both away.

"Fuck."

Oh fuck, he hadn't meant to say that out loud.

Bella sat up on the air mattress and looked at him from across the small room. "What is it? Did you hurt yourself?" The fire was dying down, and the chill in the cabin was noticeable for the first time. She pulled the sides of her shirt together and started buttoning up. "Do you need help?"

He was turned away from her, bending over his dick, paralyzed for a second. He didn't want to tell her what he'd just discovered. Yet how could he keep it from her?

"What is it? What's wrong?" she asked again, panic edging her voice as she got up and walked over to him.

He bent to the floor, picked up his pants, and tugged them on. Then he turned toward her and held her by the arms. "It tore."

"What?" Her forehead crinkled, then her eyes grew wide as understanding dawned.

"The condom. It tore."

She released a breath. "Oh. It's okay, Roman. We should be okay. I haven't missed a pill since I started two weeks ago. I mean, the doctor said to use a condom too for the first month, and we did, so it's like we had two methods on board, just like she said."

She must've seen his expression, or the tension in his shoulders, because she walked up behind him and wrapped her arms around his waist. "It's all right, we're covered. Don't worry about it."

She sounded pretty confident, and her tone relaxed him a little. Plus she'd started kneading his shoulders, which felt amazing. "Thank you for doing all this," she said. "It was magical. All of it." Her hair was wild, thick waves tumbling everywhere. He turned toward her and brushed it back, reveling in the feel of the long, silken strands. Then she dropped kisses on his chest, her curves warm and soft against him. He reached down to cup her face and tilted her head up. "I love you," he said, kissing her. He'd never meant anything more.

Who'd have ever thought that he, an orphan, would find someone to love him so completely, someone who knew all about his crappy upbringing and his quirks and loved him anyway? All worries faded as he bent down to kiss her again and press their bodies together, and whisper in her ear that he'd never let her go.

CHAPTER 7

"I need you to do me a favor," Maggie McShae, Bella's business partner, said as soon as Bella entered their shared office space right smack in the middle of Main Street. It was Monday night, and Bella was getting ready for her weekly divorced or bereaved group for seniors.

Bella detected the trace of anxiety in Maggie's voice. "Sure, what is it?" Bella asked, adjusting the thermostat so the air conditioning clicked off. The night was clear and just a little cool, and she decided that opening the big old-fashioned sash windows that faced the street and letting in some fresh air would be a lot more pleasant than the recirculated kind.

"Will you check if all the burners are off in the back? I made tea, and I—"

Bella shot a concerned look at her friend. Her blonde hair was tied back with a ribbon. Pulling her hair off her face made her blue eyes look huge, and Bella noticed she had dark circles under them. Bella suddenly remembered what was really going on—that tomorrow was the two-year anniversary of Maggie's husband's death after a prolonged battle with cancer. "No problem. You need to go home to Griffin. It's almost seven." She herself had worked until five, gone home for dinner, and was now back for her group therapy session tonight, while Maggie had never left the office.

"The babysitter took him and his friend from preschool to a movie. They're not due back for another half an hour." Maggie was putting in some long hours lately, and her OCD was really acting up, a sure sign of some other stress going on in her life. She and Maggie had known each other since grade school, so it didn't take a rocket scientist to figure that out. "If I would've known you were still here," Bella said, "I'd have brought you some of my lasagna."

"Don't worry about me. I was just catching up on paperwork." Maggie picked up her leather satchel from the reception counter and shoved her computer into it.

"Don't forget tomorrow night—dinner at MacNamara's with the girls. You promised to support me before my big date." Bella's best friends—Maggie, Samantha Spikonos, and Jessica Martin, who taught with Sam at Mirror Lake High—had each insisted on fixing her up with nice guys they knew, and for some reason she'd agreed to be their guinea pig. Her first date was tomorrow. She was counting on their support.

"I wouldn't miss it. You know how badly we all want you to stay in town."

"I'm not really sure why I agreed to this."

"Um, because we plied you with margaritas until you said yes, remember?" A look of worry flashed across Maggie's face. "Is something up with you?"

"No. What makes you think that?" Her problems weren't even worth mentioning in the face of what Maggie was going through.

"Just that I ran into Marjorie and she told me about the face-off with Vito the other day."

"Just for the record, there were no shotguns involved."

"Good to hear." Maggie shoved some papers into her bag. "Want to talk about it?"

"Gracie bolted for the water, and Roman and I got a little wet fishing her out of the lake."

"And a little hot and bothered?"

"No. Well, yes, a little." Bella picked up a pen from the reception desk and started fiddling with it. "In that same weird way as always. I may not be able to help what happens to me when he's near—but I can control the outcome, right? I'm an adult. It would be the most foolish thing in the world to get involved with him again. A huge mistake."

Maggie's frown deepened into what Bella referred to as her therapist expression. Which always meant she was going to attempt some of her psychological voodoo on *her*. "Did you ever talk to him about what happened way back then?"

"Of course not. No. Nor will I. Who would ever want to bring all that up again?"

"Because you lied to him, Bella. You told him you didn't want him. Maybe that's why part of you hangs on to him. Because of how it ended. His being back here is an opportunity to clear the air that maybe you should take."

"I've moved on. He's just still so . . . hot." The cheap pen she was holding suddenly came apart, a tiny spring bouncing to the ground. She bent down to pick up the pieces. "Anyway, sorry. Didn't mean to get into all that."

"I've got to get home. We'll talk more tomorrow." Maggie got halfway to the door before she stopped and walked back to the counter, scanning the surface. "I just wanted to be sure I didn't leave my wallet. You're going to make sure the back door's locked, right? And turn off all the lights except for the waiting room one we always leave on. In fact, I can go turn it—"

"Maggie, go home," Bella said, taking her by the elbow and steering her back toward the door. "Unless you want to stay for group. Then we could grab a bite afterward. You know the ladies always bring plenty of dessert—that'll tide you over."

"Thanks, Bella, but I'm not staying for advice from the Divorced, Desperate, or Dead crowd."

It was actually the Divorced or Bereaved Senior Support Group, but the ladies themselves tended to refer to themselves as the Three Ds. The topics of discussion they brought up might stir a private chuckle once in a while as they loved to socialize, but underneath that, they'd all survived the death of a spouse or a divorce, sometimes after many years of marriage. "Tell me honestly," Bella said. "Is there something I can do to help?"

"I just have to get through this week." She gave a smile that looked more summoned up than spontaneous. "I'll be fine."

Bella gave her a little hug. "I'm sorry, honey."

"Yeah. Sucks, you know?"

"Are you sure I can't feed you? Fix you up with a nice new pet from Ethan to keep you company? Or maybe just . . . fix you up with Ethan?"

Maggie smiled. "Not interested in a pet or a boyfriend. I can barely handle myself and Griffin."

"How about someone to fool around with?"

"You tried that with Ethan and look where that got you. The man is head over heels."

"He's not. He's just upset about his last breakup, and whenever that happens, he gets these fantasies of us being together." Maggie didn't look convinced, but she had the good sense to not say anything. "You know Dr. Maloney would see you if your symptoms are really acting up. Maybe give you something temporary—" Dr. Maloney was the psychiatrist they often consulted for patients who needed to be prescribed meds.

She'd caught Maggie going over and over her patients' charts the other day. Obsessing about ways she could help them better. Worried she might have forgotten to do something important. And Bella knew she was taking work home where she could do the same thing later, too.

"I don't want to take drugs, Bella. I took tomorrow off, and I scheduled myself a little lighter this week. I'll be fine." She added, "But if I'm not, I'll be sure to call her next week. Okay?"

Bella hugged her. "I know you'll be fine. But don't be ashamed to ask for help."

Maggie laughed. "I say that to people all day long."

Bella shrugged. "And sometimes you've got to say it to yourself, right?"

"I'll be fine. See you at MacNamara's tomorrow, for your date."

Bella walked her to the door, making a mental note to bring Maggie some lasagna tomorrow. She was too thin. A shame, because all Bella had to do was look at a pound of cheese from across the room and the calories seemed to magically migrate to her hips.

At the same time the door shut, pounding sounds arose from the direction of the abandoned office space next door. Bella had no idea who would be banging around after hours, but she hoped it would be short lived. She entered the waiting room, where she began to arrange chairs in a circle. *Boom, boom, boom.* Their diplomas on the wall closest to the door rattled in their frames as the hammering became incessant.

What on earth was someone demo-ing at seven o'clock at night? The place next door had been a flower shop, and the florist had taken most of the shelving with her when she'd moved out. What could possibly be left to tear down?

Bella put on a pot of coffee and took the tiramisu she'd made last night out of the back refrigerator. She'd found over the past couple of years that food made people more comfortable, and comfortable people talked more. Besides, in a place like Mirror Lake, her clients were also her neighbors, and she was as likely to see them on the street or in the grocery store as in her office. Being neighborly never hurt.

The office door opened. "Well, hello, dear," a white-haired woman in pink sneakers and a bright floral sweater said as she gave a little wave. Everyone in town knew Effie Scofield, matriarch of the Rushford clan. She was accompanied by her best friend, Gloria Manning, a woman in a tidy tweed suit and lovely red hair the color of Prince Harry's, a fact that she loved to mention, as she was a great aficionado of all things royal. The two of them looked back at a third woman with bold glasses and very black hair who was carting a big flowered satchel.

"We brought a friend," Effie said, taking the new woman's coat and hanging it on a hook near the door.

"Hi, ladies," Bella said, greeting them by handing them coffees. "Gloria, I love your new haircut."

"Thank you for noticing, dear. Who do I remind you of?" Gloria turned her head this way and that.

"Um, I'm not sure, but it's lovely."

Gloria pulled out her phone and showed Bella a photo.

"Oh, Princess Diana!" Bella said. "Same cut. Of course!"

The new woman held out her hand and said her name. But Bella had to ask her to repeat it due to all the hammering.

"Bella," Effie began, then corrected herself. "Er, *Doctor* D'Angelo, I should say—and by the way we are very proud of that PhD you earned—this is our friend Alethea Panagakos. She's from Greece."

Bella shook her hand. "Hi, Alethea. Welcome to the group."

The frames of Alethea's glasses were dotted with faux jewels, and she was wearing a bright-red sweater with black tights and a chunky statement necklace.

"I'm so nervous being here," she said, fanning herself. "I'm not one to confide in strangers, you know? And also I'm fifty-five." She lowered her voice and whispered to Bella, "I'm not really a senior."

"If you could get an AARP card, you're a senior," Effie said loud and clear.

"I think you'll find that everyone here is very friendly," Bella said, deflecting the age comments. "What's said here, stays here." She hoped. Knowing these ladies' penchant for good gossip, sometimes she wasn't so sure, even though she did remind them at the beginning of each session to keep their mouths shut. Not in those exact words, of course.

"Most of the people in this group are looking for companionship," Gloria said, patting Alethea's hand. "Except since I've remarried, I share an entirely different set of challenges. It's like being a newlywed again."

"You're not a newlywed. You've been married six years," Effie said to Gloria, then turned back to Bella. "She and that nice retired doctor of hers are as happy as two peas in a pod. She just likes to come and visit with everyone."

"And I feel that I have a lot to offer," Gloria said proudly. "After all, I never thought I'd be one to ever remarry after I lost my husband at thirty-one. I would hope my story offers encouragement to others, that anything can happen, you know?"

Anything can happen. Bella wished *she* could believe that. She was so ready for *something* to happen. And not with a certain man who happened to be a blast from her past, either. Not that she was thinking of him at all, of course.

"If you could find a man after all those years, maybe I can, too," Alethea said.

"Bella's thirty-one and she could use one, too," came a familiar voice. Bella looked up to see her very own Aunt Francesca walk in. Nonna had died earlier this year, and Frannie had finally retired from her job as a grade-school librarian, both of which had left her free to come to Mirror Lake for an extended visit. In the past few weeks, with her father's back surgery, Bella was more than grateful to have her around.

"I'm twenty-nine, Aunt Francesca," Bella said.

"Soon to be thirty," she said.

Oh no. If left to her own devices, Aunt Francesca would be spewing forth Italian platitudes and dropping juicy tidbits of Bella's private life in no time. Bella would have to make sure that personal comment she just made would be her last. She could feel the professional caliber of the group declining at the speed of light.

She should have made Maggie take this group. These women would soon be all over Bella's love life like a vulture on roadkill, but they'd never stoop so low as to prey upon a respectable widow.

"What are you doing here?" Bella asked Aunt Fran, hoping by chance she was just stopping by with some goodies. Fat chance, as she'd never just dropped by her office before.

"I brought cookies," Aunt Fran said, handing over a big platter.

Bella took the platter, because, well, she had to. "And?" she asked her aunt, blocking the entrance into the office with her body.

"Well, this is the support group for widowed or divorced seniors, right?"

"Welcome to the Three Ds—Divorced, Desperate, or Dead," Effie said. "The dead is not for anyone personally. It's if someone you loved died."

"It's really called the Divorced or Bereaved Senior Support Group," Bella said quickly. She didn't want anyone to think that the group was a joke. Although sometimes she wasn't sure, what with these characters showing up and bringing their friends like it was senior happy hour.

"I'm not divorced or widowed, but I've been single forever." Aunt Fran tilted up her elegant Italian chin and gave Bella that special look that only her aunt was capable of leveling on her. "Never married. And

I'm tired of it. Plus I'm thinking of moving permanently to Mirror Lake. I thought I'd come and check out the group. Besides, I helped my niece make that tiramisu and I want some."

"Okay, fine. You can stay," Bella said. "But this is a professional group." She leaned over and whispered, "Absolutely nothing about my personal life. Okay?"

"Got it," her aunt said, looking around at the waiting area. "Oh, this is a very pretty office, Bella. But where are the men in the group?"

"No men so far," Effie said. "Only women."

"Aw, that's a shame," Aunt Fran said. "I was hoping to maybe meet a nice man so I wouldn't have to do online dating."

Oh Dio. Bella tried not to roll her eyes.

"I was hoping to meet a nice man here, too," Alethea said. "I keep thinking I'll meet one through church, but all the volunteer groups are full of women. Maybe I'm going to have to try that new online dating app, Tender."

"You mean Tinder," Gloria said.

"Did you say *Timber*?" Effie asked.

"No, Tender," Alethea said. "Ten-der. You know, where you can meet a tender partner. That name makes sense, doesn't it?"

"No, dear, it's Tinder," Gloria said. "Tin-der. Like something that catches a spark."

"Oh." Alethea looked a little disappointed. "A spark. I think I understand. But I like Tender better."

"There's a lot of young men who use that app, ladies," Bella said.

"I have nothing against young men," Alethea said.

"Not me," Fran said. "I want a mature man. One who's grown up and knows what he wants."

"Mature but not old," Effie said. "Like good wine."

"That's what we could use," Alethea said, scanning the table where the dessert was. "Some wine."

At this point, so could she. "Okay, ladies," Bella said. "How about if we go sit down?"

"I'm sort of glad there aren't any men here yet," Gloria said. "We can talk about woman things without feeling like we have to censor ourselves." She wrapped an arm around Aunt Francesca's shoulders and led her to a seat. "I'm glad you could join us."

Bella guided them into the waiting room, which was stylishly decorated, if she could say so herself, in soothing colors of aqua and tan and black. The ladies settled into the comfy waiting room chairs she and Maggie had picked out themselves. A few nice lamps and throw pillows made the waiting room a quiet, serene place. So did the watercolor paintings her good friend Samantha Spikonos, an art teacher, had painted.

Effie took an Italian wedding cookie and her coffee and settled in. "I can go first," she offered.

Bella poured herself some coffee but decided to wait on the dessert. Anything could come out of these women's mouths, and she had to be on her guard. "Sure, go ahead, Effie."

"I went on a date last week with a neighbor from assisted living, and all he talked about was how many medications he was on. He told me how hard it was to keep track of them all. Then he asked me how many years I was a nurse. I think he wanted someone to help keep them all straight."

A murmur went up from the other ladies. "I'm sorry about that," Gloria said. "Seems like some men our age just want someone to take care of them."

"I took care of my husband, Hercules," Alethea said. "I did everything around the house, all the cooking and cleaning, plus worked as a bookkeeper in my family's olive oil company. And do you know what he did? He fooled around on me. Marriage wasn't a good experience for me."

"Then why do you want to try it again?" Fran asked.

"For a long time I thought it was me, that I just wasn't cut out for living with a man. That maybe I drove my husband to cheat. But my girlfriend in Greece told me Hercules just divorced his third wife. It occurred to me that maybe it wasn't all my fault. Maybe it was his, too."

"How was your sex life?" Effie asked.

"That's awfully personal," Bella said quickly. Effie was like a train. She was fine if someone kept her on the tracks, but the slightest slack in vigilance and she'd head straight off the cliff.

Alethea waved her hand dismissively. "We're among friends. It was terrible."

"Did you try any K-Y, dear?" Effie asked.

"Effie," Bella warned. Dear saints in heaven, she needed dessert. And wine.

"Honey," Effie said, "I'm a nurse. It's okay for us to be a little medical. You handle the head stuff, and I'll handle the body stuff."

And who would handle the bouncer stuff? Because Bella was about to eject Effie from the group, orthopedic tennies and all.

"It was nothing like that," Alethea said. "Our sex life was full of inhibitions and no communication. I disappointed him. I thought for a long time I would disappoint anyone. But then I read one of those romance novels Samantha left lying around the house. Those people have great sex. And the men are very considerate of the women."

And book boyfriends didn't usually annoy or talk back. Or if they did, it was usually followed by great sex. Definite pluses.

Aunt Francesca covered her eyes. "I prefer when they close the door."

"My point is," Alethea said, "Hercules never cared about what I wanted, only his own pleasure. For years I blamed myself, but now I have a new perspective. I'm ready to try and find someone new."

"That's why you should try Tender," Effie said.

"That's very brave," Francesca said. "Not the Tender part. The putting-yourself-out-there part."

"Thank you," Alethea said. "Is it time for dessert yet?"

"We haven't heard from you yet, dear," Effie said to Francesca gently. "What's your story?"

Bella almost spoke up and told Fran she didn't have to tell her story. Truthfully, she didn't *know* Fran's story. Aunt Fran had been single for as long as she could remember. And while she was always willing and eager to hear everything about the rest of the family, she tended to deflect questions about her own life.

Fran shrugged. "My family didn't approve of the man I loved when I was young," she said. "And he didn't have the patience to wait. He went off and found someone else. I was heartbroken for years, but then I accepted that I was never meant to be married. But recently, something happened. I never thought this could happen at my age, but when I was in Italy last spring caring for my great-aunt before she died, I met someone. A doctor. With royal Italian blood."

"Italian royalty!" Gloria exclaimed. "How wonderful. Maybe he's a Medici."

"A doctor." Alethea said. "Even better."

She shrugged. "Not so wonderful. He lives in Palermo. My aunt died, I had to come home, and that was that."

Bella looked thoughtfully at her aunt, whom she loved dearly. A fiercely private person, she'd always been kind and loving and the voice of reason to Vito's bursting and sometimes unreasonable passion.

But Fran, librarian and book lover that she was, had a reputation in the family for being a master storyteller. Her father told Bella that when Fran was a teenager, she'd come downstairs dressed for church on Monday nights and tell her parents she was attending the novena. As soon as she was out of eyesight, she'd take off her skirt and roll down her pants and meet her boyfriend down the street. To avoid being fixed up with a boy from the village she didn't like, she pretended to have the measles and got caught when the rash she'd drawn on herself with a lipstick got all over the sheets.

It was difficult to mesh the image of this rebellious Fran with the by-the-books, deeply religious aunt who dutifully cared for her ailing mother for years. Yet Bella herself could understand how enough heartache in life could wash the fight right out of you. Was there a doctor in Palermo? She hoped so, but who knew?

"Oh, we're sorry, dear," Gloria said, patting Fran on the knee. "Very sorry."

"I want to put myself out there a little," Fran said. "Maybe get my hair done."

"Brenda at the Curli-Q on the square is one option," Gloria said. "She'll make you feel like a million bucks. I highly recommend her."

"Change is good," Bella said, "but sometimes it might only require a change of attitude, not a makeover. A makeover from the inside out, so to speak."

There was a sudden loud *thunk* followed by the sounds of crumbling rock exploding into the room, along with a hefty male curse. A floury cloud of dust enveloped the wall adjoining the next building. When it settled, a sizeable hole in the wall gaped.

"Didn't you just remodel, dear?" Aunt Francesca asked.

Bella stood up and ran to the area of damage, cautiously stepping around the debris until she could look through the hole to the other side. The walls of the old flower shop were stripped down to bare wood and a bright single-bulb work lamp hung from a cross beam by a thick orange cord. No person in sight.

"It's a hit-and-run," Effie said, right behind her. In fact, all the ladies were crowded around, eager to check out the excitement.

"I'll be right back," Bella said, heading for the door.

"Where are you going?" Aunt Fran asked. "Don't go by yourself. He has a hammer, for God's sakes."

Bella threw open the outside office door to a lungful of cool September air and six feet two of annoying male perfection poised to knock. Roman Spikonos wore jeans and work boots and an untucked blue plaid flannel shirt rolled up at the sleeves. Bella sucked in a breath. This hot-construction-worker version of Roman was just as gorgeous as the naked-chest-in-the-lake version and the wearing-a-suit-and-tie version from the wedding. Let's just say that if he were featured on a calendar, he'd have every month covered.

"You," she said on an exhale.

"It's a man," someone said behind her.

"A hubba-hubba kind of man." That had to be Effie. For sure.

"That's Roman Spikonos," Fran whispered—loudly.

"Lukas's brother?" Alethea said, perking up. "Tell him to come in right now."

"He's too young for us," Effie said.

"But not for Arabella," Fran said. "They had a thing."

"Fran!" Bella warned. It didn't stop all the whispering and tittering, as if she were surrounded by a group of silly schoolgirls instead of mature women. Or deter the tall man in front of her, who stood with his arms crossed over his big chest surveying all the ladies with a little smirk on his face.

Bella ignored the flashing red lights and the dinging of warning bells inside her head, like there was a train coming and she'd better move off the tracks *now*. She was coming to realize that these were the usual sensations she felt when Roman Spikonos was anywhere nearby.

"Are you the person who just destroyed my wall?" she asked. In a very professional voice, she was proud to say. She was going to stay calm and not get mowed over by his sex appeal, thank you very much.

He looked unfazed. As if he had to think about the question, he tapped a finger on his chin, letting his gaze rake slowly up her—from her red heels, her legs, the length of her red sheath dress, and her little black sweater—lingering on her boobs before he looked at her face. Which she was sure had just turned as bright as her dress. He was barely suppressing a chuckle. The nerve!

She had to close her eyes to get a grip. He used to look at her with those smiley bedroom eyes, and she used to know exactly what he was thinking. It couldn't be the same now, it just couldn't. *Please God, don't let him kick my hormones into overdrive. Turn these chemical reactions off right now.* She tried to imagine him with ear hairs. Or an unsightly wart. Or even a zit, but it was too late. Her body apparently didn't care that being in sudden impending nuclear meltdown mode at the mere sight of him could only lead to disaster.

Dammit, next door times two. How did she get to be so cursed?

Lord have mercy. Roman came over to apologize for knocking through his next-door neighbor's wall, but one look at her in that red dress made him forget his name and every other thought he'd ever had.

Red heels. Great legs. That dress hugging all her curves—she always did have a spectacular rack—and red lipstick on those full lips to boot. Which were not smiling.

Bella cleared her throat, and he snapped his eyeballs up quick.

"About your rack. I mean wall. Wall!" Shit, what was he doing? Must be that a cadre of old ladies was staring at him, making him nervous, and one with a thick mane of jet-black hair was pushing up to the front of the group. She even shouldered past Bella.

He reflexively raised up his hands in defense. "Um, you must be looking for my brother Lukas. He's the famous one."

"*Panagia mou!* Look at you! Oh, those gorgeous eyes, that dimple!" She grabbed him by the cheek and squeezed kind of hard. "Yes, I see the Spikonos traits! That Greek blood running strong through your veins! So handsome!"

He knew his brother sometimes had crazy fans, but he'd never had the experience himself. Maybe a girlfriend or two who hadn't wanted to break up, but nothing like this. "Look, lady, I—"

"I'm Greek! Just like you. And your brother. Oh, he and Samantha will be so pleased. And Stavros. To have an uncle! Oh, *doxa to Theo*—praise be to God." The woman launched herself at him and hugged him tight. One look at Bella showed she was trying hard not to laugh. At least she didn't look too upset about the wall.

"Roman, meet Alethea Panagakos," Bella said. "She works for your brother Lukas."

"I really just help out after school and do some light cooking and cleaning. But with the new baby coming, there will be so much more to do. Oh, Lukas has been waiting for you. I can't wait to tell him I've seen you myself. My prayers have been answered. God brought you home so you can all be a family again."

"Actually, I just ran into—" Just then Bella decided to have mercy on him, turning around and gesturing for everyone to back away. "Ladies, let's give him some space. I'm sure, Roman, you'll want to come in and assess the—er—damage."

But all the ladies wanted to do was assess *him*. Except Bella, who ran off into the back rooms of the office, leaving him to fend for himself.

"So you're Lukas's brother," a white-haired woman said. "Sam, his wife, is my granddaughter. I'm Effie, by the way."

"Those Spikonos boys grew up like orphans," Alethea said, which led the other ladies to exclaim and shake their heads solemnly. "So sad. The parents were alcoholics, and they all ended up in different homes." She turned to Roman and patted him on the cheek. "But now is your chance to find one another again, *paidi mou*. Oh, coming tonight was the best thing I could have done!"

Great. All the women introduced themselves, and Effie handed him a piece of dessert and coffee.

"Why are you in town, Roman?" the woman named Gloria asked him.

"I've inherited my grandparents' orchard," he said. "Next to D'Angelos' Garden Center," he added, giving a nod in Fran's direction.

"Then why are you banging around next door?" Fran asked.

"I'm building a wine bar," he said.

"You're going to start making wine at the orchard?" Fran asked. "That's something different."

"Not wine. Brandy. I'm building a still on the property, and I thought it would be nice to have a place downtown for people to come and sample it. Or for sophisticated women like yourselves to enjoy a nice glass of brandy or wine after a long, hard session."

Just then Bella returned from the back, carrying a stand-up dustpan and a broom. Grateful for the diversion, he set down his cake and coffee and walked over to her, gently lifting the items from her hands.

"Here, let me take these." She looked surprised. Or maybe it was the fact that he'd touched her and felt a breathless zap of current buzzing between them that threw him immediately off his game.

Just like twelve years ago. And he could swear by the way her cheeks flushed the same color as her dress that she felt it, too. He'd known her so well back then. Seemed like he could still read her pretty easily. But he wished he couldn't.

Had he learned nothing? She hadn't felt the same about them back then. That had been a painful lesson to learn. She'd moved on, had become something, made herself a life. Why did he still seem to have a problem with letting her go? Why couldn't he move on from knowing that he'd fallen for her a lot harder than she'd ever fallen for him?

"I'm sorry about the mess," he said. "I'll patch it first thing in the morning. It'll take a couple of days, but it should look fine when I'm done." He busied himself with the cleanup. The walls were old, plaster, and he'd need to fix the lath, re-plaster, then prime and paint. Some work, but the end result would look good as new.

After he'd swept up and carried the rubble out to the Dumpster in the back, he apologized for interrupting their—session, or whatever it was—but they made him sit and have another piece of cake. Which he didn't mind doing at all.

"When my wine bar opens, you ladies will have to be my special guests," he said.

"Wine bar?" Bella asked, her finely arched brows rising.

"A place where people can sample great spirits, eat simple food like cheeses and flatbreads, and listen to some good music."

"Mirror Lake doesn't have anything like that," Gloria said. "Seems like a wonderful thing for young couples to do."

"Couples of any age, friends, tourists," Roman said. "A place to chill out after a hard day's work or just relax at the end of an evening."

He made the mistake of looking at Bella. Not that he cared what she thought about his life's dream. She didn't even know about the apple brandy that he'd created and aged and would showcase there, his means of bringing it to the world, starting right here in Mirror Lake.

She was looking at him with a perplexed expression. Narrowing her eyes a little, as if she couldn't quite figure him out. "When it's looking better, I'll give you all a tour," he said. He threw his paper plate and cup into the trash. "I'd better get going and leave you to your group."

Effie looked at her watch. "Actually, Bella, we were wondering if you'd mind if we cut things a little short tonight? It's two-dollar movie night at the Palace, and they're doing a Nora Ephron double feature. *When Harry Met Sally* and then *Sleepless in Seattle*. Fran, you should come with us." Then they all hugged Bella, told Roman how great it was to meet him, and left.

Bella collapsed in a blue armchair and blew out a heavy sigh.

"Do all your clients hug their therapist good-bye like that?"

"Only in Mirror Lake. Either that or I've completely blurred the difference between therapist and friend, and this is more of a social hour than group therapy."

"Don't underestimate yourself. They probably need someone to listen to their problems. Everyone does." He stood and looked around the office. Her diplomas on the wall. The artwork. "You've done very well for yourself, Bella."

"Well, you, too. I mean, it sounds like you're going to make the orchards into something wonderful. You always wanted to put your own spin on things."

"It's going to take years for me to get the business to where I want it to be."

"I'm glad you got out of Mirror Lake to get the know-how you needed. I know it's going to be a big success."

"It's going to take a lot of work, and a couple of business partners I don't have yet." He set down his coffee cup. "Is it okay if I come by around eight tomorrow?"

"That's when I usually get here."

"Great. I'll stop at the hardware store first. I'm sorry again about the wall." But he really wasn't. It had given him a chance to talk with her.

"Roman, I don't care about the wall." She grabbed the coffeepot and started to take it to the back. Then she stopped and said, "I'm sorry about my dad. Once he gets over the shock of having you next door, I think he'll calm down. I want you to know that whatever happened between us personally, I would never hold a grudge against your business. Hopefully over time—"

"I know you don't." For a moment, their gazes locked. That same warm feeling as always pooled in his belly and spread outward, that mixing of wanting her combined with the bittersweet feeling of things left unsaid for way too long.

How was she really doing? Why had she rejected him so forcefully, when sometimes he thought he saw something in her eyes, a hunger, a sadness . . . or was he just imagining it? Was there a man? What had really happened between her and Ethan? So many questions that he wanted answers to. He needed those answers. He opened his mouth to speak, to ask—

"Well, it's late and I—I still have some paperwork to do before I leave," she said. She headed toward the door separating the waiting room from the back hallway.

"Thanks for the dessert," he called after her. Her hips sashayed softly as she walked through the door, raising an arm in a slight wave.

That familiar old ache flared up again, spreading all over his chest and threatening to double him over. He was stricken by how much he was still attracted to her. He took a couple of deep breaths until the sensation passed, then watched her disappear through the door and close it behind her.

As he turned to leave, he had the fleeting thought that it would be nowhere near as easy to break through the shield she'd built up around herself as it was through that stupid wall. And he suddenly wished he could.

CHAPTER 8

Twelve Years Earlier

Bella forgot all about the little incident in the cabin around Christmastime.

Her heart was too overflowing with joy. For the first time since her mother had passed, she was happy. Roman was everything to her.

That secretive wink he would toss her from across the room or when he passed her in the hall at school never failed to make her knees go weak and her throat dry. He always seemed to catch her eye whenever she looked at him, and smile that charming, slightly mischievous smile that always made her feel that no matter what worries were on her mind, everything was going to be all right.

He was handsome, funny, and kind, not to mention whip smart. They had a friendly competition going between them on who could score the highest on tests. Sometimes she won and sometimes he did, with the other trailing just points behind. But a talent for academics was only a small facet of the things they had in common. She wanted to spend every minute with him, but it was hard with working and housework and driving Joey around to playdates and indoor soccer and everything else she had to do. Plus, Roman logged in a lot of hours next door at his grandfather's orchard.

Bella's dad had even relented for the first time, giving her permission to actually date Roman. It made her feel a little guilty, though, all the sneaking around they did to spend time together. Twice they'd gone back to the cabin. But usually they got together in his beat-up old car and once in his bedroom when his mom was away.

Bella hated that. It seemed so—deceitful. She couldn't wait until college next year when they would both have some independence. Not that that would be easy, either. If he got the basketball scholarship at UC Davis and she was in Chicago . . . well. She wasn't even going to think about that for now.

She simply couldn't stay away from him. He got her in ways no one else ever had—he read her moods and understood when she was tired and just rubbed her feet. And he always made her laugh, no matter how angry or upset she was.

Their chemistry was so intense, so magnetic, she never knew what overtook her when she was near him. She couldn't seem to stop herself from kissing him. And they did kiss—for hours. And talk. About everything, from their feelings about politics and family to their hopes and dreams. He thought he might want to take over his grandparents' orchard, but he had big plans: he wanted to go away to study how to make beer and wine, something far different from his grandfather's more traditional plans.

Bella wasn't sure what she wanted to do, but she knew it would involve helping people in some way. Not in a physical way, because the sight of blood made her wretch, and she didn't ever see herself saving anyone with her hands the way doctors did. Her plan was to just get herself to Loyola and figure it out from all the awesome options she would have there. If she could only get in.

Everything was idyllic until one day in late January. She'd just put a cookie sheet of homemade meatballs into the oven when her father came in from outside. It was snowing pretty vigorously. He took his muddy boots off and went to the sink to pour himself a glass of water, stopping to kiss her on the cheek.

"You look tired," he said. "You're doing too much."

"Pop, it's okay," she said, closing her AP American history textbook that she'd propped against a bag of flour. Which reminded her—Joey needed to bring cupcakes for his class's Martin Luther King Jr. celebration tomorrow. She prayed there was a box of cake mix in the pantry. If not she was going back to the store to buy one. There was no way she was baking them from scratch this time.

She *did* feel tired. But she had AP classes, and it was that cold, cloudy part of the winter where you get to feeling you're never going to see anything green again. And she was tense, waiting for her college acceptances. Well, one in particular. *The* one.

Then, the next day, something strange happened. One minute, she was listening to Ms. Hall discuss women's suffrage and the next she was running to the bathroom puking into the toilet. Which had a nasty cigarette butt in it that she didn't even have time to flush first.

After the deed was done, Bella knelt beside the bowl, stunned and shaking a little, unrolling sheets of cheap, thin toilet paper to wipe her teary eyes. Kids were dropping like flies with the flu lately, coughing, nose running, head aching. She didn't have any of that, but she had felt queasy lately, especially while she was cooking. Suddenly, a pounding on the stall door made her jump and pulled her out of her thoughts. She hurriedly stood, redid her ponytail, straightened her sweater, and opened it.

There, staring at her, was Reagan. How long had she been in the bathroom? Had she heard her vomiting? Bella noticed her lipstick was shiny and fresh looking—overdone, if you asked her, but then, what about Reagan wasn't?—so she'd probably been preening in the mirror for a while. "What is it?" Bella said, not snappily, but not super friendly either.

"Ms. Hall sent me to check on you. You okay?" Her gaze traveled from Bella's ankle boots, up her jeans, and over her long cabled sweater.

Bella's first impulse was to frown, but she stifled it. Maybe Reagan really was concerned. People could change, right? And, hey, Bella was in love. It was easy to think the best about everybody. Besides, she was never one to hold grudges.

"I'm fine, thanks," Bella said. "You can go back to class now." Something about the way Reagan was looking at her—with the subtlest little smirk that marred her otherwise pretty lips—put her on guard. She wanted a chance to rinse the sour taste out of her mouth, check herself in the mirror. If only Reagan would leave.

"Okay, I'm going. Sure hope you're not late."

"Oh, don't worry. The bell's not going to ring for another—"

Bella didn't really understand what Reagan had meant until the smirk spread into a full-blown smile. The kind the Grinch smiles when his heart is three times too small and he's planning on wreaking havoc on the Whos.

Oh God, she *was* late. But there had been so much stress lately, with school and exams and—and she wasn't the most regular of people. Her cycle had always been erratic.

Bella tried to push that thought out of her head, but like gum on the sole of a shoe, it wasn't budging. As if to mock her, her stomach squeezed and another wave of nausea struck. She took a few deep breaths and refused to give in to it. This was all just because of those gross chicken nuggets she'd snagged from Jess's plate at lunch because she was still starving after her peanut butter sandwich. It was a bad combination, that's all. *That was all.*

Suddenly, she couldn't think. Spots danced in her vision, the kind you see when you're going to pass out, and she was not going to end up helpless in front of someone who would probably leave her to die on the gross floor anyway. Bella walked quickly past Reagan, who was full-blown laughing now as she leaned against the pink tiled wall.

Sometimes Bella had a certain sense of foreboding about events, one she laughingly called "The Shining" with her friends. She could swear she knew things, like when one of her friends was headed for a breakup, or a crush was going to languish in a state of unrequited love. Now, that same spiny tingle hit her out of the blue, this time with a sense of life-altering dread. She clutched her abdomen with both hands. Oh dear God, how could it be? Fate could not be so cruel. She'd gone to the doctor; she'd taken precautions. She'd made a choice that she thought she'd been smart about, but still, this had happened.

This. A *baby*.

Her blood thrummed so loudly in her ears it drowned out all her thoughts. Her breath came jagged and fast. She tried to be calm as she left the bathroom and walked down a floor to the sophomore bathroom. It wasn't really just for sophomores, but no self-respecting senior ever got caught dead there. She did what she could to make herself presentable, but dark circles rimmed her eyes and her skin tone was greenish gray. She wouldn't have any trouble signing out sick.

Somehow they let her drive herself home, but she went straight to the drugstore instead. And when she sat in her own bathroom at home and stared at the plus sign that appeared on the test stick, she knew The Shining was real. She was pregnant. Roman and she had made a baby. And soon the world was going to know.

She knew something else, too. Her whole life was about to get ripped away from its foundations and spun around like that house that crushes the witch in *The Wizard of Oz*. Things would never be the same again.

A knock sounded on the solid wooden door that her dad had painted pale pink when she was seven. Bella dropped the stick into the trash and covered it up with toilet paper. "Who is it?" she called.

Can't Stop Loving You

"It's Aunt Fran. I've got something important for you."

Bella stood up, the queasiness returning. She wanted to cry, but tears wouldn't come. They were stuck in her parched throat. She loved Aunt Fran, but for God's sake, she wanted her *mother*. How would she ever get through this without her wise counsel? She cracked open the door. Aunt Fran was all smiles. She thrust a long white envelope through the door opening.

"I know you're not feeling well, but I thought you might want to see this. Plus I have some tea and toast for your stomach."

Oh, Aunt Fran. Shaking, Bella took the envelope. Tore it open and read it. *Congratulations!* It read. *We welcome you to Loyola.* She skimmed down the page. *Full scholarship* blurred before her eyes. Her dream come true.

"So?" Fran said, one brow raised. "What's the news? Shall I get your father?"

"I—" Bella couldn't tell the truth. Saying it out loud would break their hearts. And hers, too, because she knew beyond a doubt she would never set foot on that campus, never live in Chicago. She would have different responsibilities.

She would be a mother, carting around a baby sling when everyone else would be dragging their backpacks across various campuses in the crisp fall air. A mother, to Roman's baby. The shock was still overwhelming, but underneath it all, a tiny kernel of hope surfaced.

Roman loved her, she knew it. Together, they would make a plan, and somehow, they would get through this. She inhaled deeply and faced her aunt. "They rejected me, Aunt Fran. I didn't make it. I'm on the—um, the waiting list."

"Oh, honey. I felt so sure it would be great news. I'm sorry to have made you open that."

She hugged her aunt. "No, you did the right thing. I would've wanted to know, either way."

Then she begged off sick and spent the rest of the evening lying on her bed, staring at the ceiling. Ignoring Roman's repeated calls. Somehow, while she dreaded telling him, the image she kept seeing in her mind was of her father's face. His weathered, too-old-for-his-age face that always carried a tinge of sadness around the corners of his mouth and in his eyes. And she wondered how on earth she was ever going to stop from breaking his heart.

Roman hadn't exactly had the best first reaction to Bella's news the next day when she'd found him practicing in the gym.

He'd just shot a basket from the three-point line, and it had sailed through the net with a confident swoosh. He'd retrieved the ball and stood behind the line to do it again.

"Roman, I need to talk with you," Bella said, standing just off the court. Her voice sounded a little tight, a little urgent.

She never came to practice or met him in the gym, so her being there, right on the court, was unusual.

"It's important," she said.

"Okay, sure," he said, gearing up for another shot. "Can it wait another ten minutes? Coach wanted me to do a few more layups before I leave."

She walked up to him. "I have to tell you something. And I'm sorry if it interrupts your basketball practice, but I've been waiting an extra hour for you to be done already and I've got to get home." He shot the ball and looked at her. Her face was pale. She wasn't laughing or joking. "I'm pregnant," she blurted.

He was vaguely aware of the ball bouncing away, hitting the gym floor and rolling, rolling out of bounds, off the court, somewhere far, far away.

"What?" he said. It was suddenly hard to suck in air, and his legs felt a little shaky. "Are you sure?"

She rolled her eyes. "Yes, I'm sure. I went to the doctor. It happened the first time. You know, the condom problem."

"Wow. I mean . . . wow. That's . . . that's some news, Bella."

"Yeah, some news," she said. He'd recovered enough from the shock to notice that her voice had sounded strained. She was biting on her lip. Her arms were wrapped tightly around her chest. And he realized she was waiting. Waiting for his reaction. And for her sake, he'd better not blow it.

"What are we going to do?" she asked, her voice cracking. "I mean, I'm having the baby. That's not a question. It's just . . . I wondered what your thoughts were."

Thoughts? Fear, terror, worry—all tore through him like thunderbolts. But so did . . . awe. Amazement. The feeling that Bella was the most important person in his life and that he loved her, and that somehow they could face this together. He reached out and gripped her snugly by the arms. Looked straight into her eyes. "My thoughts are, I'm going to be a father. And you're going to be a mother. So marry me and we'll make it a family."

She still felt as rigid as an icicle. And just as cold. "How do I know you're not saying that because you feel you have to?"

"Because I love you. Because I want you every second of the day, and I can't imagine spending my life without you. This might be unexpected, but it's not anything I haven't dreamed about. It just happened a little sooner than either of us planned."

Her forehead was still puckered in worry, her skin blanched pale. She let out a suppressed breath. "This is going to cause a lot of trouble, you know that, don't you?"

"Come here." He pulled her fully into his arms, kissing her forehead, finally feeling her relax a little against him. "It's going to be okay. I promise."

"Hey, Spikonos," Ethan said, "back to practice. No distractions, okay? We want to win districts, and that takes a lot of focus."

Focus. In light of this new development, that might be harder to do than he'd thought.

It was early June, and Bella was five months pregnant. Roman had driven them through town for ice cream and then up to the scenic lookout to watch the sun set. "So I think I'm going to join the army. It's good pay," Roman said. His plan was all laid out, and he was pleased it had come together so well. "I'll have basic training done by the end of summer, and the baby's not due until September. I can take out a loan and we could get GI housing wherever I'm stationed. What do you think?"

It was a beautiful evening, the sweet scent of green things in the air, the trees bursting with fresh leaves. Despite all the chaos of the past few months, things were settling down a little. He hoped the beautiful evening would have a calming effect on Bella. He worried about all the stress she was under at home.

"What if they ship you overseas?" She put a hand to her stomach. She looked a little worried, as if she didn't like the thought of him going somewhere scary.

"No matter what happens, we'll have guaranteed housing. You and the baby would be taken care of. I think if you can work another year, we can save up for you to start taking college classes. We can make this work."

He'd done a lot of thinking, and planning. And to be honest, his mother had given him unflagging support, even when he'd given up his basketball scholarship for the army. He felt bad about that, but he was determined not to have her pay for his college. He would make her proud in other ways. She'd never given him the sense that their situation was hopeless. She understood what they were up against, but she believed they could make it.

She'd asked him if he wanted to marry Bella, and he'd told her honestly that he couldn't imagine *not* marrying her. He loved her. Their situation may not be ideal, but it was temporary, and he was going to do everything in his power to get them past this.

In front of Bella, he tried to have unflagging optimism, because she was going through hell at home, with her father acting sullen and barely speaking to her. Pregnancy wasn't tolerated at Our Lady of the Lake, so Bella had had to leave school. Graduation had come and gone, and he'd felt awful about her missing it. He'd decided not to go, either, and his mom had supported him.

His mother had helped Bella to get a job as a receptionist in a psychology practice in Crooked Creek, so she'd been working full time on top of all her home responsibilities. Frankly, he couldn't wait to get her out of this place and start a life on their own.

He smiled and grabbed her hand, which had gone cold from holding the cup of ice cream. He kissed her knuckles, one by one. "I love you, Bella," he said, and was pleased when she cracked a little smile. "It's going to be okay. We're going to get through this. Do you believe me?"

She sighed. "Okay, fine, I believe you."

He ducked his head until it was at her stomach level. "And what do you think, little one?" he crooned to the baby. "How would you like to have a little house with a room all your own? We love you, honey bunches." He kissed Bella's stomach. She had a sizeable bump now, and she hated that her belly button was starting to stick out, something he constantly teased her about. He put a hand over the baby, and she closed her eyes and placed her hand over his. He hoped his touch had a calming effect on her, too.

"I love you, Roman," she whispered. Her eyes were filled with a myriad of feelings. Mostly wariness and caution, because of the stress of the last couple of months. But he hoped trust, too. "You make me feel like we're going to be okay."

"We're going to be more than okay. We're going to be a family."

"When's your aunt getting here?" he asked. Her Aunt Francesca was coming to stay for the summer after her school let out. He couldn't wait, because he felt Bella was doing too much, under too much strain.

"Next week. But don't worry. My dad's been doing more with Joey lately." She got quiet, and he knew exactly what she was thinking. This was confirmed when she spoke. "I'm worried about Joey. I mean, I've been just like his mother for the past couple of years. I'm not sure how I can leave him."

"Bella, you're his sister, not his mother. He'll have Fran and your dad. You deserve to lead your own life, too." Her lips pursed tight. He knew how much she loved Joey, and how the decision to leave was weighing on her. "Okay, I think we've had enough heavy discussion for tonight," he said, wanting to keep the mood light. "Want to take a little stroll?"

She smiled. Reached over and soothed his brow. "I'm sorry, Roman. I know you've been working extra hours and you have a lot on your mind, too."

He helped her out of the car and they started along a wide walking path that twined around the lake. It was about an hour before dusk, and joggers and bikers were enjoying the fine spring evening.

Suddenly, she gave a little cry, clutching his hand with a vise grip. She stopped in the middle of the walking path, doubling over and falling to her knees.

He dropped to the ground beside her. "Bella, what is it?" His voice sounded high pitched, with an edge of panic. Exactly how he *didn't* want to sound.

"Something's wrong," she said, clutching her abdomen and looking at him. He hated what he saw in her face. Terror. Panic. Helplessness tore through him. Without thinking, he picked her up and carried her back to the car, murmuring quietly that she was going to be all right, that everything was going to be okay, even though he had no clue what the fuck was happening. He just wanted to keep her—and himself—calm.

Tears fell from her eyes and landed on his arm. "The baby," she whispered. "Something's wrong, Roman."

"Don't cry, sweetheart," Roman said. An insidious sense of dread wrapped its tendrils around his heart. *Please, God, no more disasters. Let the baby be all right.*

"Hurry, Roman," she whispered as he started the car and made the ten-minute drive to the community hospital.

Couldn't something go in a positive direction for them for once? It seemed that the last few months had been misery piled on misery. Too many strikes against them.

After the struggles of leaving school and missing graduation, of her angry and disappointed father, of all the uncertainty, this baby was the one thing that made sense. The one thing that might make everything okay again.

A beautiful, healthy baby that would fill everyone's hearts with love and push out all the other bad stuff. So they were young. So they were against some odds. But they had a plan. A good plan. It would get both of them away from Mirror Lake where they would start fresh, begin their own life together, and become a family.

He could take it, he could bear it all, if only their baby was okay.

―――○―――

"I want to see her," Roman said to the nurse who had entered the waiting room from the adjacent surgical suite. He got in her face. "So help me God, if you don't let me back there, I'll—"

"I'm sorry, sir," the nurse said, blocking the doorway with her body. "I'm afraid I can't let anyone back until the doctor gives permission. I came out to let you know she's doing just fine."

Roman couldn't process the words. He was only vaguely aware of his behavior. All he knew was that he needed to be with Bella. The doctors had done an ultrasound, and that had confirmed the worst, that Bella was having a miscarriage at twenty weeks. The baby had been too young to survive. Bella was taken to surgery, leaving Roman to pace the waiting room with her father and sister and her best friends. Fortunately, his mother had shown up, too, and she was a godsend, bringing everyone coffee, being the voice of reason, keeping Vito in line.

He felt the slight but firm weight of his mother's hand now on his arm. "Come sit down, son," she said. "I'm sure you'll be allowed back soon." He found himself being steered to a chair where he somehow managed to sit, his mind and body numb.

Finally, a doctor came out, a woman with a kindly smile. "Bella's asking for Roman," she said.

Vito turned on Roman, who had immediately risen from his seat. "I don't want you seeing her anymore," he said.

Months of frustration came to a head. "You just try and stop me," Roman said, walking over to stand in front of the doctor.

"Oh, for God's sake, Vito," Marjorie said. "This is traumatic enough for everybody as it is."

The doctor smiled again. "To keep Bella calm right now is our priority. So if it's okay with everyone, I'm going to allow Roman back to see her."

Roman walked through the door without a second glance in Vito's direction.

The nurse led Roman to the surgical recovery room, a large, cool room with three or four patients lying on gurneys, IV bags dripping, nurses busily recording things on charts or walking back and forth tending to business. He spotted Bella immediately, small and so young looking with her hair pulled up in a surgical hat.

"She's still a little groggy," the nurse said. "But she'll open her eyes if you call her name."

He looked at the nurse, an older woman with gray hair. "The baby..."

The nurse put a kindly hand on his shoulder. "I'm sorry, dear. She wasn't far enough along for the baby to make it. But she's doing great, and she's been asking for you."

Roman steeled his face, even though his guts felt ripped out. Bella was okay, that was the important thing, and he would be strong for her if it killed him. He went and stood by the gurney. As always, he marveled at her long lashes, thick and black against her skin, which looked chalk-pale now.

So much had happened since the cabin at Christmas, and he felt responsible for it all. Being involved with him had ruined her high school career, her scholarship, her ticket out of town. He swore to himself he'd do anything to make it up to her. He loved her with all his heart, and he'd never felt so protective of anyone, so determined to make things right.

He quietly called her name. Her lids flickered and she opened her eyes. At first her expression was blank. As if she were interrupted out of a pleasant dream. But then her eyes came into focus, and he saw the moment the curtain of sleep lifted and reality dawned.

Her eyes got misty with tears. "Oh, Roman," she said.

He reached over the metal bed railing and gripped her hand, stroked her hair. "It's okay, Bella. You're going to be fine."

"The baby..."

He rubbed her back. "Shh, it's okay."

"I'm so sorry." Seeing her tears well up and roll down her cheeks killed him.

"The doctor says these things just happen sometimes. It wasn't anyone's fault."

She gripped his hand too tightly. "I wanted the baby, Roman. Despite everything." She started to cry again, and he had no idea how to make her stop.

"It was a girl," she whispered. "They told me."

Oh Jesus. Guilt and grief tore through him. And a ferocious anger. At Vito, for making like this was the end of the world. At how she'd suffered, most of all at the hands of her own family. And at himself. In that moment, he vowed never to feel so helpless again.

Bella awakened in her bedroom the next morning to bright, beautiful sunshine. In her haze of half sleep, she wondered, *Why am I not at work?* She was about to bolt upright, when she heard what had woken her up—the sound of arguing. Two voices, passionate and angry.

"You heard me," her father said in an even tone. "Get off my property."

Reality suddenly rushed in to fill the brief, pleasant void caused by sleep and the warm beams of sunshine. Her hands moved to her abdomen. *Empty.* The events of yesterday came rushing back, all of them, in all their sad detail. Her baby, lost. Roman's panicked face. The feeling of bad going to worse. The day had started out so innocently, so normally, but within a matter of hours, everything had changed.

Her father had driven her home around nine last night. She'd still been a little groggy from the drugs. Roman had wanted to stay, but her father wouldn't hear of it. But he was back now, and from the sound of it, things weren't going well.

"I'm not leaving, sir. I love your daughter. I want to marry her."

That made tears well up. *Oh, Roman.* Even in the depths of all this despair, he was the light in the darkness, her strength. She wanted him, too, with all her heart. She needed him. Only he could understand the smothering blanket of grief, the hollowness.

Despite everything, she'd *wanted* their baby. That part of him and part of her that she'd imagined endlessly for hours on end. Whose eyes would she or he have? Whose tiny fingers and toes? Now there would be no baby. But that brought no relief. Only sorrow.

"Marry her?" Vito let out a grunt. "Eighteen years old and you're going to marry my daughter." She imagined her father shaking his head in disgust, as he'd done many a time over these past nearly five months. "No money, no job, no nothing."

"Please," Roman said. "Let me see Bella."

Bella got out of bed and grabbed her robe, forgetting for a moment that she wasn't able to run. Discomfort in her abdomen and cramping prevented her from rushing, but she did okay walking. By the time she made it to the front porch, they were yelling again.

"You can't stop me from seeing her. I—"

Her father was standing on the porch, hands on hips. Roman was a few feet away, his foot propped on the bottom step, looking agitated, ready to run past her father and break into the house if necessary.

Bella touched her father on the back. She would be calm, and tempers would cool. If anything, the fact that she'd just gotten out of the hospital would soothe her father. And now that there would be no baby, maybe he could forgive her. Sad that that was the only positive thing she could think of right now. "I'm here, Dad. It's okay, Roman. I'm glad you came, I—"

Her father turned toward her. When she saw his face, hope was crushed. His thick brows were knit down deeply, and his eyes held a mixture of pain and fury. "I've held my tongue about him these past months; I've tolerated him coming around here. But now I must speak."

"No, Dad," she said softly. "Please don't. We don't have to talk about this today. We don't ha—"

"He's no longer welcome here. He comes back here at his own risk."

Bella closed her eyes. She wished for the millionth time that her mother was here, who was so much calmer, who would never react out of such anger. At that moment, Bella felt her loss so acutely her chest ached. Her mother would have brought her up a tray, smoothed her hair back, told her that in this terrible mess, everything was somehow going to work out all right. She longed to hear that. That everything that had happened wasn't so horrific. That she hadn't disappointed her father beyond repair. That life would go on, and all the anguish would be forgotten.

"It's okay, Bella," Roman said, sensing her despair. "It's going to be okay." She loved him for saying that, for being here, for standing up to her father. Just then he looked at Vito, who stood at least six inches shorter. "I'm not staying away from her, sir."

Bella shook her head, trying to signal to Roman to back down for now. He was trying so hard to be respectful. But he didn't understand what he was dealing with. Her father was passionate and fiery and completely old school. His family had generations of a confusing history of feuds and vendettas, cousins they spoke to and others who were no longer considered part of the family.

Bella knew from her father's tone that he'd meant what he'd just said. He blamed Roman for getting her pregnant, and nothing was going to change his mind. He'd endured him these past months because of the baby, but now his plan was to get rid of Roman for good.

In that instant, she hated her father. She'd spent the past months doing everything she could to please him. She'd tried apologizing, pleading, even, but he'd cold-shouldered her for months. If it weren't for Joey, Bella swore she'd step off this porch right now and never return.

Why couldn't she have a father who could reason and be rational? Marjorie wasn't prone to flying off the handle. She'd supported her son through this, and had helped Bella, too.

"Go back inside, Bella," her father said. "I'll bring you some breakfast." He turned to Roman. "You can leave now and let her rest."

"Fine." Roman looked straight at her. "I'll leave for now. But I'll be back." He turned to Vito, his fists balled, his jaw set into a tense line. "No matter how much you might want to, you can't keep us apart."

Late that evening, Roman showed up at Bella's bedroom window. As soon as he'd climbed over her sill, she'd grasped him with all her strength, hugging him and holding on tight. As if that could keep him here. As if that would change what she had to do.

Her father hadn't wasted any time laying down the law. His words from earlier that day echoed in her head. Harsh, horrible words. *You marry him, you have no family, understand? You go with him, I'm done with you for good. You're no longer my daughter.* He meant it. She knew he did. And she couldn't bear to be cut off from Joey. She could never do that to an innocent little boy who'd already lost his mother.

Her grief knifed her over and over. With their baby gone, the only spot of happiness in the hell of these past months had been snuffed out. And with that went their future. She would never survive it without him. But what other choice did she have?

"Come with me, Bella," Roman said, looking at her intently. "Tonight."

Oh, how could she bear to tell him? Before she could answer, he pulled out a box. He dropped to one knee and took her hand in his. "Marry me, Bella. I love you; I'll always love you. We can make a life together."

She looked from his face, so sincere, so *young*, to the ring. It was gold, with a small diamond surrounded by a circle of tiny diamond chips. She loved it immediately because she loved him and what he was trying to do for her. For *them*.

For a long time, she didn't speak. She wished she could draw this moment out forever, to bask in the knowledge that he loved her, baby or no baby. She reached out and touched his cheek. Her hand was trembling as she traced his strong brow line, the square edge of his jaw. Then she dropped to her knees beside him and held his hands tightly.

"Roman, I can't marry you." She bit down on her lip. She had to get through this. A voice in her head screamed, *Of course you can marry him! You love him! He's the one!* But she blocked it out. She knew what she had to do.

"Bella, I know your father is crazy, but I don't think he'd really kill me."

He was trying to make her laugh. Even now, and that made her want to cry even more. "Listen to me, Roman," she said, grabbing his sleeve. "I can't go with you."

"What do you mean? Are you sick? Is it too soon?"

Despair rolled over her in waves. She wanted to tell him how unbearably sorry she was. Maybe if she hadn't worried so much, or worked so much, or gotten more rest . . . maybe it was all her fault.

Tears rolled down her face, and Bella hid against his chest so he wouldn't see. She clutched his shirt. God, he smelled so good, even though it was just soap and . . . Roman. Familiar, comforting. Oh, how could she ever let him go? She couldn't. She loved him too much. It would kill her, and if it didn't, staying here in this stupid, stupid town would for sure.

She had to turn away to compose herself. Took a deep breath. She couldn't do it, lie and rip apart everything they had, but what else could she do? She knew with every fiber of her being that he loved her, that he would never leave her. He would stay in Mirror Lake with her. And not attend brewing school or fulfill his dream of making his grandfather's orchards into something unique and different.

Even if he left for school and she stayed, there would be no sneaking around when he came home on breaks. She'd never seen her father so angry, never seen him give such an ultimatum. Unless she ran away for good and left her family behind, she was as cornered as a squirrel in a hunter's trap.

"I—I've been thinking, Roman. Now that there's no baby, there's no rush for us to do anything . . . hasty." The words stuck in her throat. She could barely force them out. *No baby.* Oh, she'd wanted that baby. She'd wanted them to be a family. She was never going to get through this. She needed him. He was the only one who understood the heartache. How would she face all this black, gaping grief alone?

"This isn't hasty, Bella. I've been thinking about it for a long time." He grabbed her other hand, too, and she swore the skin where he touched her burned. Oh, if she could just do this quickly and get it over with. But how could she ever do it? It was like ripping her own heart out of her chest and crushing it. "I'm completely in love with you. We get along great and we just—get each other. I know people say first love can't last, but, Bella, it can with us. I know it can."

"Roman, I know you want to swoop in and take me away from here, but I've got responsibilities. I—I can't go with you."

"Joey's your brother, not your son, Bella. And he's only six. Surely your family doesn't expect you to devote another ten years of your life to raising him. Besides, Gina's close by. He'll be all right without you."

She shook her head. "No, you don't understand. I promised my mother—"

"Bella, this is your chance to get away. You've put up with enough with your father. There's no reason for you to stay—"

"Listen, Roman. I want to go to college. I don't want to scrape and scrimp and suffer to make it. You know how it's going to be. We'll just end up hating one another. No one gets married at eighteen and has it last."

"Bella, I know we can make this work. I can't promise it will always be easy, but . . ."

"I'm not going. I—I'm sorry, Roman."

"Don't you love me?"

Oh God. How much more of this could she take before she shattered into a million pieces?

"Now that I lost the baby, things are—different. I want to know what it feels like to be young again. I don't want to be chained down with responsibilities and struggling on our own. I'm sorry the pregnancy happened, but now that it's over I need some . . . freedom." She'd barely managed to choke out that word.

"This is your father talking, isn't it?"

"No! It—it's just that I've been through a lot in the past few months, and I think we should take a break."

"A break? What are you talking about?"

"It's been a difficult time for both of us. I need some time apart."

"Are you—are you breaking up with me?"

"I guess I am. I think it's for the best."

"Bella, no. It's been a difficult week. It's too soon to—"

"I'm not going with you, Roman. I'm sorry." A dry, dead lump clogged her airway. Hot tears gathered behind her eyes, searing their way out. She turned away, barely holding it together.

Finally, finally, he left through the window. Finally, she shut it. Shut him out. And finally she could cry.

He didn't give up easily. He called and sent letters she didn't answer, until at last in midsummer, he left for basic training.

She told herself she'd done the right thing. He'd escaped town. He went to start his life. At least one of them should be free to do so.

Joey grew up, and she commuted the hour to UConn for a psychology degree while continuing to work full time. Being as busy as she could bear was the only way she'd survived losing him.

Roman never came back for his ring. For a long time, she kept it on a thin chain around her neck, tucked under her shirt. It was the only thing she had left of him. She fantasized that he'd return, would eventually figure out that she was lying, would break her down and force out the truth that she could not say. And she hoped that, in time, her father would mellow. That all of this would be temporary, and that, soon enough, she and Roman would work things out.

But time told Bella what her Shining knew all along: Roman Spikonos had left Mirror Lake for good.

CHAPTER 9

"I think they might be too much," Bella said, looking down at the red half-calf cowboy boots she wore with her denim dress, a cute blue-and-white scarf tied fashionably about her neck, thanks to the efforts of her friends. Those friends now examined her boots from their seats at a booth at MacNamara's, the quaint local bar that was owned by Maggie's family and frequented more by locals than tourists. It was moderately crowded on a Friday night, a small crowd hanging out around the big flat screen watching the Yankees game.

"What makes you think that?" Sam asked as she moved her glass while Scott MacNamara placed a pitcher of margaritas on the table. He acknowledged them all with a brief nod, more interested in the game than making conversation. He did bestow a special sibling shoulder punch on Maggie, his older sister, to which she said, "Hey!" and gave him a what-the-hell look as she rubbed it.

Bella shrugged. "I don't know . . . it's just that I'm not twenty anymore."

"None of us are, but that's a good thing, right?" Jess asked, clinking her glass with Maggie.

"You look adorable." Sam, newly pregnant, was drinking water. Or trying to, as she was still pretty queasy. "It's getting to be almost that time," she said, glancing at her phone, which had the effect of making *Bella* queasy. "Operation Find Bella a Beau is about to commence. Ready with the briefing, Jess?"

"I can't wait," Bella's sister Gina said, rubbing her hands together. "This is going to be so fun!"

Bella knew inviting her sister was trouble. She shouldn't have felt sorry for her, at home with an infant, barely getting out. All she knew was that this guy had better be nice, because if anything weird happened, the story would enter family lore and Gina would never let her live it down.

"Listen up," Jess said. "This guy I have lined up for tonight is really cute. He's visiting from Texas, because he's got family here."

Bella pushed down her panic. Jess had a history of dating a string of men who could all accurately be classified as idiots, and Bella couldn't help wondering if that propensity would be reflected in the date she'd chosen for her tonight. Recently, though, Jess had started dating a sweet physics teacher from Mirror Lake High where she taught English, and she'd fallen head over heels. Bella could only hope tonight's guy was more like Jess's current boyfriend than her past ones.

"How exactly do you know this guy, Jess?" Sam asked.

"Well, um, I don't personally know him. But he's Gertie Smith's nephew."

Bella's stomach pitched. Jess didn't personally know him? She tried to tell herself that could be a good thing.

"Wait a minute," Maggie said. "You're not talking about Gertie's deadbeat nephew who ran away to Texas after he got drunk and took an equestrian's horse for a ride in the middle of the night? Stealing someone's horse does *not* make someone a cowboy!"

Jess reddened. "I didn't know about that! Gertie told me he'd had a rough time of it but promised me he was on the straight and narrow."

Her friends stared at her. "Look, I'm sorry, okay? The pool of guys I know has shrunk a lot since I started dating Evan.

"Besides, she knows everybody in town, and I trust her judgment. Just look at all that organic produce she's been buying lately for the grocery store. High quality, you know? I figured her nephew would be nice, too."

This is what Bella got for trusting her friends to do this for her. She should have just found someone to date privately via a dating app and used her friends to keep an eye out for stalkers, molesters, convicts, or other unsavory men instead of letting them take charge. She took another slug of her drink.

"Just give him a chance, Bells, okay?" Jess said. "Besides, you don't necessarily need to meet the man of your dreams tonight. Just getting laid would be a good goal at this point."

Bella glared at her friend.

"I'm just being honest. I mean, how long has it been, anyway?"

"That's private," Bella said, feeling her face heat to the color of her boots.

"Has there been anyone since that dweeby guy three years ago? The one from New Jersey who loved fly-fishing."

"Hobbies are good, aren't they?" Bella said. "Plus he was athletic."

"Sure," Gina tattled, "if you consider drinking a twelve-pack every Saturday while pretending to fly-fish physical activity."

God, her sister was so annoying. At this point Bella was more than a little sorry she'd invited her out with her friends tonight. "I thought I loved him," Bella said as her friends cast her skeptical looks. She stabbed her straw into the slush of her drink. "I did." At least, she'd done one hell of a job trying to make herself believe that, just like she had with Ethan.

"It's just as well," Sam said across the table. "If you would've married him, you would've had to clean fish every weekend. Think how your house would smell."

"It's okay, Bella," Gina said, patting her hand as only an older sister could. "The right guy is out there. It's just going to take some time to find him."

"That's easy for you to say, Gina. You've known Manny since junior year of high school."

"Everybody has their hardships. I mean, look how long it took us to get pregnant." It had taken them a long time, eleven years to be exact, and Gina was now beside herself with joy. Bella loved Gino, her little nephew, and couldn't be happier for her sister. It was one of the great ironies of life that Bella had become pregnant so easily while her sister had to wait over a decade.

"Speaking of that sweet little boy of yours, who's babysitting?" Jess asked.

"Manny's watching him tonight. You know, daddy bonding time." A waitress set down some warm pretzel bites with cheese and some chips and dip. "Hey," Gina said, "is that the world-famous MacNamara's artichoke dip? Oh, I shouldn't. This darn pregnancy weight."

Jess passed over the dip and chips. "Gina, it's girls' night out. Indulge a little."

"Did it ever occur to you," Maggie said to Bella in her practical voice as they all dove into the appetizers, "that you always pick men you don't have a chance of really falling for?"

"I do not!"

"Yeah, you do," Sam said. "Ones who don't have a prayer of sweeping you off your feet."

"It's true," Gina said. "I've been trying to tell her that for years."

Okay, that was it. Her sister was definitely never getting invited again. "Just because you're a mom doesn't mean you have to mother me," Bella said a little testily.

"I'm not mothering you," she said, dragging a chip through the dip and scooping up a hearty amount. "I'm just trying to help you."

"It's not exactly easy to find Prince Charming like you all did," Bella said, gesturing to Jess, Sam, and Gina.

"You did, too, sweetie," Gina said to Maggie, now patting her hand. "He just died."

Oh dear. Bella shot an apologetic glance at Maggie, who gave Bella a little wink to indicate she wasn't offended by Gina's usual bluntness.

"All we're saying is keep an open mind," Jess said. "Maybe your past has made you too cautious. Afraid to surrender your heart. So maybe don't think about such high stakes—just focus on having fun. And try to be open and adventurous, okay?"

"Yada yada, whatever," Bella said. This was worse than going to the dentist. But maybe they were right. Maybe she was a little romantically constipated. She supposed she had managed to seal more than a few layers of plaster around her heart these past few years. Oh, okay, for more than a few years. After Roman, she'd done her best to try to open herself up again, but she'd felt like she was just going through the motions. Maybe it was time to put herself out there a little more.

Just then, a tall man in jeans and work boots opened the door to the bar. *Oh no, showtime.* She sat up straighter, wiping the margarita juice off her chin. Scanning from the ground up and trying to check out the newcomer without staring, Bella suddenly realized the tall, strapping man who'd just walked in was not Zeke the cowboy but none other than Roman himself.

Oh God. This town was getting more confining than Spanx in a size too small. Which she suddenly felt like hers were. She was nervous enough tonight. She could not live through her first blind date in three years with Roman armchair quarterbacking her from the bar the whole time.

"Hey, Bells," her annoying sister said, draining her margarita glass and setting it down with a loud clink. "Looks like the love of your life just rolled in."

Maggie elbowed her, and Sam immediately lowered her voice and said, "Wow, Bella. Who needs a cowboy when you've got him?"

"Hey! The cowboy's cute," Jess said. "I mean, at least I think he is from his picture. Wait and see."

Bella cast her friends a dark look. "I would never be dumb enough to open up that can of worms."

"It's a really hot can of worms, if I might say so myself," Maggie said. "And he's staring at you, just FYI."

Panic seemed to wrap itself around her rib cage, squeezing her lungs and making breathing difficult. Or maybe she really should have chosen the larger size of Spanx.

"My God, Bella, he is gorgeous. Have you talked to him yet?" Jess asked.

So much for Jess's support. Now all her friends had turned against her. "Of course I've talked with him—he's here to stay," Bella said.

"Then what are you waiting for?" Gina asked.

"He's been around, too, because he accidentally put a hole through our office wall," Maggie said. "And he came back today and put another coating of patch on it."

"That man can patch my walls any time," Jess said.

"Okay, Jess, enough," Bella said.

Between her well-meaning but ridiculous friends and Roman, who was now parked on a bar stool in front of the big-screen TV, the torture in her life never seemed to ease up. She couldn't help but notice he chose a seat next to a gorgeous woman, tall and skinny and model beautiful. Just then he turned around and caught Bella looking at him, but she didn't turn away. I mean, she was here first, right? She was going to proceed with her evening whether he was there or not. He nodded. She raised a brow and gave a quick nod back.

She could do this. Separate the past from her life now. Work on her future. Ignore him. *Yeah, right.* Just like you could ignore a blister on your foot that bled and stung with every step.

"I'm really excited for Lukas and Roman to be living in the same town after all these years," Sam said. "It'll be nice to have some family around, you know? Besides, Mrs. Panagakos is beside herself."

All three of her friends and her sister were staring at him. Bella finally snapped her fingers in front of their noses and said, "Okay, ladies, stop drooling. He is *not* my date, and I'd like to learn something about my real date before he shows up, all right? Jess, what does he do?"

"I think Gertie said he's an underwear model. Or he works rodeo. I forget." Jess stood up, glancing at her phone. "C'mon, ladies, let's get out of here before he shows. Bella doesn't need a crowd watching her."

"Yeah, looks like you've already got someone keeping an eye out," Sam said with a smile.

"I feel so much safer knowing Roman's here if this guy turns out to be a jerk," Maggie said.

"I can handle myself, Maggie," Bella said.

"I know you can," she said. "Just that it's good to be cautious."

"Have fun!" Sam said, tugging Maggie away.

"Bye, honey," Gina said, giving Bella a quick kiss on the cheek. "I'm so excited. We're going to see that new Sam Claflin flick. I actually get to stay out until eleven!"

"I'll talk to you tomorrow, G."

Gina squeezed her arm. Lowering her voice, she said, "Maybe it's fate, you know, Roman being here. Your chance to clear the air and start over again."

"About twelve years too late for that," Bella said.

"That's what Manny and I said about getting pregnant," Gina said. "We thought it was too late for us and then . . . surprise! So you just never know." Then she rushed out after Bella's friends.

Just then Zeke—or at least, someone wearing a Stetson—walked into the bar. Unfortunately, Roman zoned in on him, too, eyeballing him with hawk eyes. The man was handsome, just like Jess had said. Long and lean, wearing a blue button-up shirt with cuffed sleeves that matched his Texas bluebell eyes. Roman scowled and turned back to the game.

Bella stewed for a moment. Any decent man would leave, but he was going to be a pill. Well, what else was new? Ever since they'd run into each other, he'd managed to irritate her every nerve, between the run-in with the dog and the lost contact and the lake incident *and* knocking a hole in her wall, so why should tonight be any different? Fine. It was a public place. Let him sit there and do whatever, just so long as he left her alone.

Zeke saw her, but just as she held up a hand to wave, his gaze slid quickly over her and lit on the sexy woman at the bar. The woman next to Roman with a plunging neckline and shiny, lustrous black hair. And big red lipstick lips. And boobs. Nice ones. Bella cast a glimpse down at her own bosom, which wasn't bad, but yeah, no competition there.

Oh, she couldn't believe this was happening. Zeke or whatever-his-name-was thought that the hot woman at the bar was his date! And he *preferred* her.

Well, Bella wasn't going to give up after one glance. I mean, he'd barely looked at her. She had enough confidence not to be defeated that easily. So she got up and walked over to the bar where he was standing. Clearly he hadn't asked the woman's name yet. Simple mistake, right? One she'd soon set straight.

"Zeke?" she said, flashing her best smile. "Hi. I'm Bella."

He ripped his eyes off of Megan Foxx long enough for the truth to register. "Oh yeah, hi." His gaze raked her up and down, making her feel like he was evaluating a prize heifer. Or whatever cowboys took measure of. "Jess's friend, right? I'm Zeke. Zeke Powell."

Okay, this was worse than she thought. Not that he wasn't polite, but when he managed to tear his eyeballs off Megan's cleavage and look at Bella, in her cute denim dress and boots, the look he gave her held undisguised disappointment or, even worse—disinterest. She *knew* she shouldn't have worn those boots.

"I have a table for us," she said. "Want to sit down?"

He went with Bella, but not without a wink in Hot Girl's direction. That was strike two. Bella probably would have left at that point, but, well, Roman was still glaring at them, even as he sipped his beer. She wasn't going to give him the satisfaction of gloating that she was the loser candidate.

"So, what do you do?" she asked as Scott took their order for a pitcher of beer and some of his famous hot artichoke dip.

Zeke assessed her for a good long time, as if he'd finally made up his mind that she wasn't half bad, after all. Then he smiled a wicked, dimpled smile. "What do you want me to do?"

Odd answer. Before she could ask him if he was between rodeo jobs or underwear jobs, he asked, "Who's the guy with one eyebrow over there? He your brother?"

"One eyebrow?" That sounded terrifying. Until she followed the direction of his head tilt. *Roman.* He did not have a unibrow, but he was frowning so darkly he looked like he did.

"Yeah, he looks like he wants to come over here and take me out. And I don't mean for a date." He leaned over the table and took up both of her hands in his. "You are a pretty little thing," he said in his sexy Texan drawl. "How about we get out of here and go somewhere else where we can really get acquainted?"

His proposition barely registered, because Roman flashed her a look. It was his *I'm-going-to-come-over-there-and-beat-the-shit-out-of-this-guy* look. She knew it well.

"But we haven't even gotten our drinks yet," Bella said, disengaging her hands. "Besides, I want to get to know you better."

"In the biblical sense, right?"

"Um, no, in the regular sense. Like, what do you really do for a living?"

"Well, right now I'm between jobs."

"Okaaay. What did you used to do?"

"I worked in an office doing HR."

"Wait a minute. I thought you were a male underwear model. Or a cowboy."

"Honey, I can rustle me up any fine filly under the sheets and ride her 'til the cows come home. Wanna try me out?"

A loud scrape rent the air. Had Roman actually *heard* that? He'd pulled back his stool from the bar and was now stalking over.

"She's not trying you out," Roman said, leaning over the cowboy and resting his hands on the table. "Not now, not later. Beat it, butt-head." He turned to Bella. "Dating this guy is a big mistake."

Bella stood up to get in his face. "He's my mistake to make, isn't he?"

"I just don't like to see you underappreciated." He was close, close enough for her to notice a tic in his jaw. And the smell of his cologne, which was really nice. And how tall he was, and how broad his shoulders were. She remembered clinging on to those shoulders, smoothing her hands over the smooth hills and valleys of muscle . . . Oh what was she doing? She needed to shut the gate on Memory Lane once and for all. And being this close was not helping.

"It's not your business to . . . to appreciate me." She poked him in the chest, which was very hard from all that muscle. "Or feel sorry for me. Or whatever it is you think you're doing."

"I'm not feeling sorry for you. I'm trying to save you from a jerk."

"I don't need you to save me, Roman, that's the thing."

"Whoa," the fake cowboy said. "Do you two have . . . a thing going on?"

Roman ignored him. "I wouldn't have come over here if you would've told this guy off."

She'd been ready to, trust her. But something about Roman's high-and-mighty attitude made her ornery. "Maybe I'm not looking to reject anyone." She crossed her arms. "Maybe I'm just looking to have a good time."

His big brows dove deep over that one.

She tipped her head in the direction of the bar. "Looks like that was what *you* were out for tonight. Sitting next to Megan Foxx and all."

"I was minding my own business. She sat down next to *me*."

"Right. Right." She looked over to her right and was surprised to find the cowboy's chair empty.

"You scared my date away," she said.

He snorted. "Didn't take much."

Bella turned to see Zeke leaving the bar, his hand on Megan Foxx's back. "My date left with your date," she said, gathering up her stuff. "Unbelievable."

"She wasn't my date. She was just some girl—"

"Whatever. I don't want to know about your exploits."

"Don't 'whatever' me," he said, pointing a long index finger between her eyes. But it wasn't threatening. It was *hot*. Oh my God, she was getting turned on by his . . . his caveman behavior. All that passion. Directed toward *her*. Even though it was anger, it was . . . breathtaking. She snapped her gaze away from his nice, full lips, realizing with horror that she wanted to kiss him. Or *whatever* him. Bad. She needed some serious help.

She narrowed her eyes, unwilling to allow him the upper hand. "Excuse me?"

"I just came in here to watch the game."

"Well, I came for a date, and now it's ruined, thanks to you. Just because you're back in town doesn't mean you've got any business interfering with my life. You have—you have *boundary* issues."

He folded his big arms. Was he trying to look menacing? Because it was only making him look even sexier. "Yeah, seems like Mirror Lake's not big enough for us both."

"Stop making fun of me."

He rolled his eyes. "That guy was clearly eyeballing anyone in the bar who'd go home with him tonight. You can do a lot better."

"Oh? Just like you were hoping to do with Ms. Oops-I-Forgot-to-Wear-a-Bra- Tonight? It's not your business if my date's an idiot or not. Or if I decide I like idiots or want to go home with one. Just like it's not my business that you wanted to nail that floozy."

"I did not want to nail—"

"Good night, Roman." She yanked her purse up over her shoulder. "You can watch the game in peace now. I—I hope the Yankees win." Then she strode toward the door, red boots tapping, and left.

God, Bella was aggravating. Still, Roman couldn't seem to peel his eyes off her as she left, hips swaying, dark curls bouncing, in that hot little denim dress she was wearing and those little red boots. How every time he came within a few feet of her he wanted to drag her soft curves up against him, trawl his fingers through all that silky black hair, inhale her sweet smell like a drug, and kiss the bejesus out of her.

Oh, he knew he was letting lust-brain get to him. He couldn't seem to help it with her. Just as he couldn't seem to help himself from diving headfirst into her business.

Dickhead cowboy.

Roman hadn't even noticed Megan Foxx. He didn't even have any idea if the Yankees were winning. He'd just noticed *her*.

Oh, he didn't *want* to notice her. Or think about her. He should have just left, but he couldn't seem do that, either. He couldn't seem to develop anything close to a sense of detachment as far as she was concerned.

"Want a beer?" Scott MacNamara asked.

He could use one. To calm down. It would be nice to just be able to sit here and watch the game and try not to think about Bella. Scott suggested a locally made craft beer, and he said sure. Frankly, if Scott served him up some 10W-40 right now, he'd probably drink that, too.

Someone slipped into the seat beside him. Ethan. There went his calm-down period.

"I'll have the same, Scott," Ethan said.

"Hey, how's it going?' Roman asked.

"You got a sec?" Ethan asked.

"Sure." He looked at the man he'd played basketball with senior year. He'd been the point guard and Ethan was the shooting guard, and they'd won districts. If things had been different, they might have been the best of friends. Their feelings for Bella had changed that. And judging by how protective he was of her the other night when they'd picked up the mutt, it seemed like not much had changed.

"Look," Ethan said. "I'm going to lay it right on the line. I've been friends with Bella for a long time."

Yeah, Roman thought. *A lot more than friends.* How the hell did that come about anyway? Just thinking about them together made him want to . . . well. That wouldn't solve anything, would it? So he kept his mouth shut.

"She's been through a lot, and I don't want to see her hurt again. I have to ask you what your intentions are."

"Are you asking me if I want to get involved with her again?"

Roman looked at the icy-cold beer Scott had just set down in front of him. Touched the frosty sides of the glass. He did *not* want a relationship with Bella, mainly because he wasn't crazy. He had no desire to rekindle things with the woman who'd bulldozed his heart into oblivion.

"She had to deal with a lot after you left, and I wouldn't want anything like that to happen again."

Deal with a lot? What was he talking about? She'd broken up with *him.* She'd told him to leave. She hadn't wanted *him.* Why did Ethan make it seem like it was the other way around?

"Look," he said to Ethan. "I know you care about her a lot. You may not believe this, but so do I. I don't want to see her hurt, either."

Maybe he could chalk all these messy feelings up to nostalgia. Unresolved emotions from being dumped hard and fast long, long ago. Still, their breakup had never sat well with him. It had been so abrupt, in the midst of all that turmoil. And they'd been so fricking *young*.

He wasn't sure why he always seemed to have such a visceral reaction to her. With the cowboy, he'd simply *reacted*, plain and simple, and he just couldn't muster up any regret for it. That guy was a first-class idiot, and he would've done the same thing all over again.

But he had to somehow elevate himself beyond all this residual passion. Returning to Mirror Lake was going to force him to come to grips with this. He *had* to come to grips with it. Deep down, he *knew* Bella didn't need his help. She was a strong, competent woman. Busting into her business seemed to be more for him than for her, and he had to stop it.

They'd started off on the wrong foot. He wanted them to be friends. He didn't want them to have animosity between them. It was *important* to him. They had to find a way to live together in this small town. Once he approached this from a friendship angle, everything would settle down.

It had nothing to do with unresolved feelings or Ethan or some indefinable yearning he held deep inside him.

He would stay out of her business. He wouldn't let old feelings define him. He would start anew, make things right.

"Ethan, I'd love to talk, but I just realized I've got to do something important," he said. He tossed a bill on the counter and headed for the door. "Gotta go, man. See you around."

"See you around," Ethan said, a little disgruntled.

Roman had reached the door before he realized he'd never answered Ethan's question.

CHAPTER 10

The porch light was on when Bella returned from The Date That Wasn't. She found her aunt inside watching HGTV and nodding off over her crocheting, Gracie curled up on the couch beside Fran's chair. Fran hated when the dog snuck up on the furniture, and never allowed it, but Gracie was clever enough to wait until Fran dozed off before she tried it. Bella had nearly made it to the stairs when she stepped on a creaky floorboard and Fran's eyes flew open. The dog raised her head and blinked sleepily.

"You're home early," Aunt Fran said.

Bella walked back and sat next to Gracie, who yawned widely, then promptly turned belly up for a good rubbing, which of course Bella obliged her with. "Oh, thank you, Grace. I live to scratch your tummy. Yes, I do." Which led to a whirlwind of tail wags and much adoration.

"Spiffy boots," Aunt Fran said. "How was your date?"

Bella smiled and extended her legs. The date was a flop, but the boots . . . yeah, they were keepers.

"Roman was at MacNamara's tonight. My date was being a little bit of an idiot, and Roman sort of butted in."

Fran set down her crocheting. "Butted in as in *bar brawl*?"

"More like, the guy said something stupid and Roman rushed over, and then he and I got into it."

"You and Roman were arguing?"

"Well, I didn't appreciate his interference. It was unnecessary."

"That right? I think it sounds chivalrous!" Fran exclaimed. She pretended to be counting stitches, but Bella could tell by the quirk of her brow she was a little flustered by the excitement.

"It's not the Middle Ages. I can handle a guy who's being a little bit of a jerk," Bella said, slumping down on the couch. "I wish he'd never come back." Gracie thought she was playing a game and laid down across her chest, licking her on the face. "It was so peaceful without Roman. He's poking his nose into my business, and I don't like it."

"Why is he doing that, do you think?"

"I don't know. Maybe he's still angry after all these years."

"Are you angry, too?"

She waved her arm dismissively. "What happened was a long time ago. We've both gone our separate ways."

"But you didn't answer the question."

"Honestly, what's there to be angry about? I've managed just fine. More than fine. I've got a great education and a great job. No regrets there."

That was a great lie. She *was* angry. At her father for giving her such a cruel ultimatum. At herself for lying and then pretending for so many years that it didn't matter. And yes, at Roman, too, for never coming back. Not that he could have known. She must have told that whopper really well—well enough to crush him so badly that he never returned until now.

So yes, come to think of it, she was furious. In ways she couldn't bear to tell her aunt.

"Sweetheart," Fran said, "I never asked you how things ended between you two. Maybe I was afraid to. Your father and I were so worried you'd both run off together and get married. I must admit, it was a relief when you didn't."

Bella shrugged. She didn't mention her father's threats to disown her, or her fears about leaving Joey. "We were eighteen." So, so young. "I'm not sure what would've become of us." From twelve years down the road, it was a lot easier to imagine that their youth, and their lack of money and education, would have all been strikes against them.

She'd done all right, even if she was still here in Mirror Lake. For the most part, she'd left the pain and sadness behind her. She'd created a life of her own. Even if she hadn't found the right person to share it with yet. It was just that his return had pulled off the scab. Dredged up the waters. Stirred the pot.

She hadn't realized she'd closed her eyes. When she opened them, her aunt was looking at her with her kind Italian eyes and patting her hand. "Things happen for a reason."

How could her aunt say that? She really was a hopeless romantic. Bella must not have disguised her skepticism very well, because her aunt said, "Don't scoff at me, young lady. What I'm saying is, Roman's coming back is an opportunity. To clear the air." She made a swiping gesture in front of her. "To settle some things so the past is put to rest."

Like *that* was going to happen when they couldn't even speak two words to each other without getting into it.

If Bella stayed here in Mirror Lake, she knew exactly what would happen. She saw it in the way other women, like the ones in the bar, looked at Roman. It would only be a matter of time, but he would settle down. Find a wife. Have kids. She'd have to accustom herself to that eventually happening. And somehow she just couldn't stomach watching that play out before her eyes.

Yeah, that Chicago job was looking better and better.

Suddenly, she was very fatigued. "The past was plenty at rest before he came back and started mucking with it. Aunt Fran, I've been thinking about taking a job in Chicago. Maybe it's time for me to leave Mirror Lake for a while."

"You mean *run* away from Mirror Lake for a while."

"That's not really fair." Hadn't she done her time?

Her aunt took both of her hands and squeezed tight. "I have nothing against your leaving. You've done everything for your family and, God knows, you should be able to do what you want. All I'm saying is, Roman's here now. Don't run away from him. Face him. Only then can you truly put the past to rest."

Yes, but that was scary. Very, very scary. She couldn't bear to have her heart exposed like that again. There was a reason it had taken her years to build walls around it. The cost of having a buck-naked, unprotected heart was way too high.

Bella showered and slid into bed with a big, fat novel, something she did nearly every night, the room dark except for her bedside lamp. Tonight, especially, her mind needed the effects of a nice, calming love story to restore her equilibrium after Roman had knocked it off its shaky foundation. Besides, no matter how bad tonight had been, it was Friday. She was off the entire weekend. Except that tomorrow morning she was teaching a bulb-planting class at the garden center for her father, but that was more fun than work.

She ignored the stab of loneliness that gnawed at her heart. She was all right. She was always all right. She'd endure Roman, get Dad through his rehab and Tony through his last year of high school, then it was going to be time for *her* life to start. That was a promise.

Gracie was in her new doggie bed, flat on her back with legs up in the air snoring. She should be so lucky.

Bella heard a *ping* against her western window. She had the corner room, a room Gina had always personally coveted because of the windows facing two sides, west and south. A memory hit her, of Roman throwing pebbles at that window long ago. To save her from being alone during the worst night of her life. Until she'd turned him away.

Roman, Roman, Roman. She was sick of all the memories his return had stirred. She pushed them all aside and went back to reading her book. It was probably just an acorn or something, the result of those damn squirrels constantly chomping on them and letting pieces rain down everywhere.

Ping. Ping. More pebbles hit the window, sounding like sleet. Finally she got out of bed and raised the sash. She stifled a scream. Roman was on the trellis, a few feet under the window.

She clamped a hand over her mouth. Tried to breathe. Closed her eyes to get a grip.

"Oh good. You're still up," he said as if she wasn't still trying to pick half of her startled body off of the ceiling. She opened her eyes to see a grin light his handsome face. He let a handful of small stones fall from his palm to the ground and dusted off his hands.

She held a hand over her chest, where her heart was practically beating out of it in terror. "What are you doing here?" she hissed. "Like most people in this century, I do have a phone, you know."

He quirked up a corner of his mouth. "Somehow, after tonight, I didn't think you'd give me your number." He reached the window, both of his long-fingered hands draped over the sill. She'd always admired his beautiful hands. "I'm sorry I scared you. Can I come in?"

Everything about him invoked the romance of a clandestine night meeting. The black-as-night hair, catching a glint from the one dim light. The big brown eyes, innocently pleading. The big chest and lean, muscular forearms, so much more defined than when he was a boy. A man accustomed to labor. Who used his muscle as well as his brains. Yep, he was the whole big, irresistible package, and he was about to climb into her childhood bedroom.

Part of her wanted to haul him in over that sill and rip his clothes off and beg him to make love to her, right there on the floor.

But the other half wanted to push him out the window. Not really, but anything to wipe that cocky look off his face.

He was a tiger in a kitten costume. She'd be a fool to play his game.

"Of course not," Bella said. "You may be crazy, but I certainly am not. Go away." She crossed her arms. Mainly because she caught him looking at her boobs and realized she was wearing a pink camisole that was probably giving him quite a show. "That trellis is old. If I were you, I'd scuttle right back down it before you fall."

"I'm not going to—" All of a sudden he lost his grip.

She lunged forward. "Roman! Oh my God, Roman, no!" She leaned out the window to find he was huddling a little below the window, chuckling.

"I'm going to slam this window shut right now," she said darkly. "And I don't care which appendages I catch with it."

"Arabella. Wait." Oh, the sound of her given name on those lips. She shivered a little, and not from the cool night air. He reached out, his fingers grasping her naked arm, and they felt so—good. The warmth of him seemed to traverse up and down her arm and spread like fire into her chest and below. Far below. Oh, her traitorous body, so reactive to him, even after all these years.

She looked at him reluctantly. Her cheeks felt hot. Hell, *all* of her felt hot.

"I'm sorry about earlier," he said. "I was wrong to interfere with your date. I just want to talk with you. Will you let me in?"

She drew back, away from his touch. "Fine. Even though both of us are going to get shot if my father wakes up and finds you here."

He threw his long leg over the sill and climbed over it. The light somehow made the chiseled lines of his jaw look more severe, more menacing. In her old room, his tall, lean body loomed large. Too large.

"Wow, time warp," he said, looking around at the pale-pink walls, the patchwork quilt, the white furniture. Various clothes on the floor. Makeup tubes and containers scattered over her vanity. "And such a great watchdog, too," he said, glancing over at the dog, who was chasing squirrels in her sleep and snoring heavily.

Roman walked over and stood in front of her, his gaze doing a slow sweep, starting at her bare feet, working his way up her bare legs and PJ shorts, her cami, up to her frowning face. She expected some remark—sarcastic or borderline innuendo, but he surprised her. "I was out of line in the bar. Contrary to what you may believe, I do care about you. I want us to be friends. And since we're going to be living together in the same town, I think we should make an effort."

Friends. Right. She should feel relieved, but a wave of another feeling came over her. Disappointment? Oh, come on. What did she expect? That she was Rapunzel and he was rappelling in to save her from her life? Romeo coming after Juliet? She didn't need saving. What had she been expecting him to say, anyway?

Except it did seem anticlimactic, a declaration of *friends* after all that climbing.

"Okay. I accept your apology."

His eyes wandered around the room. What was he looking for? Did he expect to find a Chad Michael Murray poster or two? Maroon 5 or Nickelback or Kelly Clarkson or Britney Spears CDs lying about? Photos of them from prom? The tiny diamond ring he'd given her on that last night that she'd worn on a chain around her neck for years after he'd gone?

He smiled. A full, wide smile, and that was a knockout, too. Lord, did the man have no features that were unappealing to women? That smile was positively blinding. It sent her hormones spinning into overdrive. He had to leave. Now. "Well, thanks for coming, but . . ."

"I want to show you something," he blurted.

"What?"

He canted his head out the window. "Come with me."

"Down the trellis? No way." He might be into risking his life, but to her it did not appeal.

"I'll go down the trellis. You go the normal way and meet me over at my place."

Common sense had her shaking her head. "Roman, no. I'm sorry, this is—"

Lunacy. Against all sense. Going with him now would be dangerous for so many reasons, and really, her father was the least of those worries. She felt even now, after all these years, the intense, magnetic pull of him. The urge to run her hands over the hard planes of his back, touch the coarsely textured silk of his hair. Imagine the weight of him over her, the deep drive of his kisses, how he'd murmur in her ear and tell her how much he loved her, how he'd never love anyone else . . .

She opened her mouth to say no. But he turned away and tossed his leg back over the sill. "I just want to show you something—something that's important to me. Trust me."

Oh, right. They both knew how that had turned out.

Once he'd left and she was certain he hadn't broken his neck, she opened her top dresser drawer to get a sweatshirt. Impulse had her reaching to the back and fingering the bottom of the drawer until she came up with a small black velvet box. In it was a ring with the tiniest of stones. Microscopic, really. Surrounded by a circle of diamond chips. A poor man's gift. Or that of a very young man stuck in a very tenuous spot. *Marry me, Bella,* he'd said. *I love you, I'll always love you. We can make a life together.*

So much had been broken. Trust, family, their love for each other. Standing him up would tell him in no uncertain terms that that breach was irreparable. He was smart; he'd get the message. She would set boundaries once and for all.

Yet she found herself tugging on a sweatshirt and rummaging around under her bed for flip-flops.

Because, God help her, she couldn't stay away.

Roman was sitting on a wooden rocking chair on his porch the moment Bella first emerged from the woods. Seeing her caused a sudden warmth to spread all over his insides, a butter-melting-over-warm-toast kind of feeling. "You came," he said like an idiot. Then winced inside. He didn't mean to sound that excited or surprised. Or like he was an eighteen-year-old kid again.

He'd once loved her, and their parting was the most painful thing that he'd had to live through, except for being separated from his brothers. But now that they were adults, he could care about her as a friend. They could coexist.

Some little voice inside his head was laughing hysterically at that friendship idea. But he pushed it out of his head as he opened the screen door to the house and gestured for her to come in.

The inside of the house looked like a country theme from the eighties gone bad. In the kitchen, a wallpaper border of geese wearing bonnets alternating with pink and blue hearts wound around the middle of the walls, and an old beige vinyl table with aluminum chairs sat in the center. Plaques lined the walls containing more geese—wearing more bonnets and bows and surrounded by more hearts—and kitschy sayings about love and friendship and family. He hadn't thought of the décor at all when his grandparents had lived here—it was just part of their house and who they were. But now, without them, it was just—stuff.

"I'm sorry about your grandparents," she said. "They were good people."

"Thank you," he said. "I just hope I can make them proud."

"Why wouldn't you? They'd be thrilled that you're back here taking over the business."

Roman shrugged and toyed with a fake banana in a bowl in the center of the table. "My vision for the business is a lot different than theirs. I hope they would agree with what I'm planning."

Bella smiled. "They will if it's a success. Your grandpa was always about the bottom line."

That made him laugh. "You just reminded me of something. He used to quote Abraham Lincoln. 'Whatever you do, be a good one.'"

"I think I just saw a saying on the wall with that."

"You probably did." The first thing he'd done was give the place a good cleaning, but he hadn't begun removing all the knickknacks and things that lined the windowsills and numerous shelves and the big curio cabinet in the living room. It was almost as if some part of him was still waiting for his grandmother to do that. It seemed like the worst sacrilege to do it without her. The kitchen window was open, and a fluorescent light that ran over the top of the window bathed the kitchen in whitish-blue light. Roman flipped a switch that lit the fixture over the table.

"Is that fresh?' Bella asked, immediately zeroing in on the table where a pizza box sat. The faint odor of garlic and warm crust infused the room, indicating that it certainly was.

"I figured we both probably missed dinner," he said. "Hope you're hungry."

"For Santoro's? Always."

He found himself smiling. Had she ever passed up pizza? It was a strange relief to see that at least her appetite hadn't changed.

He grabbed up the box and a bottle filled with amber liquid that sat next to it, along with two snifters, and asked her to bring the two plates he'd carefully laid out. She followed him onto the front porch and sat in one of two big white rockers. He lit the candle in a lantern that sat on a little table between them. He hoped everything didn't look too preplanned. Like he knew she'd come.

He sat down and offered her the open box. "I ordered the kind with artichoke and garlic sauce. That still your favorite?"

"Oh yes," she said, clapping her hands a little. She pulled a slice off the pie, cheese trailing for a mile, and managed to get it on a plate. Then she loaded the other plate. He was happy she was excited about the pizza, but he was eager and uncharacteristically nervous for her to taste his brandy. Tell him what she thought of it.

He opened the bottle, then poured some of the pure golden liquid into a brandy snifter.

"This is the old-fashioned way to drink this, but it helps to concentrate the aromas at the top. Try it." He was about to hand her a glass, but he stopped. "On second thought, wait a minute," he said, taking the snifters and running into the house.

He came out a few minutes later and handed her a glass. It was warm.

"What did you do?" She took the glass, cradled it in her hands, and looked up at him with her soft brown eyes. Her face in the dim light, outlined against the glow of the house lights, did something indescribable to him. It made him picture lying with her by a roaring fire, or sitting with her on the couch watching TV or across the table at a restaurant . . . it made him picture forever. Crazy.

"I flamed it over the stove burner just for a little bit to warm it up. The flavors are better that way."

She was carefully examining the glass. She knew enough not to swirl it. He tried not to look like what she thought mattered. Like he was holding his breath. So he forced himself to sit back and picked up his own glass. "Go ahead. Try it."

"Is it cognac?" she asked. "Brandy?"

"You tell me," he said. Why did he feel so nervous?

"Okay." She brought the snifter up to her chest and nosed it. Then she brought it up to her chin and smelled it again, inhaling through her nose and mouth. Then looked directly at him. "Apples."

Jackpot. "Very good."

She swirled and smelled again. "I'm not very good at picking out all the different flavors."

"Just have some."

She took a tiny sip. "Wow," she said.

"Wow?" He was pleased. More pleased than was safe. And he tried to tamp down his pleasure.

"Yeah, it's good. Smooth, apple-y, vanilla-y, woodsy. I don't know. All I know is it's very good. I'm not sure what it is, but it's much stronger than wine."

"Much more concentrated. It's apple *brandy*. Applejack's the informal name for it. It's an old drink. George Washington and his troops drank it."

"Did your grandfather make it?"

"I did." The pride in his voice was unmistakable. He couldn't hide it. Didn't try to.

She frowned. "Doesn't brandy take years to age?"

"Very good, *bella dolche*."

Sweet Bella. She opened her mouth, probably to protest that he'd called her that silly endearment from years ago that was probably too... intimate. It had just slipped out. A little embarrassed, he walked over to the porch railing and looked out over the orchards in the distance.

"This bottle's XO," he said. "That's short for extra old—I made it seven years ago. It's not bad, but I've learned a lot about different flavors since then."

"It's excellent," she said. "Smooth."

"I came back here to take over the farm, but what I really want to do is start a distillery. I don't just want to grow apples and supply farmers' markets and restaurants and ship the bruised ones out for cider. I want to set up a still, fermentation tanks, the whole nine yards. Of course I need backers, and I'm working on that. And I'm trying to get some of the better restaurants in town to try these small batches I've made over the past few years. That's why I'm building the wine bar. A place where people can come and sample this and other unusual flavors. There's nothing like it in town."

"That's exciting. Different."

"Or foolish. Maybe both."

She shrugged. "I'm glad to see you're still dreaming big."

He turned to her. "I wanted you to know what I'm doing here. I wanted to share this with you. And I want you to know you'll always be special to me, Bella. We shared a lot once." If she would just talk to him, maybe they could clear the air. If she could tell him how it was for her back then. Help him to understand what had happened between them, then he could move on from these . . . unsettled feelings. This desire to be near her and hold her that he couldn't seem to break free of.

She looked at him, worry shadowing her brow like the tall ancient beech trees did his porch roof. "I'm excited for you. I know you'll make this a success." A safe answer. Said with a smile. It told him nothing about how she really felt.

She hesitated before speaking again. "Roman, I want to tell you I appreciate your being respectful to my father despite how difficult he is. And I'm sorry for what he said about the pond."

"Bella, I don't need the pond."

She looked at him with surprise.

He laughed a little. "If I need irrigation, I've got an entire lake in my backyard. That's not going to be one of my problems. But that doesn't mean I haven't got a lot more. The farm's neglected. A lot of things need to be brought up to speed. It won't be easy." He didn't want to talk about the farm. He wanted to talk about *them*.

"Bella, about us. I—"

She put down her glass and walked over to the porch railing. "I—I don't want to talk about the past. Everything worked out the way it was supposed to."

"Did it?" He walked up behind her, glancing out at the rows upon rows of apple trees that marched tidily into the distance. If only life were so orderly. He put a hand on each of her arms, holding her from behind. She tensed but didn't move away. "Did it work out the way it was supposed to?"

"Wh-what do you mean?"

He stood there for a moment, holding her, smelling her sweet scent, *wanting* her. Without thinking, he slowly spun her around to face him. Their gazes locked, and she gave a gasp of surprise. Her eyes were soft and brimming with feeling—but he had no idea what she was thinking. He was close enough to see the pulse in her neck jump, her full lips part, and in that moment he could swear she felt it too—the sizzling current that had always electrified the air between them.

"I'm sorry, Bella," he said, still holding her by the arms. Lord, he was sorry, for *everything*. For the way he'd left, when everything was still so chaotic. And for his pride, which in all his hurt had prevented him from returning sooner, from truly talking things out with her. He just couldn't stop the niggling feeling that she wasn't telling him everything. Because her eyes told him one thing while her words said another.

Or was all of this just that he couldn't stop himself from acting foolish around her, even after all these years? Seems like he always would. Sense slowly returned, and he took a step back. "For tonight," he quickly amended. "For being an ass. You may not believe this, but I'll always feel protective of you. I—I hope we can be friends."

She broke away, walking back to her chair and picking up her glass, taking a substantial drink. "I'll take your friendship, Roman, but I don't need your protection. I've done fine on my own. Life happened the way it did, and we both survived it." She smiled, that same superficial smile that made him want to shake her shoulders a little. "Thanks for the—er—fun evening. I loved the brandy." She lifted the glass. "To friendship," she said brightly.

"To friendship," he said, touching his glass to hers, forcing a smile he didn't really feel. *Friends* was good, yes? But it certainly didn't feel right.

CHAPTER 11

Nine Years Earlier

"Oh, Ethan, my favorite, thanks," Bella said one Friday night, taking the large tub of buttered popcorn that he was handing her as they climbed down the narrow aisle of red velvet seats. They were in the Palace Theater, Mirror Lake's hundred-year-old carefully preserved theater full of carvings, statues, very high ceilings, and the façade of a Moorish castle on either side of the velvet-curtained stage. A city landmark, quirky and beloved. Sort of how Bella felt about Ethan.

She was determined to enjoy herself. Even though the special program was a marathon of John Wayne movies from the fifties and sixties and she honestly couldn't say she'd ever sat through a Western all the way through without falling asleep. Ethan had been really excited about it, and for his sake, she was forcing herself to try something new. Do something for him for a change, when he always seemed to do so much for her.

That was her mantra lately. She was going to open herself up to new experiences. Live her life to the fullest. Leave the heartbreak of the past behind her even though it was so, so hard. But it was fall break of her junior year and she'd been thrilled not to have class for the past few days, and it was Friday night, the workweek behind her. She was up for a little bit of fun.

And Ethan was so nice, as he always was. So concerned about if she was having a good time, always so patient with her. They'd been sleeping together for a month, and it was good. Not exploding-fireworks good like it had been with Roman, but that had been full-throttle teenage love. She was older and wiser now.

She was twenty-one and she wanted to stop acting like she was eighty-one, in between working all week in Crooked Creek, grabbing a bite and driving the hour to Storrs for evening classes on Tuesdays and Thursdays and for her half-day seminar on Saturdays.

After the movies, which weren't that bad, actually, Ethan walked with her out of the auditorium and down the stairs into the massively ornate lobby, which was only moderately crowded. His hand was light on her back as he ushered her out the glass doors that spilled them out onto Main Street. That's why she knew he felt it when she stopped dead in her tracks.

There, on Main Street, directly in front of them, was Roman. She'd practically run right into him as he walked past the theater. He was wearing jeans and a black hoodie, his hands tucked into the pockets from the chill of the fall evening.

She felt like she did once when she was a kid and had attempted a cartwheel but ended up crashing to the ground with the wind suddenly knocked out of her. One second she was fine, the next she was hungrily gasping for air. Unable to take any in, panicked. Yet a reality check told her she was standing in the street, still breathing in and out, in and out. Inside, part of her was screaming and sobbing, yet her eyes stayed dry, her expression calm. She hoped.

He was different, but the same. Three years and his military training had made him more filled out, broader through the shoulders. His hair was buzzed short and he was standing very straight, as if good posture had become second nature. Or maybe he was just on guard because of her. He'd become a gorgeous hunk of a man, all muscle and tall leanness.

Ethan kept his hand on her back, perhaps holding her a little tighter, a little more possessively than before. Bella's first wild impulse was to shrug off his hand and run to Roman, throw herself into his arms and breathe in the scent that she remembered so clearly. Tell him how much she'd missed him, how she wished every second of her life that they could go back and make different choices, different decisions. Get a rewind that hadn't ended in tragedy all around.

"Hi, Roman," Ethan said coolly.

Roman cast his dark gaze from Ethan to Bella. Dread pumped through her veins as he slowly took in Ethan's arm around her. For some reason, she didn't want Roman to learn about her and Ethan. She knew in that moment that if Roman had the slightest inkling to talk to her, she would take him up on it. The seas had calmed after three years; they'd grown up and matured. Maybe there was still a chance . . .

"Look, Roman, Bella and I are dating," Ethan said, his arm starting to feel like it was locked around her. "We're together."

Bella felt her face color. That voice inside kept crying out, *No! No!* Yet on the outside, she somehow kept smiling. Roman said something, but for the life of her she didn't hear it. There was too much blood rushing in her ears.

"How—how are you doing?" she asked. She tried to get him to look her in the eye, but he wouldn't.

"Oh well—Bella, you remember Reagan, don't you?" He motioned to a woman behind him who was turned away in the opposite direction.

No, not Reagan. As the woman faced them, Bella noted her beauty hadn't faded at all. The same long, silky hair, the same Lea Michele thousand-watt smile. The same gorgeous boobs.

"Hey, Bella," she said. "You look"—she hesitated—"great." She wore the same superior smirk as in high school. Of course she was smirking! Bella glanced down at her own baggy jeans, plain brown sweater, and boring black fall raincoat, mentally comparing her outfit to Reagan's fashionable, funky sweater cut at different lengths, her skinny leather leggings, and her high, leopard-print heels. Oh, why had he chosen her of all people?

A few more lines of conversation might have transpired, Bella couldn't be altogether sure. "It was great to see you, Bella," Roman said. His eyes looked pained. Something deep inside her called out to him, *I'm sorry, I'm so sorry.* She wanted to grab him by the elbow, ask him if they could talk sometime? But Reagan's smugness and the look on Ethan's face stopped her.

Ethan's face. For the first time she saw it, a mixture of anger and hurt that maybe she'd been too blind to notice before. Could it be that he . . . loved her? Oh, she suddenly realized that she didn't want that, and yet even thinking it made her feel like such a traitor to the man who'd done everything for her in these hard, lonely years.

"Bella, are you all right?" he asked, touching her arm as they began walking again. Actually, she felt freezing. Her head was pounding. Was life always like this, she wondered, where the choices you make are never really choices? You just get swept away on a tide of your own creation until it drags you so far downstream you're completely lost.

Ethan was looking at her, fresh worry and concern in his eyes. She took a deep breath to hold it together for him. "I'm fine," she said with a smile. "I'm really hungry," she said. "Want to order a pizza?"

She didn't know how she would ever eat it. Or do anything else with Ethan tonight that wouldn't let him see right through her. After three years, tonight had shown her that she hadn't really made any progress at all. How could it be that her body kept moving down the street with Ethan but her heart had stayed back there on the sidewalk with Roman? And she feared she would never be whole or happy again.

CHAPTER 12

The next Friday rolled around before Bella knew it. Another Friday, another dating nightmare. Bella hated to admit the best thing about the failed cowboy date was spending time with Roman . . . which confused her even more. Still, she was determined to get back on the dating merry-go-round and give it the old one-two try.

"Oh, oh," Maggie said as she hung up her desk phone and cast Bella an ominous look across her office.

"What is it?" Bella asked. Maggie worried so much, you could never tell from her tone of voice whether things were catastrophic or just mildly upsetting.

"I just spoke to Sam. There's been a change of plan with your date tonight."

Bella stiffened. "That sounds ominous."

"Sam's got it under control. She wants me to tell you to keep an open mind."

"More open than usual?"

"Love can come from unexpected places."

"Now you're just plain scaring me."

"No, no reason to be afraid. Just . . . I'm not sure you're going to be thrilled."

"Oh, for God's sakes, Maggie, tell me who it is!"

"Look, you promised us three dates and to keep an open mind. That's all I'm saying or Samantha will kill me. Now I've got to go. Friday night awaits, and I've got a date myself."

"Who with?"

"Two very attractive three-year-old young men. And their mothers. It involves a swim at the rec center and chicken nuggets afterward."

"Have a blast," Bella said. "And if you and Sam have thrown me under the bus tonight, I'm giving up on men and joining a convent."

"Well, you do look good in black," Maggie said, shooing her out the door before she could respond. "Call me tomorrow, okay?"

Ten minutes later, Bella was standing in the entranceway to Brad Rushford's restaurant on the lake, Reflections, looking around for her mystery date, thinking that the guy, whoever he was, couldn't be all that bad if he wanted to meet her here, at the classiest place in town. Finally, after asking the hostess a zillion times if anyone had a table for two and was waiting for someone to show, she ended up sitting at the bar and ordering a glass of wine, praying that she wasn't being stood up. To make things worse, some businessman who was already tipsy hit on her.

That's when she saw Roman walking down the darkly varnished wooden floor with Brad Rushford himself. Bella's heart thunked hard against her ribs, which startled her and made her cheeks suddenly heat. Just once she wished she wouldn't have a full-blown fight-or-flight reaction to the mere fact that he'd walked into a room.

He looked elegantly handsome in a black suit, white shirt, and red tie. And was that a briefcase he was carrying? Here she'd thought nothing could beat seeing him in jeans and work boots. Women were staring at the two men, and she could see why. Tall, broad shouldered, sinfully sexy, both of them. But especially Roman, who never failed to send her heart plummeting into a free fall faster than an Olympic diver.

She'd loved spending time with him the other night, tasting his apple brandy. She was excited for his plans for the farm and felt honored that he'd shared them with her. It was a step toward closure.

How could she even begin to tell him she'd lied to get him to leave? That terrified her beyond words. Yet strangely, she was coming to believe it might be necessary, for herself. To fully face the past. To come clean once and for all, regardless of the consequences. But now that they were finally starting to become friends again, she was wary of disturbing their fragile truce. And of letting him see the truth, that she'd truly loved him. That she'd faced an awful choice. And that she'd made that choice without him.

Just then, Roman glanced her way and saw her. She smiled and gave a little wave. He smiled back, and, Lord, that smile hit her in all the right places. She pretended to check her phone, because . . . well, because she was alone and she suddenly didn't know where to look to avoid staring at him.

The two men shook hands, then Roman began walking toward her. *Easy there, lassie,* her inner voice chided. *He's probably just coming to say hi.* But her entire nervous system had flipped into overheat mode. Could it be . . . could it be that *he* was her mystery date? *Keep an open mind,* her friends had advised.

Maybe he'd decided to meet her tonight to explore whatever it was that was going on between them. Maybe getting everything out in the open *would* be the best thing for them both. This would be their first step forward, and who knows where it would lead? He really was the best damn looking man she'd ever seen, hands down. And he was walking straight in her direction . . .

Just as he'd almost reached the bar, Roman was intercepted by another man. One in a tweed jacket. A tweed jacket Bella would recognize anywhere, because she'd picked it up from the dry cleaners herself last week. *Ethan.*

Ethan pushed up his sexy-in-a-geeky-way glasses that he was wearing instead of his contacts tonight and shook hands with Roman. "Roman. Hi. What brings you here?"

"Business with Brad," he said guardedly. "How about you?"

"Oh, Bella and I were just about to have dinner."

Bella stood and walked over to them. "We're having dinner?" she asked. Somehow, she felt the need to make it clear to Roman that she was not in on this plan. Although she chided herself for feeling that way. Why should she care if Roman thought she and Ethan were meeting for a casual dinner? They were friends. Sometimes they did do just that. So why did this entire situation feel so strange?

Ethan turned around, surprised to see her standing there. "Oh, hey, Bells." He kissed her on the cheek. "Surprise," he said a little sheepishly.

Yep, it was indeed. A surprise.

"Nice to see you both," Roman said, but he was looking at her. Frowning. "I'll leave you both to enjoy your dinner." He clapped Ethan once on the back and left. Just like that.

"I got a table for us outside," Ethan said, gesturing to the outdoor patio built right on the lake.

She should be thrilled. Sitting outside at her favorite restaurant on a perfect early-fall evening with a fire pit and propane heaters to chase the chill was her idea of a fantastic evening. Then why was she . . . irritated?

Oh, she knew exactly why. Her heart squeezed a little tightly as the unwelcome realization fully dawned: *Ethan was not Roman.* For a brief moment, she'd thought Roman had arranged a date with her, and that thought had made her . . . excited. Happy, even.

As the hostess led them to their table, something made her glance toward the door. Roman was leaning against it, staring at her. When she caught his gaze, he pushed his back against it and made his exit out of the restaurant.

Ethan pulled out her chair and she went through the motions of sliding into it. A waitress appeared, gave them the evening-special spiel, and left them looking at the menus.

Their usual conversation was stilted. Ethan was painfully quiet. Their usual easy rapport had checked out for the night.

Finally, she couldn't take it anymore. "Ethan," she said quietly.

He looked up nervously. A little pang of dread poked at her insides. "Tell me what this is all about."

"Your date was a no-show. Sam was upset about it, so I told her I'd happily step in." He sounded nonchalant, casual. But she wasn't buying it.

They'd had dinner together lots of times. Occasionally they'd even gone fancy like this. But this didn't feel like any of their fun dinners. It felt gut twisting. Uncomfortable. *Wrong*. Finally, she grabbed his hand. "Why did you step in, Ethan?"

He set down his menu and finally made eye contact. Heaved a big sigh. "Because I had to, Bells. I just had to."

Bella had had enough experience with men to know by the earnest look in his eyes that he was going to tell her things she didn't want to hear. Then she would have to tell him things that would hurt him. And she would rather die than do that. He'd been her best friend, helped her out of the abyss she'd fallen into after she'd lost everything. He'd made her feel beautiful and special, and she didn't regret a single moment with him. She would do anything not to hurt this kind, gentle man.

Why, oh why, couldn't she love him? I mean, she did, but like a friend. Not like how it had been with Roman.

"I'm tired of pretending we're just friends," he said. "It's not like that for me. And don't say it's because I just broke up with somebody, because that's why I broke up with her. She wasn't you. I—I love you, Bella."

Her eyes misted over with tears. "Ethan, we should go somewhere and talk about this," she said in a low voice.

He grasped her hand even tighter. "We're so natural together. I can tell you anything. We laugh and tell stories and . . . no, Bella. Don't look at me like that. I've been thinking about this for a long time."

Guilt gnawed at Bella's stomach. "I love you like a friend," she whispered. "I'll never forget what you did for me. But I can't love you like . . . that."

"Maybe you can. Maybe you just can't admit it to yourself."

Usually she loved that he was always such an optimist. But not today. "Why now?" She couldn't help but think this had something to do with Roman's sudden reappearance.

"I've been thinking about this for quite a while. Maybe with Roman back, I . . . I don't know. I need you to know how I feel. Make it clear. It's time for me to take a stand."

"Oh, Ethan."

"Look, do me a favor. I know it's a bit of a shock, but just think about it for a while." He was beseeching her. No—begging. Ethan was an honest man, incapable of hiding his feelings. She saw everything in his eyes. She wondered if any of this had been there all along and she'd never seen it. Or didn't want to, because she'd needed him, if not as a lover, then as a friend. He'd always been her voice of reason, her cheerleader. The one to calm her down when she was upset, the one to bolster her when she needed confidence.

Shame washed over her. In her need for him, had she led him to believe things that weren't true? She'd thought of herself as a strong woman, but maybe she'd become dependent on his friendship in a way that had kept him from moving forward. Maybe both of them, because Ethan was always available, always there to comfort and soothe and . . .

"Ethan—"

"Look, I didn't mean to upset you. Let's have dinner and let that sit for a while, okay?" He released her hand and sat back, a tentative expression on his face. She forced a smile to her lips and tried to make small talk. When his phone rang with an emergency, she thanked God for answering her prayers.

He kissed her again on the cheek, asking her to think about what he'd said, hoping he hadn't put her off. But she knew what she knew—that she would never love him with the bone-crushing love she'd once had for Roman Spikonos.

And the worst thought of all—maybe she wasn't as done with Roman as she liked to think.

"Anybody home?"

Roman startled a little at the sound of someone at his back door. Unexpected visitors didn't tend to show up too often. Not that the orchards were that far from town, but the long driveway wound quite a distance from the street, through the orchards and some woodland, too. He turned from the ancient white porcelain stove to see Joey D'Angelo standing there, his prominent adolescent nose pressed against the screen.

Seeing Joey reminded him of seeing Bella the night before in Brad Rushford's restaurant. With Ethan. Suddenly, the hunger he'd felt smelling his lunch cook turned to queasiness.

"Hi, Joe. C'mon in." Roman opened the door, then went back to flip the flat rectangles of steak sandwich meat he'd been cooking for his lunch. "How you doing?" The kid stayed outside, so Roman turned off the gas and went back and held the door open.

"I have Gracie with me," Joey said.

"She can come in, too." The dog waltzed into his kitchen like she owned the joint, and promptly crotch-butted him. As Roman stooped to pet the dog, Joey looked at him warily, making Roman wonder what he'd heard about him from his dad, and how bad it was. There was a time, many years ago, when the kid had worshipped Roman. At eighteen, Joe was a much harder sell. "I'm making lunch," Roman said. "You hungry?"

"I'm just delivering some leftovers from my sister."

He hoped they weren't laced with arsenic. He'd made a real effort with that friends spiel and he'd almost believed it, too—until he'd spotted Bella with Ethan last night.

He took the container Joe handed him and cracked open the lid. The pungent scents of oregano and basil promptly wafted up. Big, round meatballs were dusted with Parmesan and sat in a hefty red sauce he was sure was homemade. A kind gesture. Mouthwatering, too. "Thanks," he said. Was she trying to mitigate her father's unneighborly behavior? Or was it some kind of peace offering after he'd seen her with Ethan?

Ethan. It occurred to him Joe might be able to shed some light on the status of their relationship, but it was pretty clear the kid didn't trust him. "I'm making a steak sandwich. Want one?"

"No, thanks." The kid was too smart to take a bribe.

The dog, however, wasn't. Entranced by the smell of cooking meat, she sat frozen in front of the stove with her nose in the air, her entire body overtaken by the one hope that someone might toss her a morsel.

"Well, I better get back," Joe said. "We just got a new shipment of mums I've got to put out. I swear, people are buying those up like hotcakes. I don't get it. I mean, once the frost comes, that's it, they're done." He was eyeing the sandwich with undisguised hunger.

Roman sawed the sandwich in half and put it on two plates, then pushed one toward the kid. "Help yourself," he said. He gave a half a piece of steak meat to the dog, who inhaled it in one bite.

Joe thanked him and sat reluctantly. For a minute, they ate in silence. Except for the sound of the dog's tail thumping as she kept an eagle eye out for a handout or a carelessly dropped bit of food. "Look, Joe, whatever your father has said, I'm not the enemy. I mean no disrespect—to your father or anyone. I just want to run my business."

"Bella said the same thing. I get it."

The dog sidled up to Roman's leg. He pulled another piece of meat out of his sandwich and tossed it to her. Because, at this point, he needed as many people on his side as he could get.

Joe put down the sandwich. "It's just that my sister's been through a lot. I don't want to see her hurt again."

Those words made Roman like the kid even more. He clearly had his loyalties, and Roman respected that. But then, Bella had essentially raised him, and who wouldn't love her? He wondered how it really was for her after he'd left. Raising Joe, working, studying for her own degrees.

"I think very highly of your sister," Roman said, then he wisely changed the subject.

"So senior year's going good?" Hard to believe Joe was eighteen. He still saw him as the three-year-old he and Bella used to take to Dairy Flip, sitting in his car seat with a stream of melted chocolate ice cream trickling down his chin.

Joe sighed. "Most of my college apps are in. But I'm looking for a second job. I want to buy a car to take to college."

"I could use a little help." The words were out before he could think. Well, why not? Joe could use a break, and maybe he could back-door into Vito's civility via his son. "It would involve clearing scrap from the roof, loading the Dumpster, some cleaning, and some painting. Hourly work. You interested?"

"Yeah, if you don't mind me working it in with everything else."

"When you're able to come, you come."

"Okay. But I want to be paid in cash. And my dad can't know."

If Roman could count the things he'd done that Vito didn't know, he'd be a rich man. But this time around, he didn't want to keep any more secrets. "Maybe you should tell him up front," Roman suggested.

"I'll handle my dad."

All right, then. "Come over when you can. I'll put you on the clock." Roman tossed the dog one last bite of meat. She ate it and then stretched out at his feet, her head on his shoe. He bent over to pet her back. Now that her coat wasn't all tangled, it was actually kind of silky.

"Sounds great." Joe took another bite of sandwich. "Bella has another date tonight."

"With Ethan?" he asked.

"Nope. Bruno Santoro."

Please God, not Bruno the Mooner. Roman tried not to grimace. Way back in high school, Bruno had suffered a bad breakup with Jess Martin and decided after a couple of beers to show the world how pissed off he was. Until the cops caught him driving past the town diner flashing his naked ass out the passenger window of his friend's beat-up Chevy Malibu, thus giving birth to his unshakable nickname.

"She said she sort of has to go."

"What does Ethan think about that?"

"Ethan?"

"Yeah. He and Bella are—er, close, right?"

He shrugged. "I guess so." Okay, that was no help.

Joe frowned. "What do you care?"

"Who, me?" Roman gestured to his own chest. He got the distinct impression he was being interrogated. "I think of your sister strictly as a friend," he lied.

"I know this girl at school," Joe said. "I want to ask her to homecoming . . ."

"But . . . ?" Roman assessed him carefully. Was he asking him for advice? Or playing him?

"But she thinks of me like her friend." He made *friend* sound sort of like the plague.

"Hey, friend is a great place to start," Roman said, a little flattered that the kid was confiding in him. "Maybe she doesn't know you're interested in being more."

"Right," Joe said, standing up. "Well, thanks for the sandwich. And the job."

"All righty, then. Thank your sister for the food. And good luck with your . . . friend." The dog followed Roman to the door. As Roman reached down for one last pet, the dog licked his hand and gazed at him rapturously. A piece of steak, a friend for life.

Joe, on the other hand, was more complicated. He rolled his eyes. Then he gave Roman a long, meaningful look, one that immediately told Roman the kid was warning him, not soliciting advice. "Even I know it doesn't work to be friends with girls. Not the ones you *like*, anyway."

Boy, wasn't that the truth.

CHAPTER 13

"Why, it's Arabella D'Angelo. Come in, come in." A short, stout woman wiped her hands on a red-checkered apron, opened the hinged countertop that separated the cashier area from the dining area of Santoro's restaurant, and hugged Bella. Patrons sat at the red-and-white-checkered tablecloth-covered tables, eating spaghetti and manicotti and pizza, the smells of sauce and warm dough filling the air.

"Hi, Mrs. Santoro," Bella said, hugging her back. "Nice to see you."

This Saturday date was a collaborative effort between the Santoros and her father, longtime friends, both families hailing a couple of generations ago from the same village in Italy. Dreams of a marriage to unite both families died early when Bella refused to date Bruno in high school, but now that he was divorced and back in town, and apparently her father was desperate to marry off his almost-thirty-year-old daughter.

She could have said no, but her dad sold their restaurant a ton of vegetables and she didn't want to upset them and lose their account.

Besides, she was due to hear back about the Chicago job any time now, then she would be done with all these dates for good. Not that she didn't appreciate the effort, but she knew the chances of a real relationship coming from them was as likely as her suddenly waking up one day blonde with blue eyes.

"Bruno's in the kitchen with his father," Mrs. Santoro said. "We're so happy to have him back to stay." Sure enough, Bruno looked up from the window between the kitchen and the counter and smiled.

"Hey, Bruno," she said, waving. He looked—nice. Tall, with combed-back black hair and a somewhat prominent Italian nose, but it suited him. Plus he was wearing a crisp white apron as he prepared food, which was actually kind of sexy. She forcibly swept away the tendency to compare him to Roman, as she seemed to do unconsciously with every man she met. Not as tall, not as lean, not as muscular . . .

Stop it, she scolded herself. He was handsome. Besides, he didn't look like he went around mooning people or pinching girls' asses anymore. People change from high school, right?

People can change, period. And she could get over obsessing about Roman. Once he was in town for a while, the novelty of seeing him again would wear off. Besides, she'd probably be long gone anyway. Either way, she wasn't going to waste precious time thinking about him.

Even though she could've sworn he was about to kiss her the other night. That she'd *wanted* him to, despite having a litany of reasons why that was a very bad idea. Tell that to her body, which seemed to react to him with all the combustibility of dry kindling confronted by a match.

"I'll be out in a second, sweetheart," Bruno said with a wink.

She looked around. Nope, no other woman in sight. That *sweetheart* was meant for her. Cute. And better than the cowboy. Mrs. Santoro led her to a quiet booth in the back corner, near the kitchen. "Sit here and let me get you something until he's done, okay? What would you like, sweetie? A Coke?"

"Oh, I'm fine, Mrs. Santoro. I'll just wait for Bruno. Why don't you sit with me for a minute?"

"You know, I think I will." She slid into the booth and let out a big sigh. "Oh, that feels good. My back is killing me today. I'm so glad Bruno got rid of that bad wife of his. Now he's finally home where he belongs."

"And I hear he's a chef now, too."

"Yes. He went back and finished cooking school after his divorce. Now that he's back, I'm going to cut down to working part time. I'm so excited. It'll be the first time in thirty years."

"Well, you deserve to slow down a little," Bella said. The Santoros had run their restaurant like her father had run the garden center—with a lot of hard work and plenty of family labor.

"So what's it like being a psychologist?" Mrs. S asked. "Do you like your job?"

"I love my job. I'm very happy."

"I'm sure you must have long hours, what with being a professional woman and all."

"Well, sometimes, yes, but it's totally worth it. I really enjoy my work."

"I see. I bet it's hard to work those hours and cook dinner and do the chores around home for your father and brother?"

Why was Mrs. S so concerned about how much she worked? "Sure, but you know how that is. Chef's hours are hard, too, right?" Besides, she made Joey toe the line, but she didn't say that.

Bruno came out. Up close, he looked just as good. Maybe a little too much gel slicking back the hair, but she barely noticed. He hugged his mother and handed her his apron. Then he kissed Bella on the cheek.

Okay. Bruno the Mooner had grown up. Maybe this wasn't going to be so bad, after all.

Bella picked up her sweater and purse from the booth. "So, where are we going?" she asked. She was glad she'd taken the time to freshen up after work and change into a black cashmere sweater and black heels with her skirt.

"Well, I was thinking we could go to the place that serves the best food in town."

He smiled widely—at his mother. Mrs. Santoro blushed. Bella glanced between the two of them. Oh dear, it suddenly dawned on her that—oh my. Every word of their date was going to be overheard by Mama and Papa Santoro. Great.

Well, he was proud of his family's restaurant. That was a positive thing, right?

He gestured for her to sit back down in the booth. "Mama, bring us a menu. And a bottle of red, all right?" He looked at Bella. "You don't mind, do you?" He lowered his voice. "It would make her so happy to wait on us."

"Sure, Bruno. Great with me." She was starving anyway. It was good food—the best pizza in town—so, why not? Family was important. Maybe not to tag along with you on a first date, but whatever.

"How about you let me bring you some wedding soup as an appetizer?" Mama Santoro asked.

"Oh no, thank you," Bella said. Yep, she was an Italian who didn't like wedding soup. It made her a little nervous saying no. If this family was anything like hers, if you refused their food, they took it personally.

"What's the matter, you don't like it? You're too skinny, you need to get a little meat on your bones, no? You'll like my wedding soup for sure. I'm going to bring you some while you look over the menu."

Bella loved anyone saying she was skinny, even though she wasn't, but she really couldn't stomach wedding soup. It was tied to an old memory with Gina and throwing up, and she'd never touched it since. Not that she could explain all of that at the moment. "But—" Her *but* was wasted, as Mrs. Santoro was already halfway to the kitchen. Fine. She was used to eavesdroppers and food forcers. It was the Italian way. In that respect, Bruno and she shared a common heritage.

"You look very pretty, Bella," Bruno said.

He was saying all the right things. And he had nice eyes, even though they lacked the intensity of Roman's, whose gaze always seemed to flame straight through her and turn her insides to charcoal. "Oh, thank you, Bruno. So tell me, how've you been?"

He rubbed his neck. "My wife divorced me. It's been a year and a half."

"Oh, I'm sorry to hear that. Do you have any kids?"

"No, no bambinos," Mrs. Santoro said loudly from the kitchen. "Thank God. After the divorce, that would be even more heartache."

"I told Louise it was time to start having some," Bruno said, "but she kept insisting that she needed to keep working, even after she had them. There was never a good time."

"Imagine that," Mrs. Santoro added with undisguised outrage, back with a basket of steaming, fragrant bread straight from the oven and the dreaded soup. Bella's stomach rumbled, for the bread anyway, and she remembered she'd had to skip lunch today because of a regional meeting with other mental health providers. "She wanted to work and put the children in day care."

"I even compromised," Bruno said. "Told her we could move back here and my mother would watch the kids during the day . . . but that wasn't good enough."

"How come you're not eating your soup?" Mrs. Santoro asked, eyeing her closely. And taking note of the fact that she was eating a piece of bread, which really was melt-in-your-mouth delicious.

Bella guiltily put down the bread and picked up her spoon. "Oh, I was waiting for it to cool." She picked up her spoon and made a gesture, like, *See? I'm going to force feed it to myself right now.* Because it was looking like she didn't have a choice. She even glanced beneath the table. Nope, no pet in sight to maybe lap it up. She was starting to stress a little. She really did hate wedding soup. In a gagging, bad way.

"I'm going to be honest with you, Bella," Bruno said, leaning in and giving her a serious look as Mrs. Santoro hustled back into the kitchen.

"What is it, Bruno?"

"I'm a certain age."

A certain age? Wait, wasn't he thirty like her? "Thirty's not ol—"

"I want to get my life started as soon as possible. I want lots of kids and a wife who'll be around to take care of them and me. In return, I can cook every Italian dish known to mankind. How's that sound?"

Did people still barter for brides? Was he . . . proposing marriage? Because it sure sounded like it. And the funny thing was, she'd do almost anything for food. She loved every Italian dish under the sun, except for that damn soup.

A vision formed in her head. Of herself, heavy with child, hanging sheets on a clothesline, chasing miniature Brunos around the Santoros' yard while Mama S chided her to eat her wedding soup. She needed to get out of here fast.

"Well, Bruno, I—"

"I'm lonesome, you're lonesome. You're pretty, you're Italian, we can make beautiful children."

She cleared her throat. "This is a little quick for me."

"Okay," Mrs. Santoro said, hovering at her side and wringing her hands with worry. "Is there a problem?" Oh my God, the woman was back *again*.

Bella forced a polite smile. "Oh no, it's just that we've been enjoying talking so much that I haven't taken the time to eat it."

"You don't like my cooking." She looked like she was getting upset. Bella forced a spoonful of the soup to her lips and tried to push the old memory out of her mind. She and Gina were in the backseat, and she'd just come from Uncle Tony's house, where she'd eaten two whole helpings of soup. But stomach flu was going around school, and just then she'd felt a rumbling in her stomach. Waves of nausea had suddenly hit her and then she'd projectile vomited all over herself, Gina, and the backseat of their station wagon. It had smelled like stinky socks for months afterward and never failed to make her feel like retching every time she got in the car, no matter how many times her mother scrubbed it or hung tree air fresheners from the rearview mirror. Sure enough, as soon as the spoon went into her mouth, she choked a little.

"I've never seen such a face," Mrs. Santoro said, now standing with arms crossed over her ample bosom.

Suddenly, Mr. Santoro walked out of the kitchen and stood next to his wife. "She doesn't like the soup?"

"It's nothing personal, honest," Bella said apologetically. "It's just that when I was a kid—"

"It's delicious, Ma," Bruno said, an offended expression on his face.

"Yes, it is," Bella said. "Honestly, it's just that I had a little childhood trauma after I ate some—"

"You've insulted my mother's cooking," Bruno said. "She, who's done nothing but wait on us."

"Oh, I didn't mean—"

"Bruno, can we see you in private for a moment?" Mrs. Santoro gestured toward the kitchen.

They exited en masse. Bella tried to slow her breathing. She took a big gulp of wine. But she couldn't help hearing their voices. "She's too skinny. She's a career woman. She'll never be around for the children. I wasn't sure about her anyway, after what happened to her in high school."

Bella set down the wine. Forced herself to swallow the liquid that suddenly seemed trapped in her throat. She couldn't have heard that right.

The wine churned in her stomach, and she really did feel like she was going to be sick. There it was again, the one thing the entire rest of her life would always be judged by, for as long as she stayed in this crazy town.

But, hey, at least they'd called her skinny.

Oh, this had happened before. Not in quite this way, but, especially in earlier years, she was used to the little whispers, the quick glances in her direction as people discussed the big scandal. She'd had enough practice that she always out of habit sat up a little straighter and held her chin up a little higher, even as she reminded herself of how hard she'd fought to get to where she was today. The years of night classes, the constant fight to become something other than *that girl*.

No, she was made of tougher stuff now.

Bruno returned, looking a little sheepish. "Hey, listen, Bella, it was a mistake to try and do this here. Next time we'll go someplace different."

"You know what, Bruno, I'm going to go. Please give my apologies to your mom about the soup, okay?"

As Bella walked out of the restaurant, she wondered what it would be like to walk down a random city street and be anonymous. To not have anyone know you or your past mistakes. Just walking to her car, she passed three people, all of whom she knew: Mr. Marks from the hardware store, Teddy Lawrence from the bakery, and Alex Rushford from Bridal Aisle. Everyone smiled and waved, stopped to make a little bit of pleasant small talk. Not that everyone wasn't nice.

Just that when she finally believed her past was truly in the past, it reared its ugly head again. It was impossible to be anonymous . . . or forgiven.

Or maybe the problem was that she simply hadn't forgiven herself.

All she knew was that moving on, having a clean slate, wasn't ever going to happen in Mirror Lake.

Roman didn't hear the knock on his door with Journey cranked up on his phone at full blast. It was only after he'd stirred the cooking macaroni from the macaroni and cheese box and finished singing along to

Can't Stop Loving You

the chorus of "Don't Stop Believin'" that he saw Bella staring at him from outside his door. Caught in the middle of a few bad dance moves, he quickly turned down the music and let her in.

More startled that she was there than embarrassed she'd caught him singing and dancing, he told her to come in, looking her over to try and figure out what was wrong. Because why else would she show up at his door? "Is everything okay?"

"Nothing's wrong," she said, biting back a smile. "Nice air guitar." He quickly set down the wooden spoon he was holding, hoping she was too busy toying with a ceramic collie figurine to notice his prop.

"You just happened to be passing by?"

"Yeah," she said, looking up. "After another bad date." He was struck by her understated elegance, as always. She wore a classic black skirt and heels, and red lipstick that looked like it hadn't been kissed off, thank God. He loved the way she had of casually hooking her hair behind her ear. She seemed a little nervous and a little subdued, but not upset. He figured he'd let her explain why she was here in her own time.

"The bad date made you think of me, huh? Like, bet you're really glad I wasn't around to tell this one off." He drained the pasta, then dumped it back into the pot and stirred in the milk, butter, and cheese packet.

She laughed. "The cowboy was an idiot. I'm grateful you stood up for me."

"Oh." He stopped mixing for a second. "You are?"

She shrugged. "I mean, I can admit now that it was nice of you to be concerned."

"Want some mac and cheese?" He held up a spoonful of the bright-yellow stuff.

"Sounds great. I'm starving."

"You've got to start going out on dates with men who like to eat." He placed the pot in the center of the table and brought over two wineglasses and a bottle of wine. He brought over bowls and spoons too but somehow they ended up eating right out of the pot. They didn't talk much while they ate, but the silence wasn't uncomfortable, either.

After a while he asked, "So, want to tell me what happened during dinner with Bruno?"

She frowned. "How'd you know I went out with him?"

"Joe told me."

"He decided we should eat at the restaurant. His mother gave me wedding soup."

"Oh no. Not wedding soup."

"So it all ended in disaster."

"Because of the wedding soup?"

She grew quiet. "That and the fact that I'm not likely to give up my career after the babies come."

She put down her wine and fingered the stem, tapping on the base.

He reached across the table and grasped her hand, held onto it until she met his gaze. "Surely that can't be what's upsetting you?"

She swallowed. "I—I'm not sure why I'm here."

She tried to tug her hand away, but he wouldn't let her. On impulse, he brought it to his lips and kissed it. "Tell me what's wrong."

This time she didn't pull away, which he took as a good sign. "I heard them talking in the kitchen," she said. "They said I was too skinny—that's a laugh, right?—and that I was too career oriented."

"I'd consider both of those compliments," he said, still holding her hand.

She looked him in the eye. "Then I heard Mrs. Santoro say it didn't matter anyway because I was the girl who got pregnant in high school."

Roman just reacted. Before he could think, he'd pushed back his chair and gathered her up in his arms. He wanted to punch someone. It would have to be Bruno to make up for the callous remarks of his mother. Instead, he held Bella tight. At first, he felt only the pounding in his chest, the sickening churn of his stomach as he imagined how someone's ignorant remark could be so hurtful.

But despite himself, everything changed. From comforting to an acute awareness of her in his arms, soft and warm and curvy. An intense gut-burning ache came over him, a desperate need to protect her and save her from pain and, dammit, to *kiss* her until she turned boneless and trembling in his arms.

He knew she didn't need his protection. And she sure as hell didn't want him tackling her to the floor. She probably just needed a friend. He cleared his throat. "You're not that girl anymore. You're an accomplished woman, a doctor."

"This is what happens when you stay in the same town your whole life. Your past follows you."

"I'm sorry for your pain. I'm sorry for ignorant people." He drew back and held her at arm's length, struggling to keep his thoughts clear. They hadn't talked about the past. But maybe now they could.

"I—I didn't come here because I needed consoling. Honestly, I could care less about Bruno or his parents." She suddenly looked up—straight at him. "I guess I just felt bad, and all I could think of was coming to talk to you."

"Why *me*?" he asked quietly, despite his blood suddenly rushing in his ears. This was important. He had to know. "I mean, why not Maggie or Jess or Sam?"

His gaze locked with hers. She looked uncomfortable, like she might bolt at any minute, but he needed to hear what she had to say. "Tell me, Bella. Why me?"

She lay one hand against his chest. The warmth of her hand penetrated through his shirt, searing him. His heart was beating so strongly he was certain she could feel it under her palm. But still, he didn't release her.

"I knew you'd understand," she said. "Not that it's really hurtful anymore, but small towns have big memories. I don't know why it got to me tonight."

"Tell me how it was for you after I left."

She shrugged. "I didn't care so much about the gossip. It made me understand who my true friends were. The worst thing was that my father took it hard. I don't think he's ever completely gotten over it."

Roman snorted. "You put yourself through school. You started your own practice. You dedicated yourself to raising your brother. How can he be anything but proud of you after all this time?"

"I'm sure he is in his own way."

"Maybe you think he's still disappointed because you're still so hard on yourself."

She looked a little startled. "Thanks for that," she said, looking like she didn't quite believe his compliments. She hesitated before she spoke again, leveling her gaze directly on him. "Really, the gossip and the whispering were nothing compared to how sad it was without you."

Her words struck him. Surprised the hell out of him, too. It was the first really personal thing she'd told him. "I thought you were relieved to have me go. So you could start over."

"Turns out starting over without you wasn't that great."

She looked for a moment like she was going to say more. But she didn't, just stood there, her eyes filled with unspoken feeling.

"You remember that time I ran into you and Ethan at the theater?" he asked.

Her forehead creased, like it was an unpleasant memory. "You were with Reagan."

"Yeah, well, I wasn't really *with* Reagan. She'd seen me on the street that night and started walking with me."

"But I thought—"

"I wanted you to think that, Bella, because I was hurt. I was jealous. You'd clearly moved on. Funny thing was, I'd come back to town that weekend to talk with you."

Her eyes filled with tears, but he kept talking. "I often thought I should have come back sooner. The way we left it wasn't—right. We were both upset, and you had so many other responsibilities tying you here. I wasn't—understanding. I let my hurt get in the way of everything else."

"Roman, I—it was complicated. The things I said—"

He cut her off by lowering his head and kissing her. To tell her now without words how sorry he was that she'd had to face such a thing alone for all these years. And because he needed to touch her, *needed* to put his lips on hers.

Her lips were soft and lush, and God, he *remembered* the feel of her. Her quiet sigh as their lips melded together, the warmth of her silky skin, the perfect way she fit in his arms. He'd meant the kiss to be quiet and tentative, or at least he thought for her sake it should be, but from the first touch, it burst into a flaming torch of a kiss, lips sliding together, tongues tangling in a hot, wet dance. He reached his hands up to thread through the thick mass of her hair, and curved them around her head, pulling her closer so their lips and bodies were flush. And still the kissing continued, deep and languorous and long, the hunger a decade in the making.

The years melted away like rainwater gurgling down a gutter after a summer storm, whisked away like no time had passed, and all he could think of was how right this felt, how perfectly they fit together.

"Bella," Roman said, his voice a muffled groan. He readjusted his hold, pulled her even closer against him, breathed in her sweet scent, tasted the wine on her tongue. The tiny, dimly lit kitchen ceased to exist, and it was just her, only her, as it had been so long ago. For those few moments, it was as if all the pain of their years apart had vanished.

She clutched at his back and stood on tiptoe to kiss him so softly and deeply he thought he might die. Her fingers tangled in his hair, and her breasts pushed against his chest, and he feared he might take her right on this ancient linoleum floor, but he was afraid to suggest moving, afraid to do anything to break this incredible spell.

She surprised him by tugging on his T-shirt, which he yanked off in one quick swoop. Her hands roamed over his chest, warm and fluttering, inflaming his need for her. Without hesitation, he lifted her up and set her on the countertop, which set the coffeepot and some stray silverware to clattering. If her sweater hadn't looked so expensive, he would've had it off of her without regard for the buttons, but he worked each one carefully, gritting his teeth for patience, until she finally shrugged it off and tossed it to the floor. Her white blouse promptly joined the sweater.

Then, Saints Above, his breath snagged. She was sitting on that old yellow Formica countertop, in her skirt and heels and a delicate, lacy bra, her hair full and thick and tumbling about her beautiful face and shoulders, and he wished to God he could capture that image forever. "You're beautiful," he whispered, stepping forward. Without hesitation, she wrapped her legs around his waist and tugged him against her.

He picked her up and carried her to the living room, dragging his lips down her sweet neck as she angled to give him better access, threading her fingers through his hair, scraping them against his scalp.

He set her down on the couch and stretched out over her. "You feel so good," he growled against her skin. Her kisses were a drug, and he was getting lost in her, running his fingers over the lace of her bra, and at last, tugging away the lace and fitting his mouth over one pink nipple. She groaned and arched into him, her touches becoming frantic as they roamed over his back and tugged on his jeans.

He'd just sucked her nipple into a taut, hard peak and begun doing the same to the other one when a phone rang. And rang. Hers. From somewhere. The kitchen.

She lifted her head, but he kept kissing her, afraid to let go. But she murmured something against his lips that sounded like, *I better get that*, and pushed against him until he moved. She tumbled off the couch and ran to the kitchen, returning with the phone at her ear. He was disoriented, his breath coming in ragged pants, and the sight of her did not help one fricking bit. Her hair was wild, completely undone, her lips swollen, her chest blotchy from the scrape of his beard stubble, breasts spilling from the cups of her bra . . . basically she was every fantasy he'd ever had come to life.

His entire body was on fire for her. Everything had felt so right, like something that's been missed for so long, and when it's finally found, you can rest and have peace. *Home.* His mind had felt it, and dammit, so had his *soul* in some basic, elemental way.

"Sure, no problem," she said into the phone. "No hard feelings, Bruno. Bye."

She threw her phone in her bag and looked at him. "Everything okay?" he asked, not really caring about Bruno. He wanted her on top of him, kissing him like that again. Judging by how hard he was right now, the rest of him did, too.

"Bruno wanted to apologize. But he called my dad's first, and he thinks my dad is worried because I'm not home yet. I should go."

He stood up and put his hands on her arms. "Don't go. Stay."

She shook her head and stepped back. Reached up and touched his cheek.

"That"—she nodded over to the couch—"shouldn't have happened. It was a lapse of judgment. A mistake." She was rubber-banding back her hair, pulling on her blouse, straightening her skirt, finding her shoes . . .

He couldn't let her leave. "It didn't feel like a mistake, Bella."

She didn't laugh, just began gathering her stuff. "I told my dad I wouldn't be out too late. He still needs a bit of help getting ready for bed." She slung her purse over her shoulder and headed to the door. She paused with one hand on the screen.

He'd screwed up big time. Just when she'd finally let down her guard, finally started really talking to him, he'd violated the friend zone. He simply couldn't help himself. Hell, she was no more his friend than unicorns pooped rainbows.

"I—um." He blew out a big breath, rubbing the back of his neck. Okay, he could do better than caveman talk. Just that most of his blood was still down south, away from his brain. "Sorry. I meant to keep it friendly between us."

But he wasn't sorry. Not at all.

"If this is how you treat all your *friends*, then we're in a whole lot of trouble." She tossed him a quick look over her shoulder. Her mouth was quirked up in the slightest smile.

Then she was gone, leaving him listening to the sound of her heels crunching on the gravel drive.

CHAPTER 14

What the hell had she been thinking? Going over to Roman's and letting her emotions get the best of her. Oh, those kisses had been terrible and wonderful, every cell in her body was on fire, and it had taken all her strength not to turn around and march right back to his door for more.

She was a train wreck. Her brain was fogged with lust, her body no better. Thank God her phone had rung, because it had saved her from a horrific lapse of judgment.

She'd almost told him the truth. About how she'd had to let him go all those years ago. But she'd chickened out, and it was probably for the best. What would be the point in stirring up old history? That would lead to imagining what could have been, dangerous ground she couldn't walk on. It had taken her too many years to *stop* imagining that. Besides, Roman had always been so upright, so sincere. What would he think about being lied to?

She did not want to start something up with Roman again, no matter how irresistible he was. First loves were always sentimental and irresistible, more based on hormones than reality. After all it took to forget him, she could not allow herself to fall for him again. The gossips would have their field day, and when things went south, as they inevitably would, she'd have to live with him in this town. Oh, and she was moving. All good reasons to stay the hell away from Roman Spikonos.

The house was dark, except for the stove light in the kitchen and one small table lamp in the living room. The typical we've-gone-to-bed lights. Bella heaved a huge sigh as she tossed her keys across the countertop. Thank God no one was up, because she really hadn't done a very good job tying back her hair or wiping off her smeared lipstick. Or calming down.

Good Lord, she needed a drink. Or a gallon of ice cream. She headed into the kitchen, where she found an open bottle of red wine on the counter and took a decent drink, not bothering to pour it into a glass. Her entire body was buzzing, wired, wanting. Roman hadn't lost his touch, or his ability to electrify her every nerve ending, just as he had so long ago.

Those few wild, uninhibited moments with him had reminded her of someone—of the girl she used to be. Before life had happened and had dimmed the good parts of her down. Like the lightbulb in the lamp next to her father's favorite chair. He kept it on the lowest setting to save it. From what, she wasn't sure. Because lightbulbs were still pretty darn cheap. And youth—well, she still had it, but it wasn't going to last forever.

"Where have you been?" her father asked.

She startled, setting the wine bottle down with a hard clink as the glass hit the granite, and wiped her mouth. Slowly, she turned. Her father was sitting in his favorite chair, a light-brown La-Z-Boy with a subtle geometric pattern she'd picked out for him. Comfortable and practical yet decently stylish, her fashion sense in a nutshell. Gracie sat at his feet, resting her head on his knee.

"I stopped at Maggie's after my date," she lied. Almost thirty years old and still fibbing. There was something dramatically wrong with this picture.

"Bruno called looking for you."

"I know, Pop. I came right home." She walked over and sat on the couch next to her dad's chair. He was absently stroking Gracie's sweet little head, his seed catalogs and today's newspaper folded in his lap. Memories hit her. At one time, she would've gotten a book and sat on the floor next to her dad. He'd pause from his reading and pat her on the head just like Gracie. There was a time when she could do no wrong in his eyes.

In some ways, she was still that little girl longing to be in his good graces. Even though she'd hated what he'd done to her and Roman, she understood how she'd disappointed him. She'd been the one to fracture his image of her as a good, obedient daughter. She'd broken his heart when it was already shattered from the loss of her mother.

But her father's love came with too many caveats and expectations. She'd failed to live up to his standards, and he'd clung to his disappointment for years. And that disappointment would linger, perhaps his entire life, no matter what she did to try and rectify it.

She wondered if penance had a time limit. She didn't think so, at least as far as her father was concerned.

Sometimes she wondered if the situation was like Roman had implied . . . that a part of all this was her *own* feeling that she'd disappointed him irreparably—that she'd projected her own disappointment of *herself* onto her father.

Either way, it was pretty messed up.

"He sounded upset," her father said.

"Oh, you know the Santoros," she said, waving her arm dismissively. "I don't think they want a career woman for their son." Much less one who got knocked up in high school. Well, they'd have to work hard to find him an Italian virgin. Good luck in finding him a virgin of any nationality, in fact.

"You're too good for him anyway," Vito said. He reached over and patted her hand. A quiet gesture. Two little pats. His hands were a bit older that what she'd remembered as a kid; they were weather toughened and mostly rough, but his touch felt good. It was a little sign of affection he had difficulty displaying otherwise.

"They were looking for someone to quit their job to take care of the bambinos," she said. "And probably to log in more than a few hours a week in the restaurant."

"He's still a mama's boy. He told me on the phone he's living with his parents. What a *persona pigra*."

Italian for lazy, the kiss of death in her father's eyes. She didn't know about the lazy part, but Bruno did like his parents enough to take them with him on a first date. "Why'd you want me to go out with him, anyway?"

He shrugged. "Italian, good family, trying to keep you away from bad influences."

"Right." *Like what he thought Roman was?* The dog had crept over to her for some petting and was sniffing at her legs. Bella wondered if she smelled Roman's scent on her. She gave her a good scratch behind the ears, and in return Gracie happily pressed against her leg, slid down and went belly up for more.

"I promised your mother I'd find you somebody good to marry."

Bella looked up in surprise. "What?"

"Before she died, she made me promise." Her father touched her cheek. "You have a good heart, Arabella. Don't ever sell yourself short."

Bella frowned. "What do you mean, Pop?"

"All I'm saying is, you've waited this long. Don't settle for someone who doesn't make you happy."

"Do you mean Bruno? You don't have to tell me that, Pop. No chemistry there, that's for sure." Thank her lucky stars her father wasn't into brokering an arranged marriage with the Santoros. The relief was palpable.

"No, not Bruno." He paused a long time. She knew it was difficult for him to talk about personal matters. Like her love life. "I mean Ethan."

"Oh." Bella was a little shocked. Her father loved Ethan like a son, and to say this . . . well. She had no words. For her father to actually talk to her about her happiness—and not have the conversation be about marrying a nice Italian boy or about encouraging her to return Ethan's affection—it was a side of her father that left her speechless.

"Gina told me he surprised you at that fancy restaurant at the marina. He's been a good—friend, hasn't he?" her father said. "But he doesn't make you happy. Make sure you marry someone who does. Or your mother will never forgive me."

"I'll do my best." She kissed him on the cheek. "Can I help you get ready for bed now?"

Her father picked up his newspaper. "I'm not tired just yet. But I'll be fine. You go on up."

"Good night, Dad."

As she and Gracie walked up the steps, Bella wondered what her father would have thought about Roman if he'd met him now for the first time. If she hadn't gotten pregnant, if there'd been no history, no drama. Vito would have admired his work ethic, thought him enterprising, and thought his applejack idea was innovative.

But there *was* a past, and she could not continue to dredge up all the pain from that time in her life again: the heartbreak of losing Roman, the loss of their baby, the anger at her father's rigidity, the heartbreak of having to live a life here that she had never planned. Roman's return had the potential to release a floodgate of emotion that she couldn't bear fully opening again. Her fresh start did not include getting tangled back up with her painful past, no matter how tempting he was.

"One more coat and it'll be good as new, ladies," Roman said, pushing the paint roller up and down Bella's office wall on Monday evening as Bella watched from behind the reception area. But tried not to. It was just so hard with all those beautiful muscles flexing before her eyes. And remembering how she'd had her hands all over them this weekend wasn't helping, either.

Bella cleared her throat, which was suddenly very dry, and went back to checking her schedule.

From behind Roman, out of his line of vision, Maggie flexed her own biceps and gave it a little squeeze and pointed to Roman, mouthing *wow*. Bella rolled her eyes and gestured for Maggie to move along, which she perversely did not do. Instead she lingered in the waiting room, pretending to read a magazine while she eavesdropped.

"So how was your weekend?" Roman asked, barely disguising the smile that threatened to break out.

"It was great, thanks." Their recent make-out session loomed large in her thoughts. She couldn't even *remember* the rest of the weekend. "How about yours?" she asked casually. At least, she tried to sound casual despite not feeling anywhere near casual at all.

"Great. The roof's coming along, and the barn is cleaned out and ready for the construction crew." It was mesmerizing, watching those big golden muscles move up and down her wall, flexing like he was pumping iron. He turned around suddenly and caught her staring. Unfazed, he tossed her a *caught-ya* smile.

She snapped her gaze back to her paperwork, which she'd reread at least three times. "Well, I'd love to chat, but our senior citizen group is starting soon."

"Oh," he said, his gaze raking her up and down. "Think I'll go home and eat some leftover mac and cheese. You like mac and cheese, don't you?" he said, his eyes dancing with laughter. "Except I read somewhere that it was an aphrodisiac."

He was clearly amused by this . . . situation. Well, she didn't think it was funny at all. Maybe making out was no big deal to him, but to her it was catastrophic. Something to be avoided again at all costs.

"Well," she said, "prepared mac and cheese is old food. We Italians tend to look for something more fresh and original, you know?"

"Oh, I don't know about that. Nothing beats quickie mac and cheese. Delicious *and* satisfying."

She scowled at his big Cheshire grin and walked back to her office.

"Good Lord, Bella," Maggie whispered, following behind her. "There's more sexual tension in the air than paint smell. Forget about the bad dates! Nail that guy. He's gorgeous and he's got the hots for you."

Bella eyed her oldest friend. "It's sort of become a problem."

"That's a problem I wish I had," Maggie said. "Someone who can't stop staring at me. Who checks out my ass when I bend down to pick up my pen."

"Listen, our past is very complicated." She flipped randomly through one of many piles of papers on her desk.

"Too complicated to give it another shot?"

Bella shot her a look. "Okay, okay," Maggie said. "Maybe you could just sleep with him."

Maggie knew she didn't sleep around and that she wasn't into flings. "Why would I want to do that?"

She counted on her fingers. "Because he's gorgeous. Because you're single. Because you're obsessed with him."

"Maggie, I have to tell you something. I heard back from the psychology practice I interviewed at in Chicago. They offered me the job."

"Oh, Bella," Maggie said, giving her a weak smile and a hug. "I'm happy for you. I think. But I'm sad, too."

"Maybe you should come, too. We can both start somewhere new. What do you say?"

"I just don't have the heart to move halfway across the country now. Besides, I know everybody in Mirror Lake. I like it here." She played with Bella's silver Chinese fortune cookie paperweight, a cool favor she'd gotten at a wedding. "Bella, I'm going to ask you something. Don't get offended, okay?"

"Okay."

"If you were just meeting Roman for the first time, would you go out with him?"

"What do you mean?"

"I mean, if you met him today, and he was handsome and charming and all, would you give him a chance?"

"I can't erase our history together. What's your point?"

"I just don't want you to run away—from him. I mean, you're a therapist. Think about what you'd tell a client in this situation. Wouldn't it be better to face this head-on?"

"I've talked about leaving long before he showed up. Be fair, Maggie."

"I know, but all I'm saying is, it's convenient not to have to deal with him. And maybe you should give him a chance."

"There's too much water under that bridge. I can't revisit all that pain—losing him, losing the baby. I would just be setting myself up for heartache again. Not to mention that my dad would never accept Roman, even under the best of circumstances."

"He would if you loved him."

"Well, I doubt it, but thanks for your concern."

A half hour later, Roman was gone for the night or out of sight somewhere and Maggie and Bella were seated around the circle with the Desperate ladies. Maggie's three-year-old son, Griffin, was spending the night at her parents', so she'd decided to stay and co-lead the group tonight with Bella.

"What's for dessert tonight?" Effie asked.

"I made banoffee pie," Gloria said. "It's British."

"And I made cannoli," Francesca said, somewhat defensively.

"Well, I'm sure we'll enjoy both, ladies," Bella said.

"Oh dear," Alethea said. "I would have brought something Greek, but Stavros had a program at school today and then a T-ball game. I'm so sorry."

"Don't apologize, Alethea," Bella said. "I think it would be less work if we just brought one dessert a week. It's healthier, too."

"And less competitive," Maggie added.

Bella was trying to steer the conversation away from the bake-off when the door suddenly swung open. A man dressed in an elegant black tux minus the tie stood in the office entrance, out of breath, eyes panicked. He was young, broad-shouldered, and darkly good looking, with an expensive haircut, shaved closer at the sides than on top, the lower half of his carved jaw darkened by a shadow of stubble. He looked like a male model who'd just walked out of a wedding photo shoot. The ladies' mouths dropped open, and Maggie even stifled a gasp. He quickly closed the door behind him but continued to stand against it.

"It's a man," Effie said. "A hot one." Murmurs of interest rose up from around the room.

Maggie stood and cleared her throat. "May I help you?"

The man cast his eyes around a little wildly. They landed on a little folded cardboard sign in the center of a low table that welcomed anyone to the support group. "I'm—here for group tonight."

"Well, are you divorced or widowed?" Effie triaged.

"I just ended an—um—long-term relationship."

"Oh," Maggie said. "Well, technically you have to be divorced or widowed. Distress from acute breakups is usually covered in individual therapy sessions."

"You said Three Ds," Alethea said. "Divorced, Desperate, or Dead. He looks a little desperate."

"And he's male and we're short on those." Effie took her sweater off the seat next to her and patted it. "You can come sit right here next to me, sweetie."

Bella wasn't exactly sure the man heard. Because he was staring at Maggie. Petite, blonde Maggie, who looked pretty and professional and . . . irritated. "You're the—doctor?" he asked, sounding a little surprised.

"I'm Dr. McShae, and that's Dr. D'Angelo," Maggie said. "You don't have a problem with that, do you?" Bella was afraid Maggie would get confrontational. I mean, maybe this guy was sexist or a misogynist, but he also could be a loose cannon who just ran in off the street and humoring him would be prudent.

"No, of course not. Just that you're so—pretty. I mean *young*. What I mean is you're *pretty young*, Dr. McShae." The man was sweating and he kept glancing out the window. Something was just . . . off. Bella wondered if she should call the police.

"Well, age doesn't matter, Mr., ah—what was your name again?"

"My name is Drew."

"Okay, Drew. Well, I'm happy to give you some information about our practice and some forms to fill out if you'd like to be seen by one of us privately. But I'm afraid you can't just join—"

"I am desperate," he said, looking pleadingly at Effie, an obvious target for someone who needed a softie. "Like what she just said." He pointed to Alethea. "And besides, I'm—anxious." He took a breath. His eyes darted to the windows. "I have anxiety."

"How long has your anxiety been an issue?" Maggie asked, beginning to write things down. Vaguely, Bella wondered if Roman was coming back tonight. This man was a wild card, and he was making her nervous. She didn't want to call for help for no reason, but still . . .

"For about the last fifteen minutes—I mean *years*. Fifteen *years*."

"Fifteen years? Well, that definitely would require an individual appointment." Maggie scribbled more down. "How desperate are you? Do you have thoughts of harming yourself or others?"

"Only the paparazzi," he mumbled. Louder, he said, "I mean, no, of course not. I'm not suicidal and I don't want to hurt anyone."

Well, that's a relief, Bella thought. Except why should she believe this nervous man who kept glancing out the windows like he was expecting someone to burst into their office right now? They had an obligation to protect their clients, and this was too strange, and a little scary.

Effie got up and took their new visitor by the arm and led him to the empty seat next to hers. Alethea cut him a piece of dessert and tucked a cannoli onto his plate and Francesca got him a cup of coffee—decaf, Bella hoped.

"Maggie," Bella whispered. "I'm calling the cops."

Maggie nodded. "I agree."

Just then the door opened. To Bella's relief, it was Roman, back with some supplies. The ladies were fussing over the new visitor and didn't even notice. Bella ran over and tugged his arm, speaking in a low voice. "I'm glad you're back. Some strange guy just ran in off the street and he's acting very . . . strange."

While Bella dialed the police station, which was only a few doors down, Roman set down his paint can and a bag of brushes and approached the group of women.

"Oh, hello, Roman," Francesca said.

Roman nodded and glanced around the small circle of women. "Hi, Francesca. Nice to see you. Ladies." Then the newcomer caught his eye and froze. Roman went white. "I can't believe it."

"Roman?" the newcomer said.

"Andreas."

The man got up, set his food down on his chair, and approached Roman. "God, am I glad to see you." The two men hugged and laughed and pounded each other on the back.

"Andreas, that's it!" Alethea said. "I know who this is! You're Andreas Poulos."

"The *billionaire*?" asked Maggie. "Who's marrying that Wall Street mogul's daughter?"

"According to my iPhone," Alethea said, waving it above her head, "he's on the lam from his own wedding. He was supposed to marry Anika Brewer at St. Patrick's Cathedral at three p.m. today."

There was a knock on the door. Everyone stopped talking and froze.

"That's got to be the police," Bella said.

"Don't let them in," Andreas, or rather, Drew, said. "I've got paparazzi following me everywhere. I'm begging you." He turned to Roman. "I just need a little time to get myself together. Please, Roman."

"It's all right." Roman smiled and slapped the man on the back. Was Roman out of his mind, helping this unstable man that he clearly was somehow acquainted with? She cast him a wary glance, ready to let the cops in anyway. But then he looked over at her, a huge smile lighting up his face. "Bella, would you tell them everything's okay? This guy's my brother."

Later that evening, Roman sat at his kitchen table, Lukas on one side of him and Drew on the other. Drew was eating an everything pizza like he'd skipped about a week of meals.

"I got your e-mail a couple weeks ago," Drew said between bites.

"Which you didn't answer," Lukas said.

Drew set down his pizza and wiped his mouth with a napkin. "I wasn't going to answer it, frankly. I was going to ignore it."

"I can't believe our family bond meant that little to you," Lukas said, tongue in cheek.

"They always come running home when there's a crisis," Roman said, pointing to Drew's plate. "Eat your pizza."

"I'll be honest with you both," Drew said.

"That would be helpful," Lukas said.

"My marriage was a business merger. I thought I could go through with it, but at the last minute . . . I couldn't."

"So you left some woman crying at the altar?" Lukas asked.

"Not *some woman*, Lukas," Roman said. "Anika Brewer. Her daddy owns half of New York. And Dubai, the Canary Islands, Cayman . . ."

"We get it," Lukas said. "Everyone knows who Richard Brewer is."

"Right," Roman said. "Plus Anika used to be a Victoria's Secret model." He looked at his brother. "Are you crazy?"

Drew shook his head. "It wasn't a love match for her, either." He paused. "And I don't want to go into detail, but let's just say she's no angel."

Lukas put his hand on Drew's shoulder. "Okay. So you ran to save yourself from a loveless marriage. Now what's your plan?"

A muscle in Drew's jaw ticked, which Roman picked up on immediately. "I actually don't have one," Drew said. "But I was wondering—I was wondering if maybe you'd let me hang out here until I get one."

"I don't know if you remember this," Roman said, "but when we were kids, Lukas used to sit me down and try to help me with my math problems."

Lukas laughed. "Don't remind me. Man, you completely lost it with subtraction. Borrowing nearly did you in."

"Thanks, Lukas, but I have an MBA now, okay? I think I finally got it. Anyway, I'd be sitting there all clueless and Lukas would be sweating and cussing a little, trying to explain, but you—you just waltzed right in there between us and took charge."

"So I was good at math."

"You were good at everything. Whip smart. So whatever you have to figure out, I reckon you'll do it just fine. And you're welcome to stay here until you do."

"Because we're brothers," Lukas said, lifting his beer bottle. "Right?"

The other two lifted theirs.

"Right," Drew said, clinking bottles. "If I knew you guys were beer drinkers, I would've shown up earlier."

CHAPTER 15

Bella was more than a little shocked that the Desperate ladies actually kept the return of Roman's long-lost brother under wraps. She attributed it to the fact that they were so man deprived they'd do anything to keep a secret for the possibility of having two hot handsome guys visit their group again. Mrs. Panagakos, especially, became staunchly threatening if any of the other ladies even mentioned spilling the beans on "her boys."

So no news was good news, right? No one had seen Drew *or* Roman all week. Which was what Bella wanted, right? She tried not to think of Roman and what had happened between them, and carry on with her life, but the blind-dating thing now held even less appeal. On Friday, Bella sat by herself on a bench in the little park in the middle of town, waiting for her final date and wondering exactly how she got talked into it.

"I'm not doing it," she'd said earlier that day just after her last client had left the office and Maggie, Sam, and Jess had gathered around her desk.

"This could be a good one," Maggie said. Jess had brought a bottle of wine and was passing around paper cups for everyone to drink with the cheese and crackers she'd brought in to celebrate that it was Friday.

"Third time's a charm," Jess said, moving a stack of papers to half sit on the edge of her desk.

"It's the last one," Sam chimed in. "C'mon. One last time. You can do it."

It reminded her of the voice her mom used to use as she tried to coax medicine through Bella's clamped-together lips when she was a little kid.

Well, she wasn't sick. And frankly, no matter how sweet her friends were, she simply couldn't take any more. "Thanks so much for all your efforts, but I'm done."

Jess was tapping vigorously on her phone. "Wait 'til you see him. He's not from Mirror Lake, he teaches high school, he doesn't fly-fish, he has a dog, *and* he doesn't live with his mother." She shoved the phone in front of her face where, sure enough, there was a photo of a very good-looking, smiling guy. Who was blond and blue-eyed. He could've climbed off a surfboard on a Malibu beach. Or been in an ad for toothpaste. Or tanning lotion. The guy was a hottie with a body, she'd give her friends that. An anti-Roman, if you will. But she just couldn't muster the heart.

"Jess, I love you," Bella said, "but I'm really having a hard time trusting you after that cowboy."

"My intel was faulty on that one. I promise this one will be worth your time."

"Let's forget all this nonsense and go out together for my birthday tomorrow. Give me his number so I can cancel, okay?"

"Hold on a second," Sam said. "You promised three dates. This is the *last one*. Finish the contract."

"Oh, come on."

"No. You need tough love," Sam said. "No whining."

She glared at her friend, who'd adopted Lukas's nephew, Stevie, in the past year, and judging by her mom voice, it was showing.

"Sam's right," Maggie said. "Unless . . . unless something's going on with your stud muffin next-door neighbor?"

"Nope, nothing's going on there," Bella said. Except for those go-up-in-flames kisses, that is. Lord, that man could kiss. He'd learned a few things over the years, although he hadn't exactly been an awful kisser when he was eighteen, either. Bella picked up an academic journal from her desk and fanned herself.

But their little passionate interlude—or anything like it—would never happen again. She hadn't even seen Roman this week. He apparently had his hands full with his on-the-lam brother. Oh, the tabloids were having a field day—they couldn't find Andreas Poulos, who'd left his beautiful socialite bride weeping at the altar and earned himself the label of rich playboy scoundrel. The Three Ds group had taken to him, however, and their lips were sealed. None of them was telling that, unbeknownst to the rest of the world, he was tucked away on a quiet little apple farm in southern Connecticut.

"Why are you blushing?" Maggie asked.

"I'm not blushing," Bella said, tossing down the magazine. It was just a warm October day. Really, really warm.

"Uh-huh, right," Sam said, crossing her arms.

Jess pretended to yawn widely. "What's that called in psychology talk . . . denial?"

"More like stupidity," Maggie mumbled. She stood up and shook Bella by the shoulders. "I have to say something as one of your closest friends, and I want you to listen."

She rolled her eyes. "Okay, I'm listening. What?"

"I want you to remember one thing tonight: Who cares what people think? You're almost thirty years old. Do what you want to do."

"What I want is to go home and put my sweats on and curl up with a good book."

"Books don't keep you warm at night, babe," Sam said.

"Look who's talking," Bella grumbled. "You, who have your own private rock star to cuddle up to."

Jess laughed. "It's just dinner, and you have to eat anyway. This guy is nice. And he's the last one!"

And that's why Bella was now sitting in the town square. Watching the late-afternoon sun set over the tree-covered hills in the distance, showing off the gorgeous New England fall colors. It was getting just a bit chilly, so she wrapped her sweater a little tighter around her shoulders.

Bella had made an effort tonight only because her friends had gone through all this trouble for her. She'd gone home and put on a long cable-knit sweater, leggings, and ankle boots, and redid her hair and put on some cute loopy earrings . . . But in her heart she knew, no matter how wonderful her friends were, no matter how badly they wanted her to stay in Mirror Lake, things weren't going to work out for her here. She would never have a fresh start in this town. She wanted out, and finally, now that Joey was preparing to leave for college, she had nothing stopping her from living her own life at last.

She checked her watch. The last night of her twenties. Tomorrow she would be the big three-oh. She had exactly five hours and thirty-five minutes left of youth, and she felt it slowly slipping away like wine in her glass. Then she would have to usher in the decade of first wrinkles, Spanx, gray hairs and chin hairs.

But tonight she was getting wild and crazy, *woo-hoo*, meeting her last blind date. She was glad to have the distraction, because frankly, she was dreading her birthday. *Thirty!* Her parents were married at twenty, Gina at twenty-one.

She was lonely. Oh hell, she was horny. And given the emotional significance of this birthday, she was a little afraid she'd do something stupid. Maybe she should ditch this date now while she had the chance.

Long ago, she'd held out for love—well, more like she'd been completely swept away by love—but look where that had gotten her. Then she'd told herself she was in love with Ethan, but looking back, he'd been there for her at a time when she'd desperately needed to feel loved. The last guy she'd given a chance was no different. It was like some part of her knew she'd never feel the intensity of emotion that she'd experienced when she was so young. And unconsciously she'd made sure to pick the kind of men that wouldn't demand of her that she even try.

Maybe something wild and crazy *would* happen to her tonight. Something to usher out the decade of her youth and bring in her thirties with a bang. Oh, who was she kidding? She wasn't the type to fool around with a stranger.

But maybe she needed to be a new type.

She checked her watch. Date Number Three was late. Not good, since with every passing minute, she was closer to bailing herself. She took her phone out and started scrolling through Sam's and Jess's texts. Jess had sent her the picture of Toothpaste Man. She looked around the square. Nope, no tanned, displaced California surfer guys anywhere in sight.

Just then, she saw a man walking toward her from across the square. She looked the other way, pretending to be fascinated by a couple of little kids kicking up leaves. Because she'd know that sweeping, confident gait, that straight-as-a-cornstalk carriage, those big, strong shoulders anywhere. And the way her limbs were going weak, the way her heart had catapulted into her stomach like a basketball and her breaths were coming raggedly, her body knew it, too. All that told her that the man striding quickly toward her was no surfer guy. It was Roman.

She glanced up to find him standing there, wearing jeans and a black sweater. Looking like sin, as usual.

"Oh, it's you," she said, trying to sound disappointed, but she couldn't help smiling a little. "I'm expecting my big, burly, blond

Swedish date." When she showed him the photo on her phone, his response was an emphatic grunt.

He sat next to her on the bench, his leg grazing hers unapologetically. He smelled like woodsy cologne and shaving cream, and it was making her giddy. Like he'd just had a shower and was going out for the night. Maybe he was. An image of him on a date with some gorgeous woman floated through her mind. Him laughing and sipping wine with someone and caressing her hand across the table.

She pushed back that image. It made her uncomfortable. Sad. It was only a matter of time before he met someone. He was too good looking, too funny, too chivalrous. Too *everything*.

His leg touched hers again, but he didn't say anything, like *excuse me* or *oops*. It seemed... intentional. Yet he sat there, focused on watching the sun sink over those gorgeous trees, that New England autumn post-card view...

She couldn't take it anymore. She moved away into her own personal space. "Oh, for the love of God, what are you doing here?"

He sat up a little straighter. Eyeballed her in a way that confused her... he seemed hesitant, very unlike him, who usually said what he meant and didn't play games. Finally he spoke. "Your date's not showing tonight."

"Oh." Great. Apparently she was being stood up based on appearance only, since Jess had told her she'd e-mailed him a photo. *That* was confidence inspiring. And worse was that Roman knew she was being stood up. Not only knew but came bearing the news. Wait a minute... She stopped in the middle of gathering up her purse. "How do *you* know that?"

He leaned forward on the bench, resting his elbows on his legs, tapping his fingers together. "Trust me, he's not your type."

"You interfered with my date? How could you? I thought we talked about this."

Roman sighed heavily. He turned toward her and spoke. "Your date's not showing because he doesn't exist."

Her heart skipped a beat. Or two. "Did you annihilate him?"

"No, I made him up. I gave Jess a stock photo to show you."

"To play a joke on me?" Why would he do that? Her throat felt lumpy. Through everything, she thought at least they were friends. "That is the lowest—"

He grabbed her by the shoulders. "Bella," he said and shook her a little. "Look at me."

She did, through narrowed eyes. When she saw his face, all the fight whooshed right out of her, like a balloon let loose before it's tied. There was something different about him tonight. A graveness. The way he looked at her was just *different*, like he was not joking or being sarcastic. In fact, he looked dead serious, those big brown eyes staring right at her, those long, lovely lashes looking sinfully angelic on such a gorgeous hunk of man.

"I did it because *I* want to be your date for tonight." She must have still looked confused, because he said, "I knew you'd never agree to it the regular way."

All Bella's critical body parts were humming. She was filled with elation, with *hope*. Maybe it was wine or desperation or the upcoming birthday, she didn't know. But she had the distinct feeling she was about to do something reckless, and like it. A lot.

She must've looked dumbstruck because he repeated, "I want to take you on a date."

"Take me on a date?" she echoed. A bright bulb, she was indeed.

"Yeah, you know"—he pointed back and forth between the two of them—"go out together, you and me. Tonight."

"I'm not so sure that's a good idea. Our history, you know." Their history was a mess, and they both knew it.

"Right, right," he said, pretending to contemplate that. "But still."

But still what? "Why me?" she asked. It came out sounding very quiet and clogged, because she was having difficulty getting the words out.

"I think you know why." His eyes dropped to her lips. Her stomach dropped to her feet. Oh God.

Date him? That would be foolish. Do him? Even worse. To her horror she realized she wanted to. A lot.

"Look, Bella, I don't have it in me to play games. It's just that I seem to be having this problem: I can't stop thinking about you. It's messing up my concentration." He made a hand gesture near his head, like his brains were being scrambled.

Yeah, so were hers. They must be if she was considering this.

He dropped his hand to the back of the park bench, where suddenly she found him stroking her shoulder.

It was so hard to think with his body heat seeping into her, with him smelling just like a wonderful man would smell, spicy and clean, and he was so damn deadly hot-looking in that black pullover sweater and jeans. "You want to go out with me because I'm messing up your concentration. That's really romantic."

He smiled, a sweet smile that made it impossible to be irritated with him. "I think I might be messing up yours, too." He turned to face her. "Let me try again. It's not a good enough reason for me to stay away from you because of our past. I want to spend time with you. I think about you all the time. I want to *date* you. And I want us to stop fighting whatever this is between us."

"I—I don't know how I feel about that." Sure she did. She felt great! Flattered, ecstatic. But also terrified.

"It doesn't have to be complicated. My brother's playing at the marina tonight. Want to go?"

Listening to some music didn't sound complicated. "Lukas?" Duh. Of course Lukas.

"Well, Drew doesn't sing. At least, from what I've heard from him in the shower, he's missed the music talent part of the gene pool." He chuckled to himself a little. "Besides, he's still laying low at my place."

"Oh. Okay. Sure," she found herself saying. Yet she knew she wouldn't be able to concentrate on any music. Even Lukas's, which she liked a lot. The realization suddenly dawned on her that she didn't *want* to listen to any music. She wanted to jump Roman's bones. Bad.

She thought about that. It wasn't her nature anymore to do impulsive things. For all these years, she'd been dutiful, kept her nose to the grindstone, and done what was right for herself, for her family. She'd never had a one-night stand or gone home with a stranger.

And wait a minute. What exactly did he mean by *it doesn't have to be complicated*? Every relationship she'd had since him had been complicated. Worrisome. Back when they were younger, everything had seemed so simple. Natural. Was that just because they were kids?

"I have to be clear about what you're proposing," she said.

"We both seem to have unresolved feelings from our past, so this is an opportunity to . . . explore them."

"That sounds very clinical. Like something I would say to a client."

The corner of his beautiful mouth turned up in a grin. "I was hoping you'd get it if I spoke your language." He sat there for a moment, drumming his fingers on the bench. Then he leaned over and kissed her.

He caught her by surprise. Just a graze of his lips over hers, but then he repositioned himself, using his hands to anchor her face and draw her closer, to slide his lips over hers and fully kiss her. And, oh, what a glorious kisser he was, so thorough and smooth, so sweet and tender. He was the Grand Canyon, Niagara Falls, and Aunt Fran's homemade cavatelli all rolled up into one.

"Um, okay," she said, trying to catch her breath, feeling him smile against her neck, which he'd begun nuzzling. She thought he was going to toss out a quip to lighten the mood, but he didn't say anything. In fact, when he lifted his head, he looked as thrown off guard as she was. "A date, huh?" she finally said. "All righty, then."

They got up and started walking through the park toward the lake. He slipped his hand in hers, but it made her almost tear up, because she hadn't felt that big hand encompassing hers for twelve years, and by God if it didn't feel exactly the same—warm, solid, safe. Some guys were terrible at walking and hand holding. Either they were too tall and the hands just didn't hang well together, or holding hands was stiff and awkward. But with Roman it was just about perfect.

An older couple passed them and smiled. In the distance, the faint sounds of a band warming up drifted across the park, the marina lights glowing softly as the day faded to twilight.

Bella was getting a little overwhelmed, so she slid her hand away and started fishing through her purse, pretending to look for something. Besides, if they showed up holding hands at the marina, their relationship status would spread faster than if she'd posted it on Facebook.

"Second thoughts?" he asked.

"No." That wasn't it at all. She stopped fishing. Something in his eyes urged her to say what was on her mind. "Do you—do you want to go to my apartment?" she blurted. She'd never propositioned a man so outwardly. Or invited one up for lovemaking. Well, she'd never turned thirty before, either. She cleared her throat and forced herself to say it more calmly. "I haven't been there for a few weeks, but it's just a couple of blocks away, and I think we can—"

"Yes." No hesitation there. His full-on gaze let her know what she'd always known, that he was a straight shooter who'd always said what he meant.

Before she could rethink anything, she led him away from the square, a few blocks south to the end of a street lined with moderate-size century-old homes. Her apartment was a nondescript brick building with metal letters lined up over the portico that read "Mirror Lake Meadows. Senior Living."

Bella loved that her apartment was in the middle of this old, tree-lined neighborhood, and that it was only a few blocks from work. There were a handful of younger tenants, too. Not that she minded the seniors—they were quiet and friendly . . . but sometimes a little nosy, too.

She took the concrete pathway to the back. In a building full of elderly widows, there was no shortage of eyes watching every move she made, and she wanted to be discreet. Because the last time she'd brought a man here had been exactly . . . never. She let them in with a key and climbed the stairs to the third floor.

She knew there would be clothes all over the bed. Shoes strewn about from her last wardrobe crisis. Mail on the table. She usually drew the line at stockpiling dirty dishes—she hoped. Roman had always been kind of a neat freak, a trait not uncommon in children with alcoholic parents. She'd just have to make sure he was too focused on her to notice.

She flipped on a switch by the front door, which lit a little table lamp. The apartment didn't look too bad, if she could say so herself.

"Nice place," Roman said, but his attention was all on her as he leaned casually against the doorframe, hands in his pockets, looking like dessert. Nope, he didn't seem like he minded a little bit of mess at all.

Dressed all *GQ*, the faint growth of beard already shadowing his jaw, he made her stomach tumble with nervous excitement. He looked faintly amused, his dark eyes holding a glint of mischief, but he didn't speak. He was letting her call all the shots.

For the first time in her life, Bella turned off all the warning voices inside her head. The ones that told her that getting involved with him again was an impossible mistake, that it could only lead to more heartbreak. Because beneath all the warnings lay this need that could no longer be denied.

She walked a few steps forward until she was standing right in front of him. He met her gaze levelly, an invisible tractor beam between them, drawing them inexorably together. But he didn't move a muscle.

She placed her hand near his jawline, felt the slight scrape of stubble there. She was pleased when he closed his eyes, seeming to savor her touch. He brought his hand up to cover hers, pulled it to his lips, and kissed the inside of her wrist slowly, softly. Then he opened his eyes and smiled.

"I'm glad you're my date tonight," she said, her voice practically a whisper. *Oh, what a dumb thing to say.* It didn't even begin to express the thunderous wave of emotion that was welling up inside her. To stop all the thinking inside her head, she stood on tiptoe and brushed her lips over his.

That was all the invitation he needed. As soon as she kissed him, he circled her waist with his hands and tugged her flush against him. And, oh, he felt so good, so big and masculine, so *familiar*. He pulled her closer, angling his mouth over hers and kissing her deeply. The absolute pleasure of his touch radiated hotly through her stomach, her limbs, making her lose her balance and her breath at the same time.

He showed no mercy, pulling her closer and dragging his lips from her mouth down her neck. She could only arch helplessly to give him better access. *More, more,* she wanted to cry out. *Take all of me.*

"Took you long enough to kiss me," he said as he was doing that nuzzling thing again that felt so, so good.

"It's only been a minute since we got here."

"That's a minute too long," he said. "You know I've wanted you from the moment I saw you again."

Oh, that pleased her, because she'd felt the exact same way. He kissed her again, and this time their tongues slid together, and Bella curled her fingers through his hair, relishing the silky coarseness.

"Why do you always wear sweaters with a thousand buttons?" he mumbled as he struggled with undoing them. She brushed his hands away and peeled the sweater over her head. He tugged his own sweater off and tossed it across the room, where it landed on a chair. Meanwhile she tugged his shirt free of his jeans. Her hand brushed his flat abdomen, and she couldn't resist running her hands up along the valleys and hills of his beautiful chest, the hard muscle, the fine covering of hair that hadn't been there at eighteen.

He was kissing her like it was their last moments on earth. Armageddon kissing, deep and hard and wet. And it felt so damn good to be kissed like that, like he wanted her more than water and food and air. As much as she wanted him.

Everything about him was so good, the warm, hard feel of him, the clean smell of his soap, the way his hands felt on her as he undid her blouse. The way he undid *her*.

It was too good. Scary in a way she'd never felt before. She had to remind herself what this was really all about. That she had to somehow prevent herself from the absolute surrender that would be so easy to succumb to.

A wave of panic suddenly welled up inside her. "Wait," she said, gasping, pushing on his rock solid chest. "I have—conditions."

He stood up, took a step back, frowning. "Conditions?"

"Yes." She could barely talk. "I'd like to keep this . . . private."

"What . . . do you mean?"

"Roman, so much has happened. I—want to keep this loose. Not a relationship. Not a couple." She forced herself not to wince. It sounded cruel in a way. But she had to protect herself. She couldn't let herself feel too much. All those lonely years she'd endured . . . all that pain . . . she couldn't risk that again. She just couldn't.

"You mean like a no-strings affair?"

Roman searched her eyes to see if she meant it. Wow, Ms. I Believe in Love was offering him a no-strings affair?

Not what he usually heard, and definitely not what he'd ever expect her to suggest. Especially now, when everything was so . . . perfect. Special. He was oddly disappointed. In the past, he would've probably jumped at the opportunity, but with her . . . it seemed wrong.

"Fine by me," he said. Anything to get back to kissing her. Which he did, starting at her shoulder, sliding down her blouse to reveal a lacy pink bra with a tiny rose sewn between her breasts. With one flick, he unclasped the bra. *Oh, holy shit.* She had gorgeous boobs. *I mean, she always did, but . . . wow.* Seeing her like this made him forget everything . . . like consonants and vowels. He reached out, his hand trembling a little, and cupped a breast in his hand, feeling its perfect weight. Slowly, he lowered his mouth to the pink tip.

He paid ample attention to both breasts, and was gratified by the little noises of pleasure she made. But he made the mistake of stopping what he was doing and looking at her.

She literally took his breath away along with his speech. With her thick, dark hair and smooth skin, she looked like the kind of woman who would grace a jug of fine Italian olive oil, a woman with a bandana over her hair and a peasant blouse hanging off her creamy shoulders and showing off the lush curves of her breasts.

His chest tightened again, and he realized he was standing there staring at her like some dumbstruck idiot.

"What is it?" she asked. Her gaze was wary, yet something in her eyes reminded him of their first time together, when she'd looked up at him with all the trust in the world. He would have done anything for her, anything, and at that moment, he felt it—that same feeling, that same desire to give her everything he had, to lay himself out before her and surrender it all.

Had she ever felt like that about him? Ever wanted him like that? He suddenly realized she was the only woman he'd ever known who had the capability to burn him, scald him to the quick, and how could he have ever been such a fool to think he could play with fire and come out unscathed?

Yet there she was, looking at him with those big, beautiful eyes, challenging him, wanting him. He couldn't resist her then, and he sure as hell couldn't now. "I—I want you so much. I—"

She cut him off with a kiss, and every thought fled. Their tongues slid together, their touches became frantic. Her clever fingers had tugged open his belt and were working on his fly.

"Take me to bed, Roman." She clutched at him, her breath coming in ragged gasps. "Make love to me." His zipper hissed, and she'd pushed his pants down far enough that he managed to shuck them off with his briefs.

Somehow they ended up on the floor. She slid her arms around his waist and pulled him on top of her. He managed to scoot them over until they were at least on the wall-to-wall in her living area. "Do you want to try a bed or something?" he asked, worried about her.

She reached up and smoothed the hair off his forehead. "I kind of like this," she said. "Reminds me of how uncomfortable it was in that old cabin." Her hand lingered on his cheek. Her eyes suddenly got soft and—was he imagining it?—a little misty. She was an enigma. She sure as hell didn't look like someone who was just doing this for kicks. Just for the sex. No. It would never be like that for him.

"Roman," she whispered, staring up at him.

"What is it?" he asked. "Tell me."

She paused a long time. Then at last she shook her head, like she was unable to speak. "Just . . . I'm glad you're back."

He wanted to say so much to her. He wanted to talk honestly about so many things, but he knew that somehow he didn't have her trust.

Instead, he decided to show her how he felt. He helped her pull off her boots. Strip down her leggings to reveal—sweet and merciful God in heaven—a tiny white thong with little pink roses on it. He rested his hand lightly on her abdomen. Felt her breath suck in as he slowly crept his fingers down, down to her most intimate places. She startled a little, but he leveled his gaze on her, questioning, and she met it and smiled. He'd take that as a green light.

Then he bent his head and gently spread her legs apart, kissing her, working his mouth slowly along her delicate flesh. She was wet and trembling, her legs shaking as he laved her over and over with his tongue. He was taking no prisoners, and he was not letting up. They had plenty of years to make up for, and dammit, he was going to show her what he was made of. Finally he placed a finger inside her, then another, using his thumb to circle her clitoris until she whimpered helplessly and bucked her hips and at last cried out his name in a pulsating, clenching release.

Hearing his name on her lips undid him inside. He rose up and kissed her on the mouth. "I want to make love to you," he said without a shade of doubt. "Not like an eighteen-year-old boy. Like a man. Like a fresh start."

"Roman." His name again, on a breathy sigh. She smoothed her hand along his arm, his chest, his abdomen, and it felt so damn good to be touched by her. "So far, this is not eighteen-year-old-boy lovemaking. Just so you know."

He reached for a condom. "Also," she said. "This time I've been on birth control for more than two weeks."

He smiled a little. "Yeah, well, if it's all right with you," he said, smiling a little, "I still don't want to take any chances."

"Double might be the best way to go with us."

He sheathed himself and positioned himself over her. Poised to enter her and gazed into her eyes. There was that look again, like she was on the verge of tears, a surprise for someone so determined to keep things light. He kissed her tenderly, hoping to convey to her with his body the things he'd left unsaid.

He pushed against her, entering her, filling her with his length, and she took him in, pulling up her hips and wrapping herself tightly around him. No words, yet their bodies understood each other perfectly.

They let go at the same time. His own release was strong, swift, and powerful. She came apart in his arms, trembling and tightening and arching toward him as he kissed away her quiet moans and whimpers.

And then suddenly there was quiet.

A strange feeling hit him in the stomach. He was not an overly emotional or sentimental man, but he had the strangest sense of . . . relief. Like something long lost had been found.

They lay together a long time, listening to nothing but the sound of the ice-cube maker filling with water and occasional knocks and footfalls from the apartment next door. Bella lay against him, her hair silky and wild on his chest, but there was a slight tension about her, in the way she held him, her arms wound tightly around him as if she were afraid he might bolt at any minute.

As Roman held her sweet, soft body in his arms, he was afraid to break the silence. But the words rose in his throat nonetheless, ones he did not want to admit or feel, but were there, fully formed and sharp. That she was his sweet, sweet Bella, and after all the years of longing and wanting, he was finally home at last.

Hours later, Bella startled awake. Her bedroom was dark, but her bathroom light was on, which was strange, because she never slept with it on. Her heart pounded, panic settling into her consciousness. Her bedside clock read three a.m. She pulled up the sheet, which was tangled around her limbs. A feeling of restfulness rolled over her in a wave. Like she'd just had the best dream ever. A quick peek confirmed that she was naked. Naked!

One quick roll to her left, making certain the sheet covered her boobs, confirmed the worst. She swept back her hair, which was undone and springing everywhere in Medusa-like curls, and stared at the perfection that was Roman Spikonos. Lying on his back, his gorgeous chest exposed, his breathing slow and even. *Roman Spikonos* was in her bed. Was this a dream?

The night came back to her fast. Their meeting in the park. The short walk to her apartment. And several rounds of frenzied lovemaking, followed by a slower round she'd enjoyed just as well.

She lay her cheek on her pillow and stared at his sleeping profile. The picture of masculinity. Bold brows and angel-kissed lashes. That nose, that perfectly straight nose with diamond-shaped nostrils. His strong jawline, already covered with bearded shadow that she recalled scraping deliciously over her most sensitive places. It seemed a marvel to see him up close after only imagining him for so long.

She never thought she'd ever see him again, much less be with him like this.

Bella knew she needed to tell him the truth about what had happened all those years ago. Why she had let him go. He deserved to know why she'd lied to him.

Part of her had hoped that making love with him now would prove that he was a fantasy, that the reality of him wouldn't measure up, but it had only gotten better with time. No other man had ever moved her as he had, and a sinking feeling in her gut told her what she was deathly afraid to admit, that perhaps through it all, she had never stopped loving him.

Worse, even after all those years of forcing herself to forget him, she hadn't managed to drive him out of her system at all.

Roman had been as confident and sure of himself in bed as he was with everything else. And tender. The way he'd touched her, what he'd done . . . oh, magic. A languor permeated every muscle, down to her very bones—the result of having been made love to well and several times over.

She couldn't stop staring. She wanted to memorize everything, record this moment in her mind so she could have it forever, it was that perfect.

His eyes opened. "Hey," he said.

Oh shit. Her hand was half raised, on its way to . . . well, maybe to smooth his brow? Or touch his hair? She hadn't really had a plan.

"Hey," she said, trying to pretend her hand wasn't dangling conspicuously above his head.

"You're not doing anything creepy, are you?" He quirked a brow in concern. "Stealing a lock of my hair, something like that?"

What on earth could she say? *You're the most gorgeous man I've ever seen, and I wanted to memorize every inch of your face. And never leave my bed.* "No, I was just . . ." He'd gripped her lightly about both her wrists, a move which brought her up against his chest, just the thin sheet separating them.

"I was just . . . okay, fine. I was staring at you." She laughed, looking down at him as he held her captive. "There, are you happy? Now let me go." She twisted her hand so he would release her.

"Okay, fine," he said. But instead, he used the strength of his muscular torso to swing her arms around and pin her to the bed.

His face was above her, his gaze boring down, searching hers, and she was unable to look away, unable to hide. He interlaced his fingers with hers above her head as he pressed his body over hers. She felt the delicious weight of him, the hair on his chest tickling her breasts, his erection demanding notice as he pressed against her inner thigh. His lips traced her skin in a fiery path down her neck, nuzzling at the base, then trailing across her collarbone, her shoulder, until at last he found her lips.

Something was happening to her, something overwhelming, making tears well up. Too much pleasure, too much goodness, too much . . .

happiness. She didn't want to feel it. She was afraid to feel it, and she didn't want him to see it. But she could tell by the way he looked at her that he saw it anyway.

He deposited several quick but thorough kisses on her lips and reached for another condom. "You can say this doesn't mean anything," he said in a low, deep voice that sounded a little sleep roughened. "And you can say this is all about the past, or even that it's all about sex, but you'd be wrong, Arabella. This is something bigger than the both of us."

"Wh-what do we do about it?" she whispered, staring up at his beautiful face.

"I don't know," he said as he slipped inside her, kissing her again to take in her soft cry. "But happy birthday."

CHAPTER 16

"What's gotten into you this morning?" Drew asked as he walked into Roman's tiny kitchen bright and early the next morning. Roman greeted him from the stove, where he was flipping pancakes on an old-fashioned griddle. Good thing Roman was in such a great mood, or he would've commented on Drew's unkempt beard, which already looked bushman wild even though he'd only been here a few days. With Drew's jeans, bare chest, and bare feet, and all that hair everywhere, he really did look like he'd been hibernating in the woods for a few days or a year.

Drew took a look at his brother and shook his head. "Up at the butt crack of dawn, making breakfast, humming 'I can't fight this feeling anymore' . . ." He leaned across the countertop, getting in his brother's face a little and grinning. "You got some last night, didn't you?"

Roman felt too good to let the brotherly ribbing bother him. Actually, for barely having slept, he felt ready to . . . well, maybe not run a marathon, but he felt pretty amazing. Ready to tackle the barn roof his brothers had offered to help him with today. And what was wrong with humming some classic REO Speedwagon anyway?

He poured Drew some fresh coffee and slid the mug across the counter. "You know, you're going to frighten people in the neighborhood if you don't get a haircut and clean yourself up."

Drew looked around, smoothing down his beard thoughtfully. "Is this a neighborhood? Because last time I checked you're pretty surrounded by woods."

"You can't hide out here forever, you know," Roman said.

"And you can't avoid the question. You slept with Bella, didn't you?"

"None of your business."

"You slept with Bella?" The screen door squeaked shut as Lukas entered the kitchen, dressed in jeans and work boots. He said a quick hello to his brothers then indicated the coffeepot in Roman's hand. "I'll have some of that if you're pouring."

Roman filled a cup for Lukas and handed it over. Lukas was eyeballing Drew out of the corner of his eye. "He's a lot taller than when he was six, huh?" Roman said.

"I was going to say hairier, too," Lukas said, "but I was afraid to joke so soon."

"He's a Spikonos," Roman said. "He can take it."

"Actually I'm very sensitive," Drew said. "But it seems like Roman will do anything to change the subject."

"I never kiss and tell," Roman said with a grin.

Lukas walked back to the door and peered out through the screen. "By the way, there's a mangy dog on your porch."

"Is he dangerous looking?" Drew asked, turning to look.

"Yeah, fierce," Lukas said. "Foaming at the mouth, ready to pounce."

Drew joined him at the door. "That's not foaming at the mouth, that's drool."

"With all that tail wagging, he's practically swept the porch clean," Lukas said. "It's almost like he's excited for something."

Roman decided to play dumb. "It's a *she*, and you can let her in."

Drew raised a brow. "Does Bella know you're sharing custody of her dog?"

Once Lukas opened the door, the dog bolted in, going right for Roman, who grabbed a piece of bacon off the counter and tossed it. Gracie caught it midair and lay at his feet, chowing down on it.

"You've been cooking bacon every morning," Drew said. "And that dog was here yesterday, too."

"Yeah, so what?" Roman asked.

"You're feeding Bella's dog."

"More like he's luring it over here," Lukas said.

"I'm just having pity on a poor, skinny animal," Roman said.

"Bullshit," Drew said. "Where the animal is, the woman follows."

Lukas frowned. "Maybe you should toss him some Lipitor along with the bacon. You're clogging that poor animal's arteries."

Roman set the platter of bacon down on the counter. "Okay, you all have had your fun. The clock's ticking. Time to get to work."

"I just remembered something," Drew said. "We used to have a dog, didn't we?"

"Not for very long," Lukas said.

"I remember ChiChi," Roman said, stooping to pet Gracie, who was now slowly but thoroughly licking his hand, lavishing him with doggie love.

"That's right," Drew said. "ChiChi. I remember coming home from school and being so excited, petting it. The little thing curled up and went to sleep with me every night. A couple of weeks later, I came home from school and it was gone." He looked down at his coffee. "I looked everywhere. Went into a panic. Lukas, you sat me down and told me it belonged to some family. The kids had been crying for their dog and they were so happy it was alive and being so well cared for. That they really, really missed their dog, and to thank us for taking care of it, they left us money for ice cream. Then you took me out and bought me some." He got a little quiet. "I'm afraid to ask, but what exactly happened to that dog?"

Roman exchanged a glance with Lukas. "You really want to know?" Lukas asked.

"Yeah," Drew said.

"ChiChi was a pit bull I found behind that old rotting woodpile in the backyard. He was shivering, just skin and bones. I took him in and hid him in my room. Our parents never even noticed, really. Drew, you were the one who really took to him. One day when I was at school, Dad somehow found it. He must've messed with it pretty badly because the dog took a bite out of his leg. Landed him in the ER for stitches. Never saw the dog again after that."

Drew cleared his throat. "Well, thanks for the ice cream. Don't know how you got the money for that, but I appreciated it."

"It was that paper route, remember?" Roman said to Lukas. "We used to deliver papers every morning at five a.m. and hide the money under that one bad floorboard on the stairs. Remember when the old man actually fixed the floor? We waited until everyone fell asleep and then pried all the nails out."

"And the money was still there," Lukas said.

"We helped each other survive. And now . . . it's nice to have you two back in my life," Lukas said.

"If you're so thankful, maybe you can have this guy come live with you," Roman said with a wink, pointing to Drew.

"Look," Drew said, "you need a ton of work done around this place, and I told you I'd work for free in exchange for room and board."

"I should've put shaving in that contract," Roman said.

"I'd have Drew stay with me," Lukas said, "but I'm afraid he'd scare Stevie with all that facial hair. What is that, dude, like three days' growth? That's incredible."

"I have a talent for hair growth, what can I say," Drew said.

"Well, I'd love for us to keep reliving our tender childhood memories," Roman said, "but there's work to be done."

A distinctive Greek-accented voice turned everyone's attention toward the door. "Yoo-hoo, boys. Open the door, my hands are full." Roman walked over to find Alethea Panagakos, her arms laden with several large tinfoil-wrapped pans, a paper grocery bag, and a few plastic bags dangling from her wrists. Coming up behind her and carrying more bags were Sam; Maggie; Lukas and Sam's son, Stevie; and a little guy Roman guessed was Maggie's son, Griffin.

"Griffie and I were visiting Sam and Lukas and found out they were heading over here," Maggie said to Roman. "Hope you don't mind we stopped by, too."

"Glad to have you," Roman said, relieving Alethea of a few items.

"Sam told me you boys were working together to help Roman today," Alethea said, "and I figured you could use some nourishment." She pulled an embroidered hanky out of her purse and fanned her face. "It's hot out already."

Roman wrapped an arm around her shoulders. "Thank you, Alethea. Will you join us for breakfast?" He gestured at the pile of pancakes he'd just made.

Her eyes lit up like she was Cinderella just being invited to the ball. "Oh, I'd love to." She pulled up a stool next to Drew. "Is that a fresh pot of coffee over there?"

Roman poured her some while Sam and Maggie unloaded a few grocery bags. He couldn't help noticing how Lukas snagged his wife and kissed her good and hard, then hoisted Stevie up and asked if he wanted some pancakes.

"Alethea, you should run a restaurant for all the cooking you do," Maggie said, pulling a few bags of pita bread out of the bag, a giant hunk of feta cheese, and a big container of fancy olives.

"Oh, it's nothing," Alethea said. "It's what I do. Andreas," she said, turning to Drew, who'd been sitting there quietly sipping his coffee. "My, all that wondrous Greek hair you have." She had no hesitation about smoothing it down and attempting to tidy it up.

"Hey!" Drew ducked away like a boy about to have his ears washed.

"Yes, it's positively lustrous," Maggie teased. Drew frowned and tossed her a look.

"Mommy, who's that scary man?" Griffin asked, hiding behind his mother's legs, his eyes big blue discs in his small face.

Maggie patted her son on his head. He had blond hair like his mother, except his was curly. Cute kid. "It's all right, Griff," Maggie said. "That hairy man won't hurt you." Roman laughed. He liked Maggie a lot. Even more when she gave his brother shit.

Drew rolled his eyes at Maggie, but he smiled at the little boy. Maybe that was his way of trying not to look so creepy, but it tended to make him look a little more so, in Roman's opinion. "You like bacon?" he asked the boy, who nodded shyly.

"Is it all right to give him some?" he asked his mother.

"Well, I don't usually feed him processed—"

Too late, because Griffin reached his little fingers out to grab a piece of bacon. Except he promptly dropped it, and as he went to scoop it up off the floor, Gracie got to it first. The dog bit off a chunk, and Griffin, unfazed, popped the rest in his mouth.

"Honey, no!" Maggie said, like he'd just eaten Drano.

"It's okay, Mommy," Griffin said. "We shared."

The horrified look on Maggie's face, and the pleased one on her son's, made Drew burst out laughing.

"What?" Drew said innocently to Maggie, who looked about to draw blood. "It builds immunity." He turned back to his plate, his shoulders shaking a little.

Maggie scowled. "Oh, why don't you just go . . . get a haircut or something?"

"Oh, *there* she is!" a voice said from the door. Roman turned to find Bella at his door. Lucky him. He was just missing her. A lot. "Gracie, what are you doing here again?" As she let herself in, she waved to everyone in the kitchen.

Roman met her before any of his brothers could beat him to it. His breath caught in his chest at the sight of her, even though she didn't have a stitch of makeup on, just a freshly scrubbed face and her hair back in a ponytail. He had to restrain himself from lifting her up and swinging her around and telling everyone in sight how happy he was to see her. He was about to at least hug her and give her a big kiss when she spoke.

"Oh, hi, Roman," she said casually. Like they hadn't spent most of the night tangled up with each other in her bed. She handed him a large, covered platter. "I made you guys a batch of cookies. I wish I could stay, but I'm helping over at the center today. Hayrides and pumpkin carving and apple cider."

She gave Griffin a little squeeze and tousled Stevie's hair. "Maybe your moms will bring you guys over for a hayride later." She looked at her dog in dismay. "Why does she keep coming over here?" Bella bent down and petted the animal. "Gracie, what is the deal?" The dog wagged her tail and basked in being petted but wasn't telling, thank goodness.

Roman thanked her for the cookies and couldn't resist putting an arm around her. "Why don't you sit down and join us?"

She smiled at him, and all he could think is how much he loved that smile. And what a relief it was to see her beaming it at him. And how he couldn't wait to give her more reasons to smile like that again. Without thinking, he bent his head to kiss her, but she quickly stepped back before he could make contact. She frowned and shook her head, like she was asking him to understand she wasn't ready to broadcast them to the world. "Hey, Lukas. Hey, Drew," she said, turning to chat with his brothers.

Roman stood there rubbing his neck. He got that she didn't want to make things public. Everything was new—brand new—and with their effed-up past, he understood her need to take things slow. But part of him couldn't help being a little hurt. Just that he was so—happy, and he wanted to touch her. Hold her. Shout out to everyone in the room she was his.

That thought startled him. He rarely felt any sort of possessiveness over a woman. God knew, if a woman offered a casual, no-strings affair, especially a complicated woman like her, he'd be kissing her feet in gratefulness, in public *or* private. *Whatever you want, honey, no problem.* Fabulous sex, no commitments, it was a dream come true.

"Bella, did you say you brought cookies?" Alethea asked. "May I have one?"

"Of course," Bella said, uncovering the platter and setting it on the counter near Alethea.

"Oh, chocolate chip!" Alethea exclaimed, taking one and dunking it in her coffee. "My favorite."

Somehow, Roman ended up next to Bella. He was trying his best not to hover, but it was so hard. Unable to stand it any longer, he took her hand and led her out onto the porch. "Come over tonight," he whispered into her ear, tempted to nuzzle her neck while they were momentarily alone.

"Your brother's here . . ." she whispered back.

"So what?"

She shook her head. "The house is too small."

"I can't help it if you're noisy. Hope we didn't give any of the seniors cause for alarm last night."

"Come to think of it, Mrs. Landerhaven did avoid my gaze at the mailbox this morning."

"We can go back to your place," he suggested. Not to be pushy, but . . .

"I shouldn't really stay the night there until I move out of my dad's."

"Why not?" he asked.

"My dad and my aunt forgot I told them I wasn't coming home last night. They were worried. But my dad finishes his PT this week, and then I'm leaving for good."

He got that she didn't want to tell them about their relationship yet, and he didn't push. But he was desperate to be with her again. "Okay, then, what are you doing tomorrow afternoon?"

"Let's see, it's Sunday." She pretended to check her phone. "Looks like I can fit you into my schedule." She said *schedule* the British way—*shed*-ule. Cute.

"I'll pick you up at the end of the drive, okay? Around one?"

She frowned. "You don't need tutoring, do you?"

"Oh, definitely," he said, then he stepped close to her and really did nuzzle that sweet neck. "I have this goal. It's to memorize every inch of your body. Want to quiz me and make sure I've got it all covered?"

"As I recall, memorizing used to be one of your strong points."

Then he kissed her. Her lips melted softly into his, and he was reassured by the fact that she gave herself over to the kiss, molding herself against him, putting all of herself into it. He was conscious of how well they fit together, thrilled to have her back in his arms where she belonged.

Where she belonged? There he went again. Dreaming of the future when he needed to reel himself back into the present. Even after the screen creaked and she tore herself away, and Drew said an embarrassed "excuse me," even after she collected her dog and walked back into the woods with a little wave over her shoulder, he couldn't stop thinking about her. How nothing was enough, how he wanted to make up for all those lost years by not missing a single second with her.

Scary thoughts.

He gradually became aware that Drew was still standing next to him on the little porch. His brother slapped him on the back. "Not sure I'd let that one go, bro."

He smiled a little. Judging by the way his heart was thumping hard in his chest, how every muscle was ready to grab her and kiss her and tell her what a great time they had, and how he couldn't wait to get her in his arms again . . . yeah, this wasn't feeling like a fling. Or anything close to casual at all.

"Where are you taking us?" Bella asked. She was sitting across from Roman in a little rowboat on a brilliant early-October day, nothing but the lake and the golden lazy afternoon ahead of them.

She could hardly believe they got to spend the whole day together. She tried to sit back and just enjoy the view—the view inside the boat, that is—how Roman's biceps flexed with every row, his simple gray T-shirt stretching across his spectacular chest. That same warm, muscled expanse she'd admired up close and personal the other night. Happiness and incredulity washed over her, and at the same time, a sense of thick, absolute panic that kept trying to crowd out the other feelings.

Roman, however, looked as tranquil as the lake around them. His lips turned up in a small, secretive smile, and he shrugged his gorgeous shoulders. "You'll just have to wait and see."

That smile nearly did her in. She kept her own smile small, but inside, it was taking over her entire insides, tearing through her head and her chest, making her heart expand and stretch in a terrifying way.

When he'd suggested going out on the lake today, she'd been excited to go. She loved being on the lake. But the privacy appealed, too. She had no experience in knowing how long flings lasted, but judging by their nature, probably not that long. Reminding herself of that would be . . . prudent.

Oh, but this didn't feel like a fling. It felt like something far more threatening. She'd hoped to avoid talking about serious things, but the weight on her chest felt crushing. It was the weight of guilt, and it had sat there squatting on her chest for too many years. She owed him honesty, and she didn't want to shy away from that. He deserved to know what had happened, even though the thought of telling him something that could turn him away for good made her blood suddenly turn the consistency of icy sludge.

"What are you thinking, Bella?" Roman stopped rowing, sat forward, and took up her hands in his big, slightly roughened ones. It reminded her of a long time ago when she used to marvel at how large and engulfing his hands were, something that had always made her feel safe. Except she wasn't safe. He was still dangerous to her in ways she'd never dreamed possible.

He stroked his thumbs over the backs of her hands. His eyes held a warmth and a playfulness that she could get lost in if she allowed herself. It was exhilarating and exhausting being with him, like being on an incline treadmill, all this fighting to keep up her pace. A fight she felt destined to lose.

He leaned in, so close she could feel his breath on her cheek. "I just want you to know that, for years, I dreamed of being with you like this," he said.

Wonderful, terrible words. She didn't dare answer. He reached up, his hand tangling in her hair, drawing her closer. Putting his mouth on hers and kissing her until her resistance melted and she got lost in the sensation of kissing him back, the feel of his eager lips, the familiar taste of him, the smell of his soap. She stopped fighting. She fell into the danger. There was simply no way she could stop.

She looked at him, so handsome, in the prime of his life, and she realized she had to stop spooking herself. Maybe the dream was too good to be true. Maybe it wouldn't last. But everything in her, every last particle and blood and marrow cell, wanted him. Like she'd never wanted another man. Life had made her wary and gun shy. It had hurt her and roughed her up a little bit. It rarely offered any certainties. But she wasn't going to let anything mar this joy. She was going to live today, live it like her last day on earth.

"Roman, I want to tell you something," she began. She wanted to tell him now, before things went any further. It was the right thing to do, and she had to act fast while her courage was up. She'd always been honest with him, until she'd hurt him so badly. She needed for her own sake to come clean.

"Hey! Your boat's drifting!" someone on a passing boat called out. Sure enough, they were headed into an inlet where straggly tree branches jutted out into the lake.

"Thanks!" Roman called, taking up the oars. Bella waved to the people in the boat, a pontoon with a middle-aged couple aboard, enjoying the sunny day.

Suddenly she did a double take. The woman had thick, dark hair. Dangling pearl earrings. And she'd been laughing with her partner. Even as she looked, the woman quickly bent over, busying herself with something on the floor of the boat.

"Fran?" Bella called. "Aunt Fran, is that you?"

"Hey, Francesca, you know that girl?" the man asked, confirming her suspicions. A gray-haired, gray-bearded, distinguished-looking man. With an Italian accent.

He was real? Her beau? From Italy? And he was here, in Mirror Lake?

"Aunt Fran!" Bella called again.

Slowly, the woman straightened. Turned her face so Bella could see it. Yep, it was Frannie all right, looking like she'd just been caught tippling in the liquor cabinet. "What are you doing out here?" Fran asked a little indignantly.

"What do you mean what am I doing out here? What are *you* doing?" Bella asked.

"Having a picnic," she said. "You should try it. It's fun."

"Hey, Fran," Roman said with a wave.

"Hello, Roman," Fran answered on a sigh. "I'll see you kids later," she said, making the *be-quiet* sign against her lips and then the slitting-her-throat sign and pointing to Bella.

"Interesting," Bella said, waving. "The Italian prince exists."

"So he does. Stranger things have happened." He full-out smiled. "But I don't want to waste our time together talking about your aunt."

"All right, then." She reached over and kissed him on the cheek, smiling brightly in return. "Roman?" she said.

"Yes, Arabella?"

"I'm so happy to be here with you. But please tell me you're not taking us to that abominable cabin."

He shrugged. "I thought it might be fun to relive the magic."

She raised a brow. "Some people might not think that fear and dread are great memories to relive."

He laughed. Stopped rowing. "I thought the part before the fear and dread was pretty spectacular, personally."

Their gazes locked. She wanted to tell him that their innocent, awkward lovemaking back then had been just as spectacular as this week's. Just as meaningful. And that scared her to death. "That cabin was falling apart back then. It's probably gone."

"Maybe, maybe not," he said. "Either way, it's a lot better being here in the daytime instead of a misty winter night."

She looked around at the gorgeous lake and the sky that only seemed to be that pure of a blue on a sunny, cloudless fall day like today. They were almost to the shore, at the same place where they'd banked all those years ago. Just thinking about that night made her stomach churn with apprehension. She didn't want to let those memories loose. Like a gift wrapped in layers of fragile packaging, once it was taken out, it could never be replaced quite the same way again.

"Maybe we shouldn't," she said. "I mean, I don't really want to see it."

"Aw, come on. We're here. It's part of our past, Bella." He gave her a serious look. A look that made her wonder if his plan included discussing that past.

That reminded her of her resolve to tell him everything. She'd lost him once with a lie, but this time the truth might make her lose him again. And expose everything she'd ever felt for him, her deepest, darkest secret. Yes, she was truly feeling nauseous now.

He rowed them to shore and banked the boat. Then he helped her out and held her hand. The hill before them was now planted with a lovely manicured lawn that could have been golf-course grade. Gone were the cattails and long, marshy grasses, the unkempt weeds everywhere. A clump of ornamental grass was in full bloom, lush and tall.

Beyond the grass, the cabin was . . . gone. In its place was a modern timber lake house, large and laden with ground-to-roof windows.

"Wow," Bella said. "Things have changed." The only thing that was the same was an uncut field between the property and the woods, full of tall grass and golden wildflowers.

Roman was looking at her. "Is that a bad thing?"

"No. I don't think it is." She smiled. "I think I've had enough, though. It's very new, but it's a little . . . boring." She pulled him back toward the lake. "Let's head back to the boat."

"You're a better view than anything else around here anyway." Suddenly, he stopped. Tugged her into the tall grass. He held her hand and kissed her knuckles, each one in succession.

Which was so romantic she almost cried. But she was so, so nervous. She had to get this off her chest. "Roman, speaking of us, there are certain things I feel we should talk about."

His face brightened. Why in God's name would it do that, right when she was about to tell him about the lowest moment of her life? She opened her mouth to speak, to get out the words, to say, *Roman, I lied to you. I drove you away on purpose* . . .

"I'm glad you mentioned that, actually," he said. "Because I have something on my mind, too. Look, I know you're apprehensive about us being together, but Bella, I feel so—great about us. I want to shout it out to everyone. Kind of like this."

"Wh—" Before she could ask him what the hell he was doing, he'd picked her up and slung her over his shoulder, spinning them around the field, letting out a few whoops. She let out a little scream of laughter from her upside-down spot, then tried to clamp her mouth shut, hoping they hadn't attracted the attention of the owners. Roman, unfazed, set her down and pulled her further into the field.

In the middle of all the golden grasses and white and yellow wildflowers waving in the breeze, he again took up her hands, gazing at her solemnly, reminding her of that look of teenage earnestness he'd worn so long ago. It made her heart flutter at the same time it made it sink with dread. She felt like she was in midair on a tightrope, close to safety yet one step just as close to plummeting into an abyss.

"I want to hold your hand in public," he said. "I want to walk down the street with you, and go to dinner with you, and kiss you in front of your friends."

Suddenly he *was* kissing her, hard, thoroughly, and she was totally under his spell, all her thoughts scattering like the grasshoppers in the field. They tumbled down into the grass, the heat of the sun warm, crickets chirping their last swan song.

Oh, she was in trouble. Big trouble, as she kissed him back, getting lost in the taste of him, the perfect slide of their tongues, the skillful work of his hands as they skimmed her body. "I'll think about it," she managed, smiling against his shoulder as she helped him drag off his shirt.

"Okay. Think about it." He looked down at her, grinning. "But not too hard."

Truthfully, she couldn't think of a thing, just *him*, the overwhelming, overpowering presence he'd always had, the ability to sweep her off her feet and make her forget everything else in the world. Then she went back to kissing him until there was nothing but the sun, the golden field, and the warmth of his body against hers.

CHAPTER 17

Roman pulled up the garden center driveway in his truck and parked in front of Bella's house. Three other cars besides Bella's father's truck were sitting in the gravel drive, leading Roman to believe the whole family was probably gathered for their traditional Sunday dinner.

He was taking a big risk coming here. But he had a plan, and now was as good a time as any to begin to scale the big, burly mountain of Vito D'Angelo. If Roman could somehow get Vito to tolerate him, Bella would feel more comfortable about their relationship. The man had wielded his power over them for too long.

Roman wanted a chance with Bella, out in the open, and he wanted them to be free to feel what they wanted. They weren't adolescents sneaking around. Besides, sitting in his living room thinking about her and watching his troubled brother eat his way through another bag of potato chips wasn't cutting it.

As a kid, he'd once lost everything that mattered to him, and as a young man, it had happened again when he'd lost her. He knew he had a tendency to be a loner, to hold tight to control, but he'd matured. His feelings for her had gotten deeper and more complex with age, like his brandy. He wanted to risk it all for her. At the same time he kept warning himself not to feel anything, but he couldn't seem to help himself. He was violating all his own rules. But it felt . . . right.

He let Bella's dog out of the passenger side of his truck and walked across the driveway to knock on the kitchen door. Laughter and voices drifted out from inside the house. Roman cleared his throat. Looked down at the dog. "Okay, so maybe this isn't the best time to do this. But maybe it is." The dog thumped her tail on the cement and stared at him with big brown eyes. "Don't look at me like that, okay? I'm going to take the first step. This is as good a time as any."

Then Bella would see that this whole situation wasn't so bad. They were all adults, for God's sake. And maybe he should have talked this over with her before he'd driven over here like this, but her family being here would be good. Vito would be less likely to lash out if other people were present. He hoped.

He was taking a step forward. Surely the old man wouldn't reject a gift. And it was finally time to get over the past. After all, Roman wasn't a serial killer.

Bella walked out wearing an old ruffly apron over a sweater and jeans—he bet it was her mother's—and holding a wooden spoon. Seeing her in the middle of just living life was unexpected, and it brought a pang of wanting. And another, surprising one . . . of jealousy. *He* wanted to be able to share something so simple as fixing a meal with her. Sitting by her, putting his arm around her, chatting with her and her family. Things most people took for granted.

The smells of basil and oregano and tomato sauce wafted toward him from the house. Her hair was pulled back, but a curl was hanging out of her ponytail. He couldn't resist tugging on it a little, watching it spring back.

He stepped forward to kiss her, wrapping his hands around her waist and pulling her close. Couldn't help himself.

She smelled like garlic and that wonderful flowery scent she always wore. The two didn't necessarily go together, but somehow it fit. And the garlic part made his stomach growl. He put his mouth very close to her ear. "You look—and smell—good enough to eat."

"Roman!" she whispered, trying to pull away, but she was smiling. She grabbed his hands and pulled them off her hips. "My whole family's here."

"Oh. Right."

When he stepped back, she noticed the dog by his side. "Gracie?" She looked puzzled. "Why does she keep wandering over to your place? The electric fence company is coming on Monday. Hopefully we'll stop this problem," she said, bending down to pet her dog and rub her nose in her silky fur.

"She can't resist me," he said, shrugging. "I tend to have that effect on women." He leveled his gaze on her. "I was hoping on you, too?"

She stood and kissed him on the cheek and beamed him a smile that told him the answer. "Why are you here?" she asked.

"Listen, Bella," he said. He hesitated, not sure how much to say. *I really want us to have a go at this* came to mind, but instead he said, "I have something for your father."

"For my father?"

He smiled. "Yeah." He found himself tensing his jaw. Crossing his fingers and toes. Maybe he'd need to turn around three times and click his heels, too, because this was important. Really important. A man like Vito D'Angelo did not forget, but Roman was about to find out if he was capable of forgiving him for getting his daughter pregnant. "Can you get him?"

Bella went a little pale. She scanned his face. "Do you think that's a good—"

He gave her hand, the one that wasn't holding the spoon, a quick squeeze. "I brought him a gift."

"A gift."

"Yeah. He's going to like it." *If he'll accept it, that is.*

"Okay, I'll get him." She paused. "I'd invite you to in, but, you know . . ."

"I understand, Bella." He made sure to smile. "I'll wait in the driveway."

Bella didn't have to get anyone, because Vito himself showed up at the door. "What's he doing here?" he asked his daughter.

"Hi, Mr. D'Angelo," Roman said, his mouth suddenly going dry. He hadn't been this nervous since he was eighteen, on that fated last day. But Roman didn't want to remember that day. This was a new day, a new life, and the past didn't get to have that control over him anymore. He walked forward, started to offer his hand to shake, but then thought better of it. No sense pushing his luck. "I brought you something."

He walked around to the back of his truck and unsnapped the tarp, exposing a bed full of crated apples. Vito eyed the crates, then levered his gaze on Roman.

"What's this for?" he asked.

Roman handed him an apple. A big, firm one, with characteristic red striations against a paler background.

"Honeycrisp," Roman said. Beautiful and round and perfect. The orchard's prize apple.

"I know what they are," Vito said. "They're very much in demand this year."

"We had a big yield this year." A great crop, considering how finicky they were to grow and pick and store. It was the most popular apple in the county—hell, make that the *country* right now—and the prices it went for were exorbitant.

And Roman didn't really give a shit about any of that. If it cost him a million dollars' loss, he'd do it if it got him Bella.

Vito took the apple and inspected it. "Very nice."

Roman smiled. "I know." He looked at the older man. "They're for you. A gift. They're extra big this year and extra sweet."

"I'll pay you for them, of course," Vito said.

"I want you to have them. As a neighborly gift." He glanced at Bella. "A peace offering."

Bella looked like she was holding her breath. Then Ethan of all people walked out of the house, the screen smacking loudly behind him, and stood beside Bella.

Vito didn't say anything.

"They're nice apples, Dad," Bella said, stepping up. "What a great gift."

Please take the damn apples, Vito, Roman thought. *For your daughter's sake. For my sake. Let's just end this right here.*

"I can't take them for free," Vito said. "I'll sell them and give you fifty percent, how's that?"

Vito scrutinized him. In his eyes, Roman saw questions, and skepticism, and suspicion. He debated whether he should insist on the gift part, but Vito was a proud man. Frankly, he was relieved he hadn't told him to take his apples and shove them.

"Deal," he said, extending his hand.

Vito didn't shake. "We live next to each other. It's okay if we do some business."

"Right. Great. Business," Roman said.

Vito turned to go back into the house. Francesca showed up alongside her brother and peeked over the truck bed. "They're beautiful, Roman. Thank you very much. We were just about to sit down for dinner. Will you join us?"

Vito frowned at his sister. Bella's face went from pale to blanched. Ethan scowled.

"Thanks," Roman said, "but I really should be getting back—"

Bella seemed to blow out a relieved breath. But Fran stepped forward and grabbed his arm. "Nonsense. Such a kind thing you've done. We've got plenty of food. Ethan's here, and Gina and Manny are inside. We insist that you stay."

Vito shot his sister another look, but he didn't protest, which Roman took as a good sign.

Fran led Roman into the house, passing Bella, who stood there, lips pressed tightly together. This wasn't what he'd planned, but what could he do? He telegraphed her an *I'm sorry* look, and she shrugged. He'd just have to prove to her that he could behave himself in front of her father and Ethan, too.

The house hadn't changed much from how he remembered it all those years ago. Oh, the furniture was different, thanks to Bella, no doubt, but he recognized the same hundred-year-old built-in mahogany cabinets on either side of the fireplace in the living room, the same heavily carved bannister on the steps, and the same antique Victorian buffet in the dining room, where everyone was sitting down for dinner.

Fran guided him to the table, and he thanked her, but he ended up following Bella into the kitchen where she was gathering together the food. "I'll go if you want me to," he said. "I only intended to drop off the apples."

She handed him the salad bowl and smiled. "Nonsense. You're staying. It'll be all right." But she looked worried. "Thanks for the apples," she said. "It was kind of you."

"I did it for you, Bella."

"I know you did," she said quietly, then quickly kissed him, glancing around to make certain no one had seen.

"It's going to be all right," he said, leveling his gaze at her. "You'll see."

Fran instructed him to take a seat between Joey and Ethan, who were talking about cars. Bella brought the lasagna out from the kitchen and sat next to Manny. Gracie, the traitor, had parked herself at Ethan's feet, making Roman wonder if he kept dog treats in his pockets on his days off.

"Where's Gina?" Bella asked.

"Feeding the baby," Manny said. "She'll be back in a little while."

"Go ahead and start without me," Gina called from the living room. "This kid always seems to sense when it's time for me to sit down and eat a meal."

"I'd breast-feed for you if I could, sweetheart," Manny said, digging into his food. "Well, I would," he said, specifically to Bella and Fran, who were looking at him funny. "She does that and then I get to change the diaper afterward. It's all good."

"I just got the engine on my Jaguar tuned up," Ethan said. "It purrs like a kitten now. I was thinking, Joe, it's yours if you want to use it for homecoming."

"No way!" Joe said. "I mean"—he looked over a little apprehensively at his father—"only if it's okay with my dad."

Vito waved his hand. "Okay by me."

"Ethan, thank you for bringing that delicious coconut cream pie," Fran said.

"Oh my God, there's pie?" Gina called from the living room.

"Homemade pie," Bella said. "Ethan made it himself."

"Speaking of cars," Vito said to Ethan. "I'm having problems with one of the tractors. Mind having a look at it later with me?"

"Sure," Ethan said in his usual good-natured way. "I brought my toolbox."

Figures. Animal lover, a whiz in the kitchen, fixer of tractors. He must've learned a thing or two in the past twelve years. And now he was just one of the family.

Gina returned, burping the baby, but before she could sit down, Bella came over to her sister and took the baby from her. Bella bounced and patted her nephew's back as she walked back and forth near the entrance to the big dining room.

"Bella, your dinner's getting cold," Gina said, shoveling her food. "Sit down and eat."

"I have all night to eat, G. My little nephew and I are bonding." She kissed the baby's head as she burped him over her shoulder. "Aren't we, you little stinker, not letting your mother eat her dinner?"

The sight of Bella holding a baby hit him like a punch in the gut. He used to imagine, years ago, what it would be like, the two of them—just kids themselves—with a baby. Them rocking on a porch swing holding a baby, or lying in a real bed, a bed of their own in their own place, the baby between them, spending hours being amazed over every little milestone. Those were fantasies that never came to fruition. Dreams that got cut short.

This was different. Not that he understood much more about the realities of raising a child, but somehow he could envision her being a mother, smoothing her hand over the baby's soft hair and then looking up at him lovingly . . . teaching a child. Hugging a child. *Their* child.

"Cute baby," Roman said, distracting himself from the direction of his thoughts.

"I mean, parenthood is amazing," Manny said, "but sometimes I miss the good old days when we were young and single." He turned to Roman. "Speaking of being young and single, I didn't know you two were dating."

Suddenly, all eyes were on him, including Bella's.

"You two are dating?" Gina asked, her finger pointing back and forth between him and Bella. "Bella, why did you not tell me?"

Vito's fork hit the plate with a loud clatter. Fran put her hands on the table, ready to get up and intervene at any moment. Even Ethan stopped chewing.

Bella laughed. A strange, high-pitched laugh. "We're not dating, Manny," she said, a little too emphatically, raking her fork through her salad. Not bothering to spear any lettuce. Not looking at Roman, either.

Bella wasn't making eye contact, but Ethan was. And his gaze was full of daggers.

Manny was still running at the mouth. "Mrs. Landerhaven said Roman's truck was parked in your lot all night the other night. And Saturday morning she saw—"

"We're *not* dating," Bella said, cutting him off, staring at Manny from across the table. "End of story."

"Well, okay, then," Gina said. "I'm sure that would be complicated anyway since you're planning on moving soon."

Moving? Surely Roman must have heard wrong. One glance at Bella showed him she'd closed her eyes and pressed her fingers to her forehead. Not a good sign. "Gina, that was private," she said. "You weren't supposed to share that."

Shit. It was true. But, really, she was *moving*?

"I didn't think it was a secret," her sister said. "Sorry."

"You're moving for sure?" Fran asked.

"I applied for a job with a group of psychologists in Chicago," Bella said quietly. "I'm still thinking about it. It's not—definite yet." This time, she looked directly at Roman.

"What is this, Chicago?" Vito said. "You don't tell your own family you're leaving?"

Or him. It didn't make Roman feel better that she hadn't told her family. He'd been under the mistaken impression that they'd shared something special. Special enough that she would have at least mentioned her plans.

Clearly, he was wrong.

Silence fell over the table. Everyone seemed to be concentrating on eating. Even the baby was quiet.

"Look, I've been in Mirror Lake my whole life," Bella said. "Maybe I need a little change."

A little change? Just when they'd reconnected and it had been so . . . explosive between them. Or maybe he was the only one who thought that.

"I'm going to cut the pie," Bella said.

"I'll help you," Ethan said, hurrying to stand up.

Roman stood and addressed Vito. "I wanted to thank you for having me over, Mr. D'Angelo." He looked over at Fran and nodded. Then he caught Bella's eye, just for a second. But he couldn't read what she was thinking.

"I'll see you out," she offered.

"Don't bother," he said. "I'll see myself out. It's no trouble."

But she followed him to the door. He spun to face her in the tiny foyer. As a rule, he tried not to speak when he was upset. But he had to know. "Why didn't you tell me you were leaving?"

"I haven't decided for sure yet. That decision's been in progress for a while. I guess I—I wasn't sure of what we have, Roman. It happened so suddenly." Her gaze flicked up at him. "What *do* we have?"

The question caught him off guard. Her refusal to acknowledge him over dinner, coupled by how Ethan was everyone's favorite son—how even Joey gravitated to him—had made him testy, so he said, "A communication problem, obviously." He stopped in front of her. "Yeah. I get it. You aren't sure of what we have."

Funny thing was, he thought he'd known *exactly* what they had. Something great. Which she obviously didn't get, did she? He walked past her and out of the door, feeling like he was eighteen again, rejected and wanting her far more than she'd ever wanted him.

CHAPTER 18

Roman sat on the couch in his living room opposite his brother and tented his fingers together in thought. Drew sat slumped, watching a baseball playoff game and eating his way through a bag of something crunchy and orange that smelled a little like gym shoes. He pointed the open mouth of the bag in Roman's direction. "Want some?" he asked.

"Thanks, but I'll pass." Roman pretended to check out the game, but it didn't really register. He couldn't seem to concentrate on anything other than Bella.

It didn't sit well with him that she'd pretended to her entire family that she wasn't seeing him.

And the Chicago thing had really blindsided him.

Oh, he understood about her father still hating him, and Ethan being the son-in-law he wished he had, and even Joey seemed to love Ethan, too. Maybe Vito would never forgive him for the past. Roman was no stranger to not belonging. But, dammit, he wanted a chance to prove who he was. And that was not someone to be embarrassed of. He'd always treated Bella with respect, and whatever had happened between them, he'd always wanted the best for her. So why in God's name would she deny that they were seeing one another?

He'd been blindsided and hurt when she'd let him go the first time. Now, all these years later, he'd been more than eager to sweep those hurt feelings under the rug, explain them away as being from a time when they were both young, that losing the baby was such a trauma, the anger of her father was so all encompassing, and Bella's obligation to her brother was so strong. Bella had certainly suffered in the aftermath of the pregnancy as far as the town was concerned, and he felt a sense of guilt for that.

She'd been so reluctant to give them a shot again that he hadn't pushed her for explanations. Maybe he hadn't really wanted to know why she didn't want to plunge full speed ahead into a relationship.

He'd known from the beginning that it would be a huge mistake to want something bigger out of this. With their past, all those messy feelings . . .

Yet he'd still wanted to shout her name from the rooftops, and he couldn't for the life of him understand why she didn't, too.

"There's another game on after this one, bro," Drew said, still chomping on his snack. "Go grab a beer."

His brother needed an intervention, but for right now that was beyond his capabilities. Too upset. He debated calling Bella, but he wasn't sure that was a good idea right now. Plus his pride was a little wounded.

A knock on the screen door had him jumping up. As soon as he saw Bella's pretty face peering at him through the door, crazy relief washed through him in a big wave. Maybe everything was bothering her, too. They would talk it through once and for all. Just holding her in his arms would make it better and bring some clarity. Then he could take her back to his bedroom and plant kisses all over her sweet, soft skin until they both forgot all about this nonsense.

As soon as Roman opened the door, her dog flew into the house like it was Christmas morning and shot directly to Drew's side, where she zeroed in on the cheese curl bag and sat there thumping her tail.

Drew tossed a couple of curls, and the dog snatched them up faster than a baseball player snapping up a ground ball off a line drive, just as Bella said, "Oh, please don't feed her any . . . oh well." She smiled a little at Roman and shrugged as she set two glass storage containers on the counter. "I brought some leftover lasagna. And some dessert. The coconut cream pie."

He didn't care about the food. All he wanted was to make everything good again between them. Because he was so afraid it wasn't.

The hope of real food got Drew off the couch to come and peek under the lids. "I'm starving. Wow, that looks amazing. Thanks, Bella."

Roman cut his brother a glare, but he was too busy inspecting the food and talking about how wonderful it was to notice.

"Um, maybe we could go for a walk?" Bella asked Roman.

Drew must have sensed the somewhat tense vibe between them. "I tell you what," he said. "I'll just take a little of this back to my room and watch television with my headphones on and not disturb anybody." He snagged the lasagna container with all the subtlety of Gracie with the cheese curls. "Have a good night, folks."

"Let's go out on the porch," Roman said, steering her away from Drew. Not that he didn't like his brother, but Drew needed a shower. And another place to live.

"So dinner didn't go so well," Bella said, sitting down on the top porch step. Gracie plopped herself down beside her, edging closer until her head rested on Bella's leg. She seemed to realize she'd hit the jackpot getting Bella for a mom and was more than happy to display eternal doggie gratefulness.

Suddenly, he found himself a little jealous. Of the dog. And of the sitting-next-to-Bella part.

"Your dad seemed to like the apples," Roman said, because it was the only positive thing he could think of right now.

"He did. But I'm talking about the rest of it."

"Yeah. The rest of it." He stood leaning against the house, his hands drilled down into his pockets, trying not to act hurt or pissed off. But the simple truth was, he was a bit of both. Okay, a *lot* of both.

"I'm sorry about today, Roman. But I didn't think that was a good moment to go public with our . . . with our—"

"Seems like you don't think it's a relationship or you wouldn't be avoiding the word." He sat down next to her so he could see her face. Her lips were drawn in a tight line, and she was fidgeting her hands. Other than knowing she was uncomfortable, he had no idea what she was thinking, but it was time to find out. "You were the one with the rules, Bella. You were the one who decided to be secretive. You were the one who wanted to keep it casual."

How ironic that the roles were reversed from every relationship he'd had since her. That he'd never gunned for a relationship like this since he did for her twelve years ago. None of the other ones mattered. But he couldn't force his will on her. He couldn't make her love him. Was that what he was trying to do, the typical child-of-an-alcoholic behavior, wanting to have control?

Bella's hands dropped to her lap, where he noticed she clenched them tightly together. "I came here so we could have a talk and get things out in the open. I have a few things to say to you that I feel are important, and maybe might help you understand why I didn't want to come out and tell my family about us. Frankly, it's kind of a miracle you and my father were under the same roof just now and I didn't have to call 911."

He didn't care about what her father thought. And he certainly wasn't going to allow Vito to control their relationship. "Why are you so afraid of what your family thinks? You're thirty years old. I don't understand why you can't do what you want." He paused. "And if there's any doubt about it, you're more to me than just a good time. But it seems to me you're still kowtowing to your father, even after all these years."

Bella froze. She sat up too straight, her posture rigid. "He's my father," she said with a halfhearted shrug. "I have to be respectful of him."

Fine. He got that, but where did he fit into all this? She seemed to want to please everyone but him. "And Ethan, too? After all these years, you haven't seemed to be able to get rid of him, either. Maybe there's something more going on there."

"Ethan and I are just friends."

"Maybe you should tell that to him. Because the man has it for you bad." Oh boy, he was really putting his foot in it, but he couldn't seem to stop.

"Ethan's been a good friend to me for all these years. When coming back didn't seem to cross your radar."

"You made *sure* I never came back. You made it clear you were done with me. And maybe I just didn't get the hint. But it's okay. I get the hint now. I'm not even someone you consider important enough to tell that you're leaving town." Roman sighed heavily. "Truth is, I need someone to meet me halfway. I need you to be invested. I wanted us to have a real chance this time, Bella, but I can't do it by myself. And frankly, I'm done living the past. I want us to be about now, about the future."

"Sometimes, it's not just about you and me," Bella said quietly. Her face held a deadpan expression, so unlike her usual animated passion.

Roman frowned. "What are you talking about?"

"I—things were very confusing back then. I want you to know I did love you with all my heart."

"Bella, we have a hell of a past together, but I want it to stop defining us. I want something with you in the here and now, but if you don't want that too, what good is it?"

Exasperated, she threw up her hands. "Fine, you want me to meet you halfway? I will." She sat there, frozen, as if she were about to speak, but no words came out.

Puzzled, he watched as she walked over to lean against the porch railing, sucking in the cool night air. She was acting so strangely, so hesitantly, so unlike herself. What the hell was wrong? What was she about to tell him?

Slowly, she turned to him, grasping the top of the railing tightly with her fists. "After I lost the baby, I never wanted to let you go. When I told you I'd had enough and I needed a break, it was a lie. Letting you go was the hardest thing I've ever done."

"I—I don't understand." A lie? She'd *lied?*

"My father threatened to cut me off from the family if I saw you again. From Joey. I couldn't let that happen. He was too . . . young. Too dependent on me. Too alone from not having our mother." Her voice cracked and tears began to well up in her eyes. Part of him wanted to run to her, hold her, kiss her. Take all of this pain away. But he was too damn shocked. He couldn't quite process what she was saying.

"Why didn't you just tell me the truth?" he asked. "We told each other everything. Why did you lie?"

"I knew how stubborn you were. How you were always so upstanding, such a rescuer. I knew you'd stay here, in town, and I knew I wouldn't be able to stay away from you. And I knew you wouldn't get to do any of the things you'd dreamed of doing—go out West to school, study brewing and distillation. See the country."

Roman leaned against one of the porch columns and stared at her. Tears rolled down her face, her makeup running right along with the tears, and out of desperation she wiped her nose with the arm of her sweatshirt.

But he couldn't comfort her. A great wave of anger welled up inside of him, made him actually tremble. All the hurt he'd felt! He felt the searing slice of it as much now as then. All the years he'd tried to forget her but couldn't, not really. What was it all for? Wasted years. All because of her father's manipulative threat.

"Say something, Roman. Please." She looked devastated. "I didn't want to get involved with you again. It took me years after you left to move on. The men I moved on with were ones I could never love like I love you."

The *love* part barely registered. She loved him? How could she say that after years of deceit? He shook his head. "I've never been anything but honest with you. You lied to me—a lie that lasted twelve years. How could you do that, Bella? Did you think so little of me that I wouldn't understand? Did you even realize you cut off my choices just like your father cut off yours?"

Oh God, his harsh words made her cry more, and he knew he was being an asshole, but his fury would not abate. "Roman," she said, her voice hoarse, barely a whisper. "I'm so sorry."

The pieces fit together a little bit more now. Her reluctance to get involved, to speak up about their relationship. But he felt so betrayed. For being the woman he'd loved more than anyone, how could she sustain such a lie over such a long time? It was a horrendous breach of trust.

He trawled his fingers through his hair. Every time he breathed, a stabbing pain knifed him in the chest. "Look, maybe we were wrong to start this up again."

Her eyes widened in shock. "Is that what you really think?"

"Yeah." Too complicated. Too messy. Too much hurt.

Her eyes were swollen and red. She kept swiping at them and wiping her hands on her jeans. He had to stop looking at her, because doing so blunted his anger, and he didn't *want* his anger to die down. His shock and hurt were too raw. Instead, he crossed his arms and looked out across his orchards. Those damn trees, all in tidy, precise lines. Funny, but everything in his carefully ordered life was scattered to the winds now.

"Are you . . . are you breaking up with me?" Her voice sounded small and far away, but she stood straight, the posture of a woman who'd endured her share of pain. And who didn't think enough to share it with him.

"I guess I am."

"Okay, fine, then." She walked over to where Gracie lay curled up on a cushioned chair, and tugged her by the collar. "Come on, Gracie." The dog jumped down and immediately started to head over to Roman. But he had nothing for her in his pockets today. He was empty. Bella had to tug again, because the dog's legs were practically cemented to the floor, but she finally got her off the porch. And both of them disappeared into the woods.

CHAPTER 19

"Arabella."

She'd almost made it to the stairs again without making a sound. And she'd tried really, really hard to be absolutely silent because she did not want to talk with her father. Or anyone for that matter. If it weren't for that darn dog lapping up her water so noisily, Bella would've turned the corner from the kitchen to the stairs and been home free.

She paused with one hand on the bannister. "Yes, Dad?"

"Come here for a minute."

Dammit, no. Not now. Her head was splitting and her eyes were leaking and she probably—make that definitely—looked like a raccoon from her makeup running. "Do you need anything?"

"Yeah. I need you to come in here."

Bella rolled her eyes. Wiped her eyes and nose again on her sweatshirt sleeve. Took a deep breath. Walked into the living room to face her father.

It had stung her when Roman said she'd been kowtowing to her father for years, and when would it ever end? He was right; she hadn't been honest with Vito, either. She'd never dared to talk with him about her feelings for Roman. She'd been too afraid of his anger, of losing the little scraps of approval he occasionally tossed out.

Her father was sitting in his usual chair, the stick lamp beside it the only illumination in the room. He folded his paper and peered at her over his reading glasses. She didn't often think about how her father looked to the rest of the world, but he was still relatively young. He was strong. Some might even call him handsome, in a weathered kind of way.

"You were with him, that Greek." It was just a simple statement. Not said in anger, exactly, just with a twinge of his usual pass of judgment on the fact that Roman was not, nor would he ever be, Italian. Nothing she hadn't heard many a time before.

But it made her stiffen. "Yeah, Dad, I went over there to talk to Roman."

"You're involved with him again?"

"No, I'm not involved with him again." That was the truth, as of ten minutes ago anyway, and saying it made tears flow again. "If you don't need anything, I'm going to bed." *Walk away now,* a voice inside her head said.

"Good. I knew you were too smart to go down that road again."

She tried to turn away—honest, she did. Maybe it was that his words had rubbed that newly chafed part of her, already raw from losing him again. Or the fact that she was thirty years old and he still had too much power over her decisions. Either way, something inside of her snapped, and words rose up in her throat that she couldn't keep back.

"Roman's grown into a good man. He's working really hard to rebuild his grandfather's business and create his own dream. I—I want you to be nice to him. I want you to treat him like a good neighbor."

"You talk like you have feelings for this man."

She closed her eyes. When she opened them, her father was still staring at her. "I've done my best to be a good daughter to you for all these years. I'm truly sorry for what I put you through back in high school, but when is it ever going to be enough? All that I've ever wanted is for you to love me for who I am, but it seems the choices I make will never be the right ones for you."

She walked over to her father and stood in front of his chair. Looked him in the eye for what felt like the first time in twelve years. "I have feelings for Roman. I love him." Hearing herself say it out loud caught her off guard. Oh, she did love him, with all her heart. "But it didn't work out. And I'm going to leave. I'm going to move to Chicago and start over. Joey will be gone and I'm going to begin a new life. I hope you'll accept that. I've tried hard to make you proud, to make up for my mistakes, but I'm done apologizing. I need to live my life to make *me* happy now, not keep trying to make the decisions that you approve of."

She was blubbering now, really crying. Lord, she'd cried more in the past half hour than she had since Roman had left. She'd held that in for a lot of years.

Her father set the paper down on the floor and folded his hands together. She braced herself for a big godfatherly pronouncement, something to the effect that she was officially not his daughter anymore. But she was ready for it. She wasn't going to bend to his will this time. Like Roman had told her, love was a two-way street. It wasn't just one person bending to the other's will.

Her father heaved a sigh. "I know you were upset with me back then when I forbade you to see him. I know you probably hated me. But I didn't want you to get married at eighteen. I wanted you to go to college, to be able to get a decent job. You were too smart to not have the opportunity to get an education, and I swore that all my children would have what I didn't. Maybe I was too tough on you, but I couldn't see anything but your life getting ruined any other way."

"I loved him. You took away my choices for what you thought was best for me." Like what she'd done to Roman. She'd made the choice about their relationship for him, just as her father had done for her.

"When you were young, you were always full of such joy. After this happened, you hardly smiled again. I was angry at myself. I was angry at your mother for dying and leaving me here to raise you alone, and look what a bad job I was doing. I thought you would get over him."

"I didn't get over him. I tried to, but I couldn't."

"Don't ruin everything you've worked so hard for by getting tangled up with him again. You're a doctor now, and you're just getting your practice up and running. You can do a lot better than him."

"No, Dad. *I* have to decide what's best for me. Who I love, and who I want to be with. You did the best you could on your own with Mom dying, but I'm an adult now. I have to live my own life, and you have to allow me to do it."

She let out a breath she felt she'd held for twelve years. Finally, she'd said the things she should have said long ago. Finally, she'd stood up for her own feelings. She could not lead the life her father wished for her, and she hoped he accepted that. But if he didn't, she was going to live it anyway. Despite all her pain at losing Roman for good, that was very freeing.

Her father, for once, had no words. His bushy brows were knit down hard, concentrating, worrying. The old Bella would have begged forgiveness, perhaps, or offered an apology. But not this one.

She turned and walked up the stairs, bracing herself for her father's wrath. But the funny thing was, he didn't say a thing.

"Thanks for letting me bring Gracie after work to get her stitches out," Bella said as Ethan let her into his veterinary office after hours on Thursday. He had that same Ethan smile on his face as always, lovely, nonjudgmental, and a little sad. It made her try to push all her own worries aside. She was here for the dog, but she was here for Ethan, too. It was time to have a long-overdue chat.

Bella hadn't been able to eat or sleep since the weekend. Everything reminded her of Roman. The apples her dad kept talking about, which were selling like hotcakes. The good-as-new wall in her office. Her apartment, which she'd moved back into, at least until she could find another one in Chicago. Even looking at the clear, calm surface of the lake reminded her of Roman. What they'd almost had.

If she weren't so afraid to be honest with him, maybe they *could've* had it.

She'd been so afraid to show him her true self. So afraid to tell him how much she'd loved him, how many years she'd suffered after losing him. And how she'd fallen in love with him again from the first moment she'd seen him outside the reception hall.

"Anything for you, Bella," Ethan said as he propped open the door for her and Gracie to pass. But it wasn't with his usual cheekiness. It sounded tight, like maybe he was tensing up his jaw when he said it.

She walked Gracie into the exam room and watched while he sat down on a stool and rolled over to his cabinets to take out a suture-removal kit. Before he could get the dog up on the exam table, Bella spoke. "Stop saying that," she said, shocking herself a little.

He looked up in surprise. "Stop saying what?"

Okay, she was on a roll. Now she just had to summon the courage to keep going. "Stop being so accommodating to me all the time. Stop being so damn *nice*."

"Do you want me to stop being your friend, too?"

"You've always been my friend. You've never *failed* to be my friend. You've picked me up after every major crisis in my life for the past twelve years. I just can't help feeling that . . . that . . ."

He was frowning now. "You can't help feeling what?"

"That you're angry with me." His face was a little impassive. "And maybe you *should* be angry with me. Not just because I didn't tell you about Roman or Chicago or any of that."

"What you do with Roman is your own business."

She couldn't tell if he meant it or not. But she had to be honest with him. It was all she could give him now.

She cleared her throat. "Are you in love with me, Ethan?"

He rolled his stool over to her and took up her hands. Squeezed them. Looked into her eyes. She forced herself to meet his gaze, but she was so afraid of what he would say.

"I've always loved you, Bella. From the moment you sat down in the cafeteria with that geeky Jewish boy who didn't have any friends. You always saw me for who I was. You never expected me to be anybody but myself."

She shook her head. "I've used your friendship like a crutch instead of standing on my own. I—I took advantage of your loyalty. I clung to you out of my own fear of facing things on my own." Ethan had buffered her from the criticisms and scrutiny of the town. He'd loved her unquestionably.

He smiled, but it was a sad smile "Ah well. Maybe I understood that you needed someone, and I was more than happy to be that person."

"You always seem to think I'm a better version of myself."

The dog was licking his hand. He reached inside his lab coat and pulled out a piece of dog biscuit, which the dog made a lunge for and then ran under the exam table to eat.

"I *was* angry the other night," he said. "I just couldn't believe you'd go back to Roman. Not after everything that happened. I mean, I've been trying for years to get back together with you, and he shows up and within the week you're sleeping with him."

"I love him." The words hung in the air, shocking her again. "I think I always have. But I let the past get in the way of the present. I messed things up between us pretty badly. And this time my father had nothing to do with it."

He laughed a little. "Oh, come on. You can be truthful with me, so why not be truthful with yourself? You're not eighteen anymore. You're not a victim of circumstance and a stubborn father anymore. You have the power to change your destiny."

"I've decided to go to Chicago. Clean slate and all that." She couldn't stay here anymore, live in the same town with Roman, see him on the street every day and pretend to smile as they said hi . . . "I wanted to say thank you for always being there for me. And I'm sorry if I took advantage of your kindness to me."

"You sure you want to do that? You don't have to go to Chicago to find out who you are. You can do that right here."

"Yes, I'm sure." In the old days—yesterday—she might have stayed and cried on his shoulder. Asked him for reassurance. She owed him more than that now.

He got up and hoisted Gracie up on the exam table and snipped the sutures in her leg while Bella held her paw. When all was said and done, he lowered the dog down and tossed her another biscuit. "You know, I have something to tell you, too. I've taken a job in Montana."

She laughed as she wiped her eyes. "You're funny. I thought you just said Montana." If it were a few weeks ago, she would have said, *Aw, c'mon, Eth. You don't mean it. Stay. We could get pizza and see a movie and* . . . He wasn't laughing. "You're serious, aren't you?"

"Big Sky country. Why not? I'm still young. I want an adventure."

Oh no. So far away. What would she do not seeing his smiling face, hearing his laugh or his dumb jokes? Or not picking up his dry cleaning every week?

She gave him a hug and kissed him on the cheek. "You're the best friend I've ever had," she whispered. "You pick the best sushi places, and the weirdest movie marathons, and you're the only person I know whose desk is messier than mine. Please say we'll always be friends."

"Yeah, yeah, yada yada," he said. "Now take your cookie-fanatic dog and get out of here."

"I love you, Ethan." She hugged him. "I wish you the best."

"I love you, too, babe. Love you, too."

She forced a smile, determined to show him a happy front. She didn't want to hold him back any more than she already had. It was a small thing to do for all he'd done for her.

Bella turned and headed for the door so he wouldn't see her cry. Which it seemed she was doing in spades lately. She'd just gathered her dog and her keys when her cell rang. It was Aunt Fran.

"Stop everything! Come quickly!" she said.

"Frannie, what is it?" Bella asked, gesturing to Ethan that something was wrong.

"It's your father. He's in the fields, trying to pick those damn pumpkins himself."

"What?"

"Your father's going to kill himself and throw out his back again and ruin all his hard work after surgery. Nicoletti stole away the pumpkin pickers. He's trying to do it himself, fool that he is. And he won't listen to me. We have to stop him."

Her dad was in the field picking pumpkins? Four weeks after back surgery? The man's pride was more important than his health. Why did that not surprise her? His pride was bigger than ever admitting he was wrong, too.

"Guess you can't get rid of me that soon," Ethan said. "How about if I drive?"

A few minutes later, Ethan pulled her car up to the field where her father was lifting a big-ass pumpkin into a wooden orchard bin. Smoke-gray clouds hung low in the sky, and the wind was rustling the leaves on the trees and stirring the yellowed leaves on the pumpkin vines that lined the fields.

Bella got out and grabbed hold of the pumpkin with both hands. "Pop, are you crazy? You just had back surgery!"

"That bastard took my crew."

Bella tossed the pumpkin into the bin. She took hold of his arm and pointed to the tool in his hands, which was essentially a big pair of pruners. "Give me the loppers."

Her father threw up a hand in that Italian way of his. "Arabella, leave me be. I know what I'm doing."

She snagged the loppers and put them behind her back. "Tell me what happened. Where's Raul and his crew?"

"Tony Nicoletti's paying him more than I can pay. I told you he was out to ruin me. And I'm not going to let him."

"We can match his price and get the crew back. I'll kick in the difference."

"It's too late."

"What do you mean it's too late?"

"Bad weather's coming. Maybe hail. Nicoletti paid prime price to get them to leave my job and go to his fields instead." He paused, which was never a good sign. "And besides, Raul and I had . . . words."

"Oh no, Pop, you didn't." She put her hands on her hips. "You told Raul off, didn't you?"

"Of course I did. How many years has he worked for us, that traitor? Then he goes running off because Nicoletti offers him blood money. I don't ever want to see him again." He waved his arm in a dismissive gesture.

In that moment, Bella looked at her father. Stooped over a little from the back problems, the outdoor light showing every weathered crease and wrinkle, his thick, wavy hair graying. There were many, many adjectives she could use to describe her father, starting with stubborn, obstinate, proud, and completely unreasonable.

But he was something else, too. A very hard worker. And somehow he kept everything going as it should—the fields, the flowers, the business. The equipment worked, the books were balanced. This garden center was his life. And he was not a quitter.

Bella got her amazing work ethic from him. And maybe more than a dash of his stubbornness. And even if this whole thing with Roman was killing her, just *killing* her, it was not going to define her. She was going to survive this. She wasn't eighteen anymore. She wasn't a delicate flower. When she was a girl, she hadn't understood what love was. She understood it much better now. Enough to know it was hard and it could hurt like hell, but she also knew that it would not destroy her.

And her father, giant pill that he was, was just a man. A man who made mistakes and who had his own trials to bear, and who had borne most of them alone since her mother had died. Somewhere under his gruff exterior, he probably did love her, even if he didn't approve of her imperfect life.

Well, if she wasn't perfect, neither was he.

She flung the loppers over her shoulder. They landed in the field a few rows over.

"What are you doing?" her father said, outraged.

"We will get these pumpkins picked. But you, personally, will not be picking them."

"You don't tell me what to do, young lady."

"I do if I'm the one who nursed you back to health these past few weeks. What would Mom say if she saw you ruining yourself out in these fields? How are you going to run the business if you're off your feet for months because you were too stubborn to listen to anyone?"

A truck came rolling down the dirt road that edged the field. A black pickup truck, followed by an old maroon van. The truck stopped behind Bella's car, and Roman himself got out.

At the sight of him, in jeans and an old flannel shirt, Bella's heart contracted hard, like a fist had wrapped around it and was squeezing all the blood out of it, leaving her lightheaded and empty. His handsomeness struck her as it always did, and the fact that he looked tired, and maybe a little bedraggled, like maybe these last few days had been just as hard for him as they had been for her.

She wanted to run into his arms, rub her cheek against that old, soft shirt, and feel his arms wrap around her, comforting and forgiving.

He gave her a cursory glance, then focused on her dad. "Mr. D'Angelo, I heard your pickers left. I brought some guys to help."

"Where did you find them?" Vito asked, always suspicious.

"They're my apple pickers."

"I can't take your apple pickers. Bad weather's on the way. Get your crop picked." Vito knew it was full picking season and time was money. Besides, if hail pockmarked the apples, they'd be ruined as eating apples, which were expected to be without blemish.

Roman shrugged. Caught Bella's eye, which made her heart skip, but his expression was maddeningly neutral. She'd hoped he was a little less angry. That maybe he'd come over not just as a neighbor but also because of *her*. "We'll get this done today and worry about the apples tomorrow."

Before Vito could protest, Roman walked to the maroon van. A crew of men were climbing out of it, several of them with loppers. A gray-haired man, clearly in charge, came forward to confer with Roman. After a minute, he signaled his crew. "Okay, men. Let's get to it."

The crew spread out in pairs, one of the guys lopping the pumpkins off the vines and the other lifting them and placing them in bins on a bin hauler positioned between the rows of the field. The bin hauler was a tractor capable of scooping up several bins at a time and hauling them all back to the garden center together.

"I can't thank you enough for this," Vito said. He sounded humble, for the first time Bella could ever remember. Was this really her dad? Or was this the version the aliens left behind?

"That's what neighbors are for," Roman said, but he was looking at her.

"Thank you, Roman," Bella said. She tried to let him know with her eyes how much she meant it. How sorry she was for not being honest with him from the beginning. Oh hell, she hadn't been honest with *herself*. She'd been so protective of her heart, but for what? She'd lost him anyway.

"It's no problem," he said, pleasantly enough. Their staring contest was broken by the sound of more cars—Joey and a carload of his buddies climbed out, and Gina and Manny. And Roman's brothers Lukas and Drew, and Sam and Stevie. Ethan had driven up to the house and gotten Fran and Gracie, too.

Over the next few hours, there were no signs that Roman had had a change of heart, or wanted to talk. No more subtle glances or smiles in her direction, which seemed to indicate just how hurt and angry with her he was.

On the other hand, Roman talked freely with her father, even laughing once or twice, and her father was nothing but grateful, even ordering pizza for everyone after the field was clear. So Roman and his father had finally come to terms. Too bad she couldn't say the same for them.

CHAPTER 20

Roman walked into his house after dark, muddy and a little achy in the back from hauling all those pumpkins. He'd worked his ass off today for Vito D'Angelo.

That wasn't true. He'd done it for *her*.

At least the worst of the storm had passed over. The hail never came, and his apples would be fine. All he wanted now was to be alone in his house, but wouldn't you know, he found Drew and Lukas in his living room eating a pizza.

Whatever had happened to his love of solitude? His life of contemplation in the country? He'd gained brothers and lost his quiet life, and he wasn't quite sure how he felt about that.

Or about anything, really. Being so close to Bella all day without talking to her had made him really cranky. It felt wrong. A couple of times she'd approached him, and he'd purposely feigned busyness. He'd been an ass, and he knew it.

"We were still hungry so we found a twenty on the kitchen counter and used it to order more pizza," Drew said.

"Have some," Lukas offered. "You're an ass, by the way."

"No, thanks," Roman said, propping himself on a couch arm. He didn't want any pizza. He wanted Bella.

"I mean, I get that you've had your share of rejection in your life," Lukas said. "When we were split up as kids, with Bella . . ."

"You sound like my mother," Roman said. "Please don't go there."

"I'm sensing a pattern," Lukas said. "I just think you've got some issues."

"Maybe we all do," Roman said, glancing at Drew, who was polishing off a piece of pizza in three bites.

Drew looked up to find his brothers shaking their heads at him. "What? Hey, this isn't about me." He pointed to Roman. "It's about him."

"Look," Lukas said. "We lost our parents and each other. Those are hard losses to recover from. It's hard to trust people when you've been hurt that badly. I just think you might be missing the point here."

"I already lost Bella," Roman said. "So that's a moot point."

"You can't give up without telling her how you really feel about her," Lukas said. "Tell her how much you care."

"I've done nothing *but* care about her." For about a thousand years. "You don't even know what we fought about."

"I don't care what you fought about. Have you told her you love her?"

"It's a little hard to do that when you're seriously pissed off at someone."

Roman wasn't used to having heart-to-hearts with anyone, let alone with long-lost brothers, but he understood that they were trying to be there for him.

"Think about what happened with us as kids," Lukas said. "You always shut yourself off when you were hurt, told yourself you didn't need anybody. But now you've got an opportunity for a do over. How many people actually get that?"

That hit home.

He should've figured it out, way back then. That she'd been young and frightened and faced with an impossible decision. What choice did she really have but to pick her baby brother? He shouldn't have left her to face everything on her own. Lukas was right. He'd shut down, tried to cut her out of his life. Left and never came back.

Hadn't he done the same thing this time? Thought more about how their breakup had hurt him than what she was left to deal with?

Trouble was, leaving didn't make a person forget. It didn't make him stop loving her.

And he did love her, with all his heart. He was sick of their relationship being about the past. It was time to turn that page for good.

"Sure you don't want any pizza?" Drew asked, reaching for another slice.

"I'm okay," Roman said. "But, Drew, I have something to say."

"What is it, bro?" Drew asked.

"Since we're being brothers tonight, I have to tell you something that I mean in the nicest possible way."

"Sure. What is it?" Drew asked, setting down his plate.

"You need to leave," Roman said. "You need to go back and face whatever you did back in New York. Time's up for hiding out."

Drew sighed. "I know."

"It'll be okay," Lukas said, squeezing his shoulder. "Whatever it is, you can handle it."

"Hope so," Drew said. "Um, we sort of have a proposition for you."

"For me?" Roman asked.

"Yeah, about that," Lukas said. "We want to be full partners in your brandy business. That way we can invest some capital and you can be up and running sometime this century."

"I don't want a handout from anybody."

"It's not a handout," Drew said, rolling his eyes. "It's an investment. Based on a hunch that you're going to be very successful."

"And based on the fact that we're brothers," Lukas said.

"Wow. Thanks," Roman said, genuinely floored. "I may take you up on that." But truthfully, his mind was somewhere else. "I've got to go now. It's Thursday night."

"Thursday night?" Drew asked, puzzled. "Is that code for time to drink? I'm all for starting the weekend early."

Roman smacked him on the back. "Time for group therapy. It's a special session tonight because it's Effie's birthday next Monday."

"They cancel group here if it's someone's birthday?" Drew asked.

"If you're Effie Scofield and it's Mirror Lake, yes," Lukas said. "What are you waiting for?" he asked Roman. "Except don't forget to go wash that stink off of you first."

Roman gave Lukas a friendly shove, just to get him back for that. Then he got serious. "Look," he said. "I just wanted to say . . . thanks." Not the mushiest sentiment. He tried a little harder. "I'm glad you guys are back in my life."

"Welcome," Lukas said. "I always wanted to do backbreaking pumpkin-picking labor all day." He flashed a smile. "Especially since we never got to pick any as kids."

Drew laughed. "Yeah. Beats making millions on Wall Street any day."

"Hey," Roman said. "I did buy you guys a pizza."

"Don't worry," Drew said. "While you're gone we'll stay here and finish it for you."

Roman rolled *his* eyes. Brothers. Gotta love 'em.

"Roman sent over a handful of men and his brothers and worked all afternoon with us, but he barely spoke to me," Bella told Maggie as she pulled the chocolate sheet cake out of the fridge in the back of the office. "Before I got in the shower, I threw the batter into a baking pan, and here it is. Nothing fancy."

"Hey, it's chocolate," Maggie said. "It doesn't have to be fancy. You didn't even have to bring anything. Are you all right?"

Bella shrugged. "Been better, but I'm okay."

"That was really nice what Roman did."

"He's a nice guy," Bella said. A guy who'd dropped everything to help her crotchety father. Who went out of his way to help her to rescue a mangy dog and gave her brother extra work and rescued her from a string of bad dates.

"You sure he didn't have an ulterior motive?"

"He barely spoke to me all day."

"I'm so sorry, Bella. You sure you don't want me to run group tonight? Griffin loves his new sitter. If I called and asked her, I bet—"

"Go home to your son, and quit worrying about me." She paused before walking out into their waiting area. "I'm glad I told the truth. It needed telling. Maybe someday he can forgive me for deceiving him."

"Maybe you just shocked him, you know? And he was hurt and angry over that. Maybe he loves you enough to get over it."

Bella shrugged. "He felt betrayed, and I don't blame him. But I'm okay. I came clean with him and my father. Finally, I'm going to put the past behind me for good."

Maggie gave her a hug. "Rest up after all that the pumpkin picking, and we'll plan something fun for next week, okay?"

"As long as it doesn't involve fixing me up on any more dates."

Maggie held up her hands. "I'm done with matchmaking."

"Promise?"

"I wish there was something else I could do to stop you from leaving, but I understand."

"You're a good friend, Maggie, and I love you." Bella took a moment to hug her, then picked up her chocolate cake and walked out to the waiting room. The ladies had already put all the chairs into a big circle, and the coffeepot was chugging, sending the rich odor of fresh coffee everywhere. It appeared that circle time had already begun, because they were already talking.

"This is a group of healing," Effie was saying. "We want to hear all about what you have to say."

Uh oh, looked like they'd started without her. Bella put the cake pan on the foldout table she and Maggie had set up, next to the napkins and paper plates. She'd just slid over Alethea's baklava to make more room when she heard a familiar voice.

"I loved my girlfriend as much as you could love anyone when you're eighteen. I believed what we had could last. But what do you really know at eighteen?"

Oh God. That voice. She'd recognize it anywhere. It was deep and male and *Roman*. Her back still to the group, she froze, unable to turn around.

"Eighteen is so young. It's babies," Effie said. "I've seen a lot of young mothers in my time as a nurse. It's very difficult to get your feet on the ground and get an education once you have children to support."

"My girlfriend in Greece was married at eighteen to a tycoon," Alethea said. "Thirty years older than she was. When he died she inherited everything. That was her version of financial planning for the future."

Fran sighed. "Eighteen is just so young."

"When Queen Elizabeth married Philip," Gloria said, concurring, "she was twenty-one. And a half."

"Go on, Roman," Effie said. "Tell us the rest of your story."

"I really shouldn't burden everyone with my problems."

"Now, now, dear," Effie consoled in that sweet little voice. "That's why we're here. You can feel free to say whatever you want."

Bella turned to see Effie patting him on the knee. Roman. He was *here*, sitting in the circle wearing a charcoal gray V-neck sweater with his jeans, his arms folded across his big, broad chest. Her dog was parked happily at his side. Gracie even shot her a guilty look but didn't budge from where Roman was calmly stroking her fur.

"Roman—" Bella began and immediately her throat felt clogged with Kleenex. Oh, she needed to tell him how much he meant to her, that he meant *everything*, and beg his forgiveness, and she didn't care if every old lady in Mirror Lake heard. Or if they shouted her story to the whole damn town or the world for that matter, as long as he listened. As long as he gave her one more chance.

"Shhh, Bella, we're *listening*," Alethea said a little testily.

"Let the man talk," Fran said, waving her away.

"So, anyway," Roman continued, looking at her from his seat in the circle as she managed to pull out an empty chair from the circle and sit down. "I had this plan. I was going to join the army, and after basic training, she'd come join me wherever I was stationed, and we'd be okay. But she said no. She said now that there was no baby, there was no reason to rush into marriage. She wanted to go to school, and she had obligations at home. But then she told me she needed her freedom."

"No! She didn't!" Gloria said, clutching her chest.

"I loved you more than anyone or anything." The words poured out of Bella's mouth, unstoppable. She had to make him understand. "The day I lost your baby was the day I thought my life would end. Because it was the day I lost you, too." Her voice cracked. Her eyes flooded. She was not sure she could do this.

"Go on, dear," Effie soothed.

"Telling the truth is always best," Alethea said.

"Her father threatened to cut off his you-know-what if he ever came near Bella again," Fran said with a knowing nod.

She stood up. "Joey was so young, and my father was so—powerful. I thought when I lied to you I was being noble, but I was really being stupid. I was miserable without you. I thought of you, dreamed of you, for years. And when you came back, I was so afraid that I would fall for you all over again, and if I had to endure that heartbreak again it would kill me. So I told myself I wouldn't fall again. I'd keep it light. That's why I wanted to keep you a secret from my family."

"He's too gorgeous to keep a secret, dear," Alethea said.

"Problem is, I fell in love with you again the second I bumped into you at that wedding." The tears were waterfalls now, but she forced herself to finish. "I love you, Roman. I'll always love you. Forgive me. For taking away your choices. For lying to you. I promise, if you take me back, I'll never keep anything from you again."

Suddenly he was *there*, wrapping his hands around her waist and lifting her up so that her feet left the ground, planting his lips possessively over hers. She didn't see him very clearly through the tears but God, she felt him, his lips sliding over hers, his arms holding her like they'd never let her go. "I love you," he said when the kiss was done. He leveled his gaze straight at her and gathered up her hands in his. "If I would have known, I never would have left you. You know that, right?"

"I know." She was gripping his hands right back like they were joined together by superglue and she would not be putting them down anytime soon. But he didn't seem to mind.

"I've been an ass. I felt hurt and betrayed, but I was thinking of me, not you. I understand now that you had no choice. Hell, I should have put it all together way back then, but my pride was too wounded. You were afraid and alone, and I left you to shoulder everything by yourself. I'm sorry, Bella, for all the pain in our past."

The soft gray walls blurred again, as did the cute lamps and the faces of all the women. She did happen to notice that Maggie was there, too, tearing up from the doorway.

Roman dropped to one knee. "Arabella, I've never stopped loving you." He pulled a ring out of his pocket. "I want you to be my wife. So we can build a family together. I promise that I'll do everything in my power to make up for these years we've been apart."

"I love you, Roman," she said, throwing herself into his arms and kissing him like this was their last kiss on earth. She wrapped her arms around his neck, threaded her fingers through his thick, silky hair, and clung to him. He held her tight, wrapping his big, strong arms around her and pulling her to him so there was not an inch of space between them. Then his mouth was on hers and he was kissing her back, his hand circling gently around her neck to tug her even closer, like he was in no hurry at all. A full, wonderful kiss that wasn't gentle or careful but soft and slow and possessive, like they belonged only to each other and had all the time in the world, an entire future, ahead of them.

Gracie trotted over, wanting to get in on the action, and began nudging between them, even going so far as to crotch-butt Roman until he finally rubbed behind her ears and told her she was a very good dog and, yes, he loved her, too.

"Excuse me," said a heavily accented male voice. "But I am looking for Ms. Francesca D'Angelo."

Everyone looked up. In the doorway was a distinguished-looking, gray-haired man in a suit and tie, holding a classic fedora to his chest.

"Dominic!" Aunt Fran stood and walked over to the man. "Dominic, what are you doing here?"

"Who is that?" Alethea asked. "He's handsome, too."

"Why is this family so secretive?" Gloria asked. "Hiding all these gorgeous men."

"He's a doctor," Effie said.

"He's Italian," Gloria said. "Maybe he's a prince."

"He's real," Bella said. "Thank God." It was the man from the boat they'd seen Fran with. As real as could be. And judging from Fran's blush, he meant something important to her. She prayed that Fran would get the opportunity for the happy ending she deserved.

"I thought you were on your way back to Palermo," Fran said.

"I couldn't leave without you, Francesca. Will you marry me?"

"I love group therapy," Alethea said, clapping her hands.

"It's better than the movies," Gloria said.

Effie nodded. "And the best part is . . . more weddings."

EPILOGUE

Roman and Bella were in the new house before the baby was due the next September, which was a great blessing. A Victorian-style house, with a turret and a big wraparound porch that looked out over the lake in one direction and the orchards in the other. With a side yard big enough to plant a big, long strip of irises and tulips and daffodils. Which Bella was certain her father would help them with, as soon as it got cold enough to plant some bulbs.

"Beautiful," Bella said as they sat on their porch on a quiet August evening, right before apple season. Except Bella was having trouble getting comfortable, considering she felt like she was about ten months pregnant when she was really only almost nine.

"Yes, you are," Roman said, the corner of his mouth turning up in a smirky half smile that she loved.

She smiled back, grateful for the compliment, before shifting again on the glider. He always told her she was beautiful, and it never failed to touch her, especially now when her ankles were thick and her toes resembled little cocktail sausages. He also tried hard not to complain when she slipped and forgot to put her clothes in the hamper, or when the mail pile got out of line, and she bit her tongue to not tease him at the way he insisted on lining up all his shirts and socks and underwear in color-coordinated order.

Because mostly it felt so good to finally be together, and she thought that maybe they understood better than most new couples how little any of that stuff really mattered, and what a miracle it was that they'd found each other again. "It's so peaceful here," she said. "Who'd have ever thought we'd have our own place on the lake one day?"

"And it's not even a beat-up one-room cabin," he said. "And we have real beds, not air mattresses."

"Roman," she said.

"Yes, dear?" He'd slouched down a little bit and had stretched out his long legs, using them to keep the glider swinging a little.

"I've been thinking a lot about this baby."

"That's a good thing, no?"

"Well, yes. But I just worry . . ."

"The doctor said everything's fine, sweetheart. Don't worry."

"Yes, I know, but I just want you to know something."

"What is it?

She gripped his hand kind of hard. "I love you so much," she said, her voice a little breathless.

"I love you, too." The death grip made him look up.

"That and I think my water just broke."

Vivienne Rose Spikonos made her appearance late that night in Mirror Lake Community Hospital. Roman felt very, very blessed to have possession of a healthy baby girl, who was now being admired and showered with love by friends and family.

"Joey, come say hi to your new niece," Bella said, patting a spot beside her on the bed. Roman knew she wanted Joey involved from the very beginning, that she'd always feel that he was in many ways her child, too.

"Um, Bella, I love you and all," her brother said, kissing his sister on the top of her head and studying the baby from a safe distance, "but I think you should start calling me Joe."

"I helped raise you," Bella said. "You'll always be Joey to me."

"Here, Uncle Joey," Roman said with a wink, handing him the baby.

"Uncle Joe to you, thanks very much," Joe said to the baby as he held her rather like a football, and looking like he wanted to pass her back as fast as possible. "Hey, Dr. Rushford," Joe called out to the doctor standing at the foot of the bed. "Can I come shadow you on my fall break?"

"Sure, kid," Ben Rushford, the doc who'd ended up delivering the baby in the ER, said. "You sure you don't want to stick with engineering? Better hours for sure. Maybe even better pay."

"I'm sure," Joe said.

"Hey, doc," Drew said, holding up a brown paper bag. "Is it okay if we all have a drink in here?"

Ben plugged his ears. "I didn't hear you, and if I can't hear, I can't inform you of the hospital drinking policy." Then he added in a low voice, "Just don't let the nurses catch you."

Drew started lining cups up on the window ledge. Maggie brought over the bottle of brandy. "Here you go," she said. Running a hand over her cheek and then pointing to his trimmed beard, she said, "Get tired of the Wolverine look?" She sniffed the air. "You may have even showered. Wow, why the change of heart?"

"Guess I'm done hiding," Drew said, handing her a couple of cups to pass around. "Hope I didn't distract you, being as I'm so good looking with a groomed beard." Maggie rolled her eyes and passed out the brandy.

"Congratulations, bro," Lukas said, hugging Roman and giving Bella a kiss on the cheek.

"I'm glad you're here, Lukas," Roman said, clasping his brother's hand.

"Wouldn't miss it," Lukas said, giving him a slap on the back. "We're family."

"Look at all that black hair," Sam said, smoothing down the baby's cowlick. "She's so beautiful, Bella."

"Greek and Italian genes," Alethea said. "What a beautiful combination. It does ensure that there'll be plenty of mandatory hair removal in her future."

"Thanks, Alethea. We'll be on it," Bella said as Roman handed her a cup with brandy in it.

"Just a sip," Bella said. "I'm going to breast-feed."

"Oh, that'll help you get the baby weight right off," Gina said with a sigh.

Manny handed his wife a cup of brandy and kissed her. "You're beautiful just the way you are, babe." Gina rolled her eyes, but she blushed, too.

Roman held up the brandy bottle to show his wife. "I wanted you to see this."

Bella looked at the label, then gave him an incredulous look. Her eyes started to do that misting-up thing they did. "You named your brandy after me. Oh, Roman."

"You'll always be my *bella dolche*."

She smiled and he kissed her tenderly. His sweet Bella. To have her and to have this healthy baby and be surrounded by family meant everything. Just a short time ago, he would have never believed it possible.

Marjorie asked to hold the baby. "I think she's got Roman's eyes, and Bella's pretty mouth."

"Those are D'Angelo eyes if I ever did see them," Vito said. "And the D'Angelo chin."

"Vito," Fran said, "it's a baby, not a genetic competition."

"Hey, you can't blame me, Frannie," Vito said, smiling widely. "I'm just proud." He walked over to Bella and kissed her on the forehead. "I'm so proud of you, sweetheart." He looked at his son-in-law. "And you, too, Roman."

Roman smiled at Vito. He was still a pill in many ways, but he had his moments.

"Vito, how about you do the honors?" Lukas said, raising his cup. Everyone else followed suit.

Vito raised his cup and beamed at his daughter and her husband. "I wish you both many years of happiness. *Salute. Viva la famiglia.*"

"*Viva la famiglia,*" Roman said, and kissed his wife again.

Later, when everyone had gone, Roman lay next to Bella in the hospital bed, watching their endlessly fascinating baby daughter, who was asleep in his arms. The room was dim, and outside the window, a few lights across the lake twinkled in the darkness. For Roman, the familiarity of the lake always brought about a sense of peace. And so did this rare break when the baby wasn't crying. Bella scooched a little closer to him and asked, "What are we going to tell our kids about . . . you know? Our past?"

Roman tore his gaze from the baby to look into his beautiful wife's eyes. "That maybe we met when we were a little too young, but we got a second chance to get it right."

"I love you, Roman," Bella said, circling her arm around him. In that moment, his heart overfilled with a happiness he'd never known.

"I love you, Bella," he said. "Always have, from the moment I first saw you." He smiled, then bent his head to kiss their little girl on the head. "And you, too, Vivienne." Then he kissed Bella softly on the lips. He'd never dreamed they could ever be together again after what had happened so long ago, but life is funny, sometimes. The painful past can heal and can even open up into a life you'd never dared to dream of.

"To second chances," Roman said, kissing Bella again.

"To second chances," Bella said. "The best kind ever."

ACKNOWLEDGMENTS

I'm so fortunate to be surrounded by amazing people who have enabled me to pursue this dream job.

Jill Marsal, you are awesome. To Alison Dasho and the Montlake Team, thanks for all your support and work. Thanks to my editor Charlotte Herscher, who has such a feel for getting into the heads of characters and often understands their problems better than I do. I'm so fortunate to have you edit my Mirror Lake books!

Thanks to my writer friends who I can call at a moment's notice with any kind of writing crisis—Sandra Owens; the Sunshine gals, Wendy, Vicki, Chris, Anna, Mary, and Sheri; My Lucky 13 Sisters; and my darling hubby, who knows all my characters and their many problems by heart.

Thanks to my family for the emotional and psychological support that are needed when one sits or stands in front of a computer all day. And for dragging me away when necessary so that I don't forget to live my real life.

Thanks to Lisa Graf of Graf Growers, Akron, Ohio, who took the time to explain to me about running a garden center, irrigators, emitters, and loppers. And how pumpkins are harvested.

Thanks to Dale and Peg Vodraska, owners of Rittman Orchards, who gave me a tour of their beautiful property and taught me about drip irrigation, apple graters, and bin haulers and sent me home with a big beautiful pie and a giant sack of the most delicious apples I've ever tasted.

Thanks to Laura L.K., who allowed me to borrow her beautiful baby's name to bestow upon Roman and Bella's child.

Lastly, to my readers, I love every note you send, every message and kind thought. Sometimes in the lonely hours, writers may feel that we're writing into a vacuum . . . thank you for reaching out and telling me when something I've written has made you laugh or cry, for liking my characters, and for letting me know that that is not the case.

ABOUT THE AUTHOR

As a girl, Miranda Liasson was a willing courier for the romance novels her mother traded with their next-door neighbor because it gave her a chance to sneak a peek at the contents. Today, Miranda writes award-winning romances herself, creating stories about courageous but imperfect characters who find love despite obstacles and their own personal flaws. In 2013, Miranda won the Romance Writers of America's Golden Heart Award for Best Contemporary Series Romance. *Can't Stop Loving You* is the first book in her Spikonos Brothers romance series, and she is also the author of three Mirror Lake romances: *This Thing Called Love*, *This Love of Mine*, and *This Loving Feeling*. Along with her husband, three children, and Posey, a rescued cat with attitude, Miranda makes her home in Northeast Ohio. Follow her on Facebook at www.facebook.com/MirandaLiassonAuthor and on Twitter @mirandaliasson.